Thunderbird Chosen

JORY STRONG

ELLORA'S CAVE
ROMANTICA PUBLISHING

What the critics are saying...

ဢ

SPIRIT FLIGHT

4.5 Lips "Jory Strong gives us a captivating tale of greed, resentment, love, desire, and Native American legend and spirituality. Rare is the reader who will not mark this one as a re-read. The plot is tightly woven, the heroine and hero divine, and the Thunderbird myth and magic is an essential and integral part of the story. Reader, do not miss this one!" ~ *Two Lips Reviews*

SPIRITS SHARED

"Jory Strong is a talented author indeed. The ability to form genuine relationships between two characters is a difficult enough task, make it three and things can easily spin out of control. But with a masterful grasp of emotional and erotically charged writing, the author makes this threesome work beautifully. The sequel to SPIRIT FLIGHT, SPIRITS SHARED is nonetheless a stand alone read. Jory Strong has once again proven why she deserves a place on any paranormal fan's must-buy list. Stop by Ellora's Cave and get your own copy of SPIRITS SHARED today." ~ *Romance Reviews Today Erotic*

TWO SPIRITS

4.5 Stars "I thoroughly enjoyed this book from the first page to the last. Ms. Strong kept me enraptured with these two men. Normally male-male novels are not something that I usually enjoy. Nevertheless, I found myself enthusiastically pursuing each page as these two people came together in understanding and love. This book was written with a sure hand and the plot never faltered, the story line and dialogue flowed smoothly. The emotional attachment is just what I needed while reading. [...] Overall, *Two Spirits* is a very memorable and dynamic story in the beautiful *Spirit* Series. Each one gets better and better. I would also recommend that *Spirit Flight* and *Spirit Shared* be read for greater enjoyment and understanding." ~ *Sensual EcataRomance Reviews*

An Ellora's Cave Romantica Publication

www.ellorascave.com

Thunderbird Chosen

ISBN 9781419957673
ALL RIGHTS RESERVED.
Spirit Flight Copyright © 2006 Jory Strong
Spirits Shared Copyright © 2007 Jory Strong
Two Spirits Copyright © 2007 Jory Strong
Edited by Sue-Ellen Gower.
Cover art by Syneca.

This book printed in the U.S.A. by Jasmine–Jade Enterprises, LLC.

Trade paperback Publication June 2008

THUNDERBIRD CHOSEN

෨

Spirit Flight
~11~

Spirits Shared
~57~

Two Spirits
~193~

SPIRIT FLIGHT

ຂ໑

Acknowledgements

Many, many thanks to Susan White who was kind enough to read this story and offer insights from a Native American perspective.

Trademarks Acknowledgement

The author acknowledges the trademarked status and trademark owners of the following wordmarks mentioned in this work of fiction:

Jeep: Daimler Chrysler

Chapter One

 හ

Marisa Lacoste doubled over as pain sliced through her side.

Run. Keep running. Run. Run. Run.

The words pounded through her in time to a heart that felt like it was going to burst out of her chest. She panted. Sucking in air while the pain in her side kept her still for a minute.

She had no idea if they were behind her. At this point she had no idea if they even realized she was no longer out sketching impressions of the mountains.

Stupid! She'd been so stupid. So unaware. So naïve.

A different kind of pain twisted through her. How could Ethan be involved in this? And for money. He knew the most important thing to her was her art. It was all she'd cared about since she was old enough to hold a crayon.

Tears threatened, from the emotional pain as well as the physical. She tried to quiet her breathing so she'd be able to hear them if they came crashing after her. Tried to force herself to breathe through her nose, realizing as she did so that her throat and lungs were starting to ache from gasping the cold mountain air of the Cascades.

A rumble sounded in the distance. Thunder to go with the darkening sky as the gray clouds were starting to gather.

Tears trickled down her face and Marisa brushed them away impatiently. Tears wouldn't do any good now and she couldn't allow herself the luxury of them.

Maybe later. When she found her way off the mountain. When she flagged down a car or found a call box. When she got back to the last town they'd stopped in. Hohoq—so small it wasn't even on the map.

They'd eaten at a tiny home-style diner there and anyone who'd seen them together would testify they'd been in great spirits. A man and two women. Enjoying themselves the way people do when they're on vacation. Laughing. Teasing. Probably in the area for rock climbing or hiking, or just to camp. She and Ethan resembling each other so closely with their black hair and blue eyes that they were obviously related. Not that Kaitlyn wouldn't have drawn her share of appreciative glances with her blonde, fashion-model looks.

Fresh pain ricocheted in Marisa's chest. They'd played her so well. Not just for the last couple of days, but for months.

The beautiful tabletop books with pictures of the Cascades. Talking her into taking a rock-climbing class. All of it done so this trip wouldn't seem out of character and her *accidental* death wouldn't seem suspicious.

Stupid! She'd been so thrilled to be included!

But now she could see the exact moment when this thing had been set in motion. When she'd realized that slowly, over the years, she'd begun living only on the proceeds from the sales of her paintings. When she'd casually mentioned that she wanted to put the money she'd inherited from their father, the money her brother had been managing, into a scholarship fund so other artists could "make it" as she had.

She wondered if any of the money was left. If Ethan had been embezzling it all along. Or only since Kaitlyn came into the picture.

Marisa pushed thoughts of her brother and Kaitlyn aside. Forced herself to straighten. The air around her was getting colder and the sky darker.

A different fear gripped her. Its fingers icy dread.

Lost, her skin slick with sweat from running, exposed to the elements overnight with nothing more than the clothing she was wearing, she could as easily die from hypothermia as from a staged fall while rock climbing.

It'd be so easy for them to claim she'd gotten lost while she was hiking. Gotten so absorbed in her surroundings, in the beauty and colors she'd try to pull into her art later, that she hadn't been paying attention to where she was going. They would say she had panicked and run when she finally realized she didn't know where she was or where camp was.

Anyone who'd ever seen her when she became immersed in her work would testify that she could go days without answering the phone or opening the mail, would barely remember to eat. It wouldn't take any great leap of imagination to believe she'd gotten lost.

Marisa shivered. The sweat starting to chill underneath her shirt and jeans.

They'd still want to find her body, just to make sure she hadn't used her art pencils to leave a note behind. A record of what she'd overheard them planning and why she'd run.

The breeze picked up. Bringing with it the scent of impending rain. Distant thunder rumbling in confirmation a storm was on its way. It's threatened arrival turning both the mountain and time into deadly enemies.

She wouldn't last the night if her clothing got wet. She knew it with a certainty that came from being a news addict, not an experienced camper.

Marisa surveyed her surroundings. Took in the vast panorama of rock and pine, brambles and juniper. Breathtaking beauty and terrifying solitude at the same time.

In that moment she would have given every penny she had just to spot smoke curling upward from a cabin tucked away in the landscape. But there was nothing. No indication anyone lived in the area though the presence of the rough dirt road and the *No Trespassing* signs she'd seen a short time ago had given her hope that she'd find someone to help her.

Another rumble sounded, this one sending adrenaline and terror coursing through her. All doubt as to whether or not they'd realized she was missing answered by the sound of the off-road motorcycle.

There was a grove of pine and oak ahead but she wasn't sure she could get to it before being seen. And even if she did, the trees and undergrowth might slow her down and trap her instead of offering her shelter and protection.

She'd returned to camp earlier than expected and overheard them deciding to find her and kill her *now*, when the storm would work to their advantage. But despite the pain and panic and fear she'd experienced since that horrible moment, Marisa had tried to keep her wits. She'd stuck to roads leading downward, though early on she knew she wasn't on the one they'd taken to get to the remote campsite. It had become too narrow, too overgrown, barely more than a footpath in places before opening on a harsher, wider track.

Where it had become a wider track again was where she'd seen the *No Trespassing* signs and a short distance beyond those, the totem poles. So exquisitely carved that she knew she was looking at something created by a master craftsman. The animal figures carved in detail, the thunderbirds on the top of each pole ferocious, magnificent, the epitome of raw power and the primal acknowledgment of forces greater than man. Even in her flight to reach safety she couldn't go past the totem poles without stopping long enough to run her fingers over the designs etched into the wood, her artist's spirit aching to linger, to try and capture on paper the essence of what was in front of her. The image of the great thunderbirds — their wings outspread, their attention focused outward, claiming everything for as far as the eye could see — filling her with profound emotion.

The rumble of the motorcycle grew louder and for the first time since she fled the camp, she left the road and confronted the mountain directly. Scrambled over rock, grabbing with her hands and trying to gain purchase with her feet while pebbles tumbled like small slides down the steep incline.

She was trying to get out of sight from the road. Praying that whoever was on the bike was simply following a possible escape route rather than tracking her specifically. Her only intention was to find a place where she could cling safely until the bike had passed and then passed again, returning to camp.

But as the bike drew near, its engine roaring, echoing in the canyon, the rock under Marisa's hands and feet gave way and sent her hurtling downward, clawing desperately, each wild grab dislodging more rock and earth so that a tide of it heralded her descent.

For the first few seconds there was only wild panic, a desperate awareness of speed and motion, of being momentarily airborne. But then came pain. Legs, ribs, arms, back as she landed hard on an outcropping, the debris in her wake striking her face and arms and torso before bouncing and continuing the journey downward.

When the last of it had passed and the sound of the slide faded, only the purr of an engine remained. Marisa opened her eyes and watched as the motorcycle stopped far above her and the rider slid the helmet off to get a better view — or maybe it was a gloating show of victory. Either way, for long moments Kaitlyn looked down at where Marisa lay, and then with a wave, she put the helmet back on and drove away.

There was nothing but pain afterward. Emotional. Physical.

Bleeding, killing wounds inflicted to heart and soul.

Breaking, tearing wounds done to bone and flesh.

Marisa faded in and out of consciousness. Aware on some level of the darkening sky, the rapidly approaching storm, the feel of cold rain pelting against her exposed skin when it finally arrived. The wetness of her clothes. Their sodden mass a heavy weight on a frame barely able to sustain life.

The thunder was directly overhead now. Lightning flashed, its brilliance flickering against Marisa's eyelids.

She forced them open, knowing she was dying and yet *choosing* to see the beauty around her. The magnificence of the storm. Far more powerful and real than anything she'd ever been able to capture in her art—though sometimes she came close, and those were the paintings she treasured.

A crash sounded, followed by lightning. Jagged streaks illuminated the sky and Marisa gasped, her pain forgotten as the thunderbird image from on top of the totem pole hovered above her.

His powerful wings beat the air with such force that clouds swirled around and under him. The bright colors of his feathers reflected off gray rock, painting it red and white with splashes of yellow and blue woven in. His beak open in a soundless scream as lightning sparked from coal black eyes.

Marisa knew she was hallucinating and yet she embraced the hallucination, even managed a small laugh of sheer joy as she felt herself floating upward, toward the thunderbird, the wind catching the sound of her pleasure and carrying it away.

But then the great bird turned its eyes on her and swooped. Its dive sending the clouds scattering and rushing away, driving Marisa's awareness back to her body. To pain and cold. And finally—nothingness.

Chapter Two

ဢ

There was the sound of a solitary drum beating in the rhythm of a heart. A voice accompanied it in a chantlike song offering prayers in a language Marisa didn't understand.

Instead of pain, there was only heat. Moving through her. Over her. Building in intensity as the song built, peaking, fading. The process repeated over and over again until the voice stopped. The drum stopped.

Into the sudden silence came the eerie sound of water dripping in the distance. The sensation of being watched. The hint of a woodsy scent that coiled in Marisa's womb and gave her the strength to open her eyes and struggle to her elbows.

It took her a minute to see him, and even then she blinked. Licked lips that were dry as she forced herself into a sitting position. The movement made her lightheaded for an instant, warned her that she shouldn't try to scramble to her feet.

He rose from where he was squatting next to a small fire and her fingers clenched involuntarily—not with the need to defend herself, but with the urge to draw him. To capture him on paper.

He was a vision from history. A warrior. His muscles toned from a life where only the fittest survived. His skin bronzed, revealed except for the area covered by the loincloth he wore.

The bulk of his black hair was a curtain flowing over his shoulders and down his back. But on either side of his face beads and feathers decorated tight, narrow braids.

"Drink this," he said, kneeling next to her and offering her a cup she hadn't noticed him carrying. His voice deep, confident. His words English, firm.

She shook her head in confusion as the memories flooded in, of overhearing Ethan and Kaitlyn plotting to kill her, of running, of being injured, of knowing she was dying and seeing the thunderbird swoop down from the sky.

"Drink this," he repeated, gripping the back of her head and holding her still as he pressed the cup to her lips. She struggled instinctively, wondered if she was drugged.

Her captor set the cup down and quickly subdued her. His arms around her torso all that was necessary in her weakened condition.

A different kind of awareness ripped through her when skin came into contact with skin. When she realized she was completely naked.

"Easy," he said, as if sensing her rising panic and her intention to renew her fight. "Easy. I'm not going to hurt you."

Marisa's attention flitted wildly around her, taking in the rock, the darkness, the campfire and finally her clothes. Torn and bloody, dripping from a peg pounded into the wall. The sight of them calmed her as nothing else would have.

Her gaze returned to the man holding her. Seeing the dark eyes. The thunderbird's eyes. The colorful feathers braided into his hair. Red and white and black with splashes of blue and yellow. The thunderbird's colors.

"You rescued me," Marisa whispered, understanding dawning. She must have been delirious when he found her, her mind lost in the last piece of art to make an impression on her. The totem poles.

Marisa pulled away from him and this time he let her go. Wonder flowed through her, disbelief as she gazed down at her body and saw no open wounds, felt no broken bones even though the state of her clothing attested to the fact that she *had* been injured and bleeding.

She glanced up and her nipples tightened in reaction when she saw his gaze travel over the same territory hers had just explored. His eyes darkened with masculine appreciation at the sight of her exposed nipples and cunt.

His nostrils flared as though he could scent her sudden wetness and Marisa's womb fluttered in response. Her hand went to the apex of her thighs in an attempt to shield her mound and arousal from his view. The other hand dropped to the material underneath her and she realized it was thick fur, a hide tanned and softened.

"No," he said, his fingers going to her wrist, stilling her when she shifted, intending to free the fur and wrap it around herself. "I will bathe you first."

Marisa's breath caught in her throat. Her entire body hummed at the words, at the possessive way he was looking at her. At the command in his voice.

He picked up the cup and once again held it to her lips. "Drink this. It will help you gain strength, Marisa."

She opened her mouth to ask him how he knew her name and he used her response to his advantage, tilted the cup and left her no choice but to drink the contents or choke on it. She swallowed, expecting something cold and bitter. Finding instead something warm and thick and tasting of honey.

Almost immediately the heat of the drink spread out from her belly, going first to her cunt and breasts and making her whimper. She licked her lips and groaned as warmth spread there too.

"You've drugged me," she whispered, her eyes meeting his then going to his mouth, her upper body leaning forward, following the direction of her gaze.

He laughed, a small husky sound, and once again took her into his arms, this time brushing his lips across her temple. "You are feeling the call of our spirits to one another. The drink was to aid you, nothing more."

She allowed herself to simply luxuriate in the feel of hard muscle and hot flesh, to soak in his strength and breathe his scent. A shiver went through her and another whimper escaped when his hands smoothed over her back, slid down to her hips and pulled her more tightly against him. Her breath caught when she became aware of what his loincloth was concealing. "I don't even know your name," she said, wondering how she could be naked and yet so at ease in this stranger's arms.

"Ukiah," he said, rubbing his cheek against Marisa's, giving her the name the townspeople and guests at his lodge knew him by. The name he went by in the physical world.

He tangled his fingers in her hair in order to keep her from turning her face away as he settled his mouth on hers, coaxed her lips into parting so his tongue could slip into the wet heat of her mouth, tasting her essence along with the drink the Creator had directed him to give her.

She was lush and sweet, utterly desirable. His. Given to him by the one who had called up the storm and drawn the thunderbird into the air. Leading him to where Marisa lay dying, her soul ready to flutter away.

It was not Ukiah's place to question the Creator's choice of a wife for him and he had no desire to do so. She was beautiful. Long-limbed and exquisitely feminine. Her breasts tipped with large dusky nipples, her pubic hair trimmed into a small dark triangle left to arrow downward toward a delicate clit and bare cunt lips.

He hadn't known what reaction to expect from her. Had thought only of carrying her to the cave and stripping her of the wet clothing, of starting a fire and beginning the sing, offering up prayers and supplications and promises that he would accept her and care for her and teach her so that she would answer the call as a thunderbird.

Until she opened her eyes and became aware of her surroundings he had tried to respect her privacy, to not stare at her naked body where it lay on furs, warmed by a fire that was created by the Creator's will, just as the drink Ukiah had given Marisa was.

Ukiah groaned as his cock pressed against the loincloth. His heart soared as her tongue twined with his. As her arms wrapped around his neck and she clung to him, the smoothness of her skin and scent of her arousal tempting him to lay her back down on the furs and cover her with his body.

He ached for her as he'd never ached for another woman. Wanted desperately to peel away the loincloth and bathe his penis in her wetness before pressing into her, merging his body to hers.

He'd waited so long. Had dreamed of having a woman at his side. A helpmate and companion. A mate who would fly with him when the thunderbird was called to the sky, who would winter with him when the snows came and celebrate with him when spring kissed the land.

But even as his cock demanded to be sheathed in her wet heat, Ukiah wanted to finish caring for her. As he'd promised to do. He wanted them to know each other better, to have their first joining be more than an urgent, mindless rush toward physical release. He wanted her to welcome him into her body as a soul mate, not simply as the man who had rescued her.

It took all of his strength to lift his mouth from hers. "I need to bathe you first."

"No, I need this more," she whispered against his lips, her arms tightening around him as her tongue forged into his mouth, as she became the aggressor.

Marisa knew she was reacting to the betrayal, to the wild run which had very nearly ended in her death. A part of her mind argued for her to pull away from Ukiah and put some distance between them. But that part of her seemed powerless against the deep anguished cry of her soul, the clamor of her body for warmth and comfort, for the security he represented.

She shivered when he responded, when he moaned and eased her backward so she was once again lying on the luxurious pelt of fur. His body straddled hers, making her whimper and arch in a futile attempt to rub her pelvis against his. She slid her hands down his sides and settled them on his hips with the intention of removing his loincloth. But he grasped her wrists and held them to the ground above her head.

"No," he said, lifting his mouth from hers, the rich waves of black hair a curtain on either side his face. The narrow braids with their beads and bright feathers brushed against her cheeks, overlaying the present with the past in a burst of déjà vu that made her think they'd once been like this before, in another lifetime.

His eyes widened slightly and she wondered if he was experiencing the same thing, but before she could ask him he lowered his head and her breath caught in her throat. Need pulsed through her cunt at the glimpse of herself reflected in the dark pools of his eyes. Her naked body made golden and sensuous, wanton, in the flicker of a fire that seemed too small to provide so much light.

Ukiah's tongue traced her bottom lip before sucking it into his mouth. His knees tightened against her hips to keep her from arching high enough to rub against him. He altered his grip, shifted so he could hold both of her wrists with one hand while the other moved to her breast, cupping it, worshipping it with his touch. A thin sheen of sweat formed on his upper torso as the ghost drums sounded in his mind, as ancient, long-dead ancestors joined their voices in a prayer for fertility rather than a healing song.

He groaned as he slanted his mouth, penetrated hers with his tongue. His testicles heavy with seed. His cock pulsing in time to the mystical drum beat.

Images of other lives fluttered past with the swiftness of a falcon, whispered voices called him by names his spirit had once answered to. Whispered the names he'd known Marisa by.

The tempo of the ghost music increased, built, urged Ukiah to consummate his union with Marisa. Filled his chest with echoes of a long ago emotion, the fierce pride of ownership. She'd once been his captive, his war prize.

The drums and songs and whispered voices blended, so tightly knit that they stripped him of control. He freed her wrists and kissed downward, no longer able to separate the man known as Ukiah with the ones who had come before him. From the thunderbird who knew this woman as its mate and wanted to reclaim her.

He circled and laved her nipples with his tongue until they were ripe and hard. The sounds of Marisa's moans and the sharp sting where her fingers buried in his hair, tugging as if she would pull him into her very skin, only made him feel *more*. Only made him crave her more.

He bit and suckled as his hands roamed over her breasts possessively. Exploring their fullness. Imagining the sight of them hanging free beneath her like ancient symbols of fertility when he took her on her hands and knees.

With a groan he forced himself away from them, kissed down her belly and buried his face between her thighs, doing nothing at first but inhaling her, filling his lungs with her unique scent. She whimpered and arched into him, a primitive plea for succor and pleasure and protection. A submissive yielding as if she too was locked in a long ago role where she lived or died at his will.

Ukiah tilted his head so he could see her face, wanted to watch her expression as he took the first taste of her, his tongue gliding along her lower lips, dipping into her slick channel in a primal claiming.

Her skin glistened, her eyelashes were delicate black crescents against taut skin. He wanted to command that she look at him but he couldn't bring himself to leave her silky wet cleft.

She gasped when he pierced her with his tongue, tightened her grip on his hair, her luscious breasts flushing a deeper color. He thrust again and the muscles of her sheath clamped down, trying to draw him deeper even as she drowned him in arousal.

The cadence of the ghost drumbeat demanded that he thrust again, and again. His hips jerking in time to the press and retreat of his tongue. His cock pulsing, rigid and confined, making him as much of a captive as she was.

Her cries of pleasure filled the cave and he could imagine them drifting upward and rolling through time like a supernatural thunder. Carrying a message, a scream of victory, a promise for the future.

Ukiah spread her thighs further, bent her knees and tilted her pelvis so that every inch of her was exposed, open, his to lick and suck. To fuck with his tongue.

Her clit was swollen, as rigid as his cock, its hood pulled back just as his foreskin was. Its head nearly purple.

"Please," Marisa said, her voice hoarse, her back bowed as though she could force him to swallow her whole, her hands trying to guide him to her clit. "Please," she begged again. Her skin coated with a sheen of sweat. Her heart racing, pounding so fast that it made her think of drums beating on a dark night, of ancient fertility rites and gods so old they were no longer named.

Ukiah licked over her swollen knob and she convulsed with pleasure, the icy-hot shards of it spearing through her, making her buttocks clench and her breath so scarce that she felt lightheaded. He closed his mouth around her clit and the tears came. Mixed with whimpers and cries as he sucked, hard and fast, aggressive now, somehow knowing she needed a violent release in order to cleanse her of the horror of what had happened to her.

He pinned her to the fur. Held her down as if she was his captive. The feathers and beads and silk of his hair making him seem primitive, savage. The shadows on the wall dancing like some ancient people around a timeless campfire.

Over and over again he swirled his tongue across her clit as he sucked. His lips firm, resistant, driving her higher and higher until she came, shuddering and writhing. Ecstasy rolled through her like a fierce storm and Marisa rode the pleasure until the last of it passed into distant rumbles and short bursts of lightning, leaving her feeling cleansed, calm, like the earth after a rain.

Color flooded her cheeks when she finally forced her eyes open. A sudden shyness at having taken so much from him but given nothing in return.

Ukiah's skin felt stretched tight and his cock ached with the need to sheathe itself in her wet heat. He could feel the dampness against his flushed foreskin where the head had leaked in preparation for coupling with Marisa.

For long moments his chest rose and fell in sharp pants, only gradually did his heart slow as the drum beats and singing faded, leaving him the choice as to when to join with her.

He kissed his way up her body, stroked her heated flesh as he did so, cupped her breasts, lingered to suck before once again claiming her mouth. This time sharing the taste of her pleasure with her.

She wound her arms around his neck and even that simple gesture filled him with a contentment he'd never known before. A sense that all would be well. That there was no need to hurry or rush.

He rose to his knees and lifted her into his arms before standing. Carried her to the cavern next to the one they were in and settled her into a small indentation in the floor that was filled with heated water.

Ukiah smiled when she squeaked, her eyes widening with surprise and confusion. "There are still volcanoes in this range," he reminded her, though in truth the water running down the wall and into the shallow pool was heated at his command, as was the cavern itself. Everything within created and maintained for her safety and comfort.

They were not abilities he had in his mortal form, only in this one. When he was both thunderbird and man, a creation of magic and belief.

Ukiah squatted by the natural bath, grimaced as his cock and balls pressed against the loincloth. He dipped his hands into the water before reaching for a crudely made bar of soap. Tumbled it over and over until lather coated his fingers.

Chapter Three

✖

"I can do it," Marisa said, her voice husky, low, nearly breathless.

"But *I* will do it," he said, his tone telling her it was his right and nothing she said would dissuade him.

Heat stole into her cheeks and remained there as he smoothed his palms over her neck, her shoulders, the slopes of her breasts, her arms.

He stroked every inch of her. Claimed every inch of her.

His touch was possessive, caring, so erotic that by the time he'd rinsed the last of the lather from her skin, Marisa was shaking with need. Her labia flushed and swollen. Her nipples and clit tight hard knots.

Nervousness fluttered through her and she licked her lips. He inhaled sharply and her gaze went to his face. Confidence returned in a heated rush at the sight of his taut features, the coal black eyes focused completely on her, the erection that strained against his loincloth, framed by thighs strung tight with tension and self-control.

She touched him then. Slid her hand along the muscle of his thigh, watched through lowered eyelashes as his nostrils flared and his jaw clenched. Felt the silent command to move higher, to free him from the loincloth in the way he held himself completely still.

Anxiety pitted in her stomach when her fingers arrived at the suede-like material stretched tightly over his cock. Its construction unfamiliar.

Ukiah's fingers covered hers, gently guiding them, explaining without words how to remove the loincloth. Her breath caught when the garment fell away, revealing his length and thickness, his penis—uncircumcised, his testicles heavy sacs underneath it, making her think of a stallion.

She stared in fascination, licked her lips again, only barely aware of his groan when she did so. Tentatively she reached out to touch him. To stroke his foreskin, to explore what she'd only seen in studio models and in finished art, untouchable examples of man as he'd been created by nature or god or maybe both.

Ukiah's masculine beauty appealed to her on so many levels. But as she stroked his shaft, it wasn't the artist who prevailed, but the woman.

Desire shivered through her at how soft he was. Her cunt throbbed, clenching and unclenching when arousal escaped the blood-filled tip of his cock. She grasped him in her hand and he hunched forward, burying his fingers in her hair as she'd done earlier. Pulling her to him.

She rose from the shallow basin of steamy water and kissed his chest. His nipples. Laughed softly when they became hard, tiny peaks on a sculpted chest.

"Marisa," he whispered, and her name sounded like a prayer on his lips.

Happiness filled her. Joy. Something more than lust.

Her kisses trailed downward. One hand going to cup his testicles, to weigh them like sacs of gold, to explore them while the fingers of her other hand wrapped around his cock, stroking up and down until his hips were moving to the rhythm she imposed on him. His breath coming in short pants.

His fingers tightened on her hair and Marisa didn't resist when he guided her mouth to his erection. She nuzzled it, her tongue darting out. Tasting. Feeling. Learning him as he'd learned her.

Waves of jagged pleasure rippled through Ukiah. Spikes of painful ecstasy like fractured bolts of lightning with each touch of her tongue to his heated flesh. He was helpless in her hands. Unable to do anything more than pant, and shake, and hold her to him as she tortured him with her tongue, with her fingers and lips.

Beads of sweat rolled down his neck and chest. Every muscle in his body strained to remain still, afraid that any movement would shatter the last of his control and he would hold her to him and spew his seed in the wet depths of her mouth instead of her cunt.

He cried out when her soft mouth left his shaft, her tongue like the kiss of the sun against his sac, burning him with heat, then immersing him in a river of fiery sensation when she sucked first one testicle and then the other.

Ukiah bucked against her, his body strung so tightly that between one heartbeat and the next he knew he'd reached his limit. "No," he said, the word so guttural it was barely recognizable. "No more."

He used the grip on Marisa's hair to pull her away from him, his buttocks clenching when his testicle slid from between her firm lips. The drumbeats which had faded began again, only this time they were the thunder of his own heart.

He picked her up, heedless of the water adhering to her skin and splashing onto his. Uncaring of anything except returning to the other chamber with her and spreading her out on the furs.

"Look at me," he said, coming down on top of her, his fingers intertwined with hers, holding her hands to the floor as his thighs roughly opened hers.

He groaned when his cock encountered the slick wet heat of her swollen vulva. Very nearly plunged in and impaled himself to the hilt in one fast, hard stroke. But he managed to hold himself at her entrance. To meet her gaze and then slowly, an inch at a time give himself to her—just as slowly, an inch at a time, he claimed her for his own.

"Ukiah," Marisa said, her fingers tightening on his as he pushed deeper, his name filling her soul as completely as his cock filled her channel.

She shuddered when he reached the end of her, wrapped her legs around him as if afraid he'd try and leave her. She rejoiced in the heavy feel of his testicles against her buttocks. Wanted to close her eyes but his coal-black gaze commanded that she keep them open, that she see the possessive way he gazed at her. Acknowledge the ownership he claimed as his hips began moving, first in short, forceful jabs, and then in long, full-length strokes that left her mewling and whimpering, crying for him.

He covered her lips with his and began thrusting in earnest. Made her scream in climax as he filled her with his seed. His release a violent hammering that had him going lax against her before rolling to the side and gathering her in his arms.

The sound of their breathing was harsh and ragged. Loud in the small cave. It drowned out the drip of water and the crackling of the fire. Masked even the far away droning, the continuous undertone that made Marisa think of chanting but was probably the sound of wind through rocks, or more ominous, deep shifts in the mountain range.

She cuddled against him, content as she'd never been before. Then made a murmur of protest when he released her and stood. But a moment later he'd once again scooped her into his arms and carried her to the sunken indentation filled with heated water.

"This is wonderful," she said when he sat, positioning her so that she was straddling him, her head on his shoulder, the water covering her legs and lapping at her lower back. The pool only barely large enough to hold the two of them.

Ukiah brushed his hand along her spine. His heart filled with not only the beauty of the woman in his arms, but at what they'd already shared. Even without the Creator guiding him to her, gifting him with her, he would have been drawn to Marisa.

"How did you end up on these lands?" he asked. "When I was in Hohoq earlier today, no one mentioned there were visitors staying in town."

Marisa's eyebrows drew together in surprised confusion. *Hohoq?* That was the name of the town where they'd stopped for lunch days ago. And after they'd left, it had taken them hours to get to the campsite.

She reached for one of Ukiah's narrow braids, finding comfort in the feel of the smooth beads and soft feathers. "Am I close to there?" It occurred to her that she didn't really know where she was, other than in a cave. "Am I close to where you found me?"

He chuckled, a rumble that vibrated against her and made her smile. "Yes to both questions." His fingers skimmed over her backbone again and made her shiver and press more tightly against him. "So you were lost?

Her hand clenched on his braid. Then she forced herself to release it in favor of touching his skin, of curling her fingers around his biceps. "I was lost. Mainly I was trying to get somewhere safe."

Overhearing the conversation to kill her. Running. Her terrified escape. It seemed like a nightmare now. Unreal. Unbelievable. Something that had happened to someone else. While this...being here with him... It felt like they'd always been together. Not in the same way as people who've known each other years, but in the way of people whose souls are linked.

Marisa remembered her earlier thoughts, of knowing him in another life. Of belonging to him then. She shivered then laughed silently at herself. Attributing her flight of fantasy to artistic temperament.

Ukiah leaned back and in the process forced her to shift position so he could look into her face, his hand tangled in her hair held her still for a lingering kiss before he pushed her for answers.

The tension in her body a moment earlier—along with the motorcycle tracks on the road above where he'd found her— told him the safety she'd been seeking was more than shelter from the storm or the approaching night. "Someone was chasing you?" he whispered against her lips and she immediately jerked in his arms.

She met his eyes and everything inside him responded to the fear he saw in them. His cock stirred where it lay snug between her wet thighs, filled, grew ready to offer physical reassurance that she was safe, cared for.

Marisa's fingernails dug into Ukiah's biceps. Tears formed at the corner of her eyes, and a quiet sob escaped when he leaned forward, kissing them away. Nuzzling her, rubbing his cheeks to hers and finally taking her mouth again. His tongue twined with hers, reassured, eased the ache in her heart until the pain of betrayal gave way to heat and warmth, the beginnings of love.

When they separated, she made him smile by guessing at the source of his question, by asking, "You saw the bike tracks?"

"Yes. Who was chasing you? And why?"

Marisa exhaled on a long shaky sigh. "My brother and his girlfriend. Kaitlyn's the one who finally caught up with me, but not before I'd already taken a fall down the mountain. Though I guess that turned out to be a good thing. It fit with their plans perfectly so they were willing to leave me there and let nature take its course rather than help it along." She leaned in, shaking despite the heated water they were sitting in. Hugged him tightly. "If you hadn't found me…"

Ukiah slid his arms around Marisa and held her to him, glad her face was buried against his neck so she couldn't see the rage in his expression, the utter determination to destroy those who wished to harm her. Who had left her to die. "Why were they trying to kill you?"

"Over money." She shuddered, a soul-deep protest of betrayal and Ukiah thought she wasn't going to say anything more, but then she seemed to force a calm into her body. "I'll know more when I get back home. But for the last couple of years my brother Ethan has been managing the money our father left me. At first I got a monthly allowance, but as my art started to actually pay for my apartment and anything else I needed... It was stupid not to pay attention, but Dad left Ethan the business. He trusted him with that. So I trusted Ethan too. I wanted to believe we were a family."

"You were close?"

"Our father left his mother and married mine — while she was pregnant with me. So no, we weren't close when we were growing up. But after our father died..." She shrugged. "But maybe that was all pretend, even if I'd like to think Ethan changed because of Kaitlyn. That she somehow convinced him to do this for her."

Marisa took a deep breath. "They were planning on a rock-climbing accident. Only once we got here... There were so many images I wanted to capture on paper. And then when I saw where they wanted to climb... It made me feel scared. Maybe part of me guessed what they intended to do."

She closed her eyes and Ukiah speared his hands in her hair and tugged, the sharp little pain making her lift her face so that once again he could cover her lips with his.

This time his tongue coaxed hers, tempted it to enter his mouth so he could hold it, suck on it, a gentle offer of sympathy as well as an acknowledgement of the rawness of her emotions. An offer of closeness and safe haven which she accepted with the softening of her body, with the opening of her thighs and the press of her swollen cunt lips against his engorged penis. When she whimpered he abandoned her hair in favor of grasping her hips and lifting her, settling her on his cock as he held her tongue captive in his mouth.

Marisa was helpless against Ukiah's sensual assault. There was no protest in her mind. No thought other than to invite him further into her body, their movements synchronized to his sucking, so subtle that the water barely rippled and yet each tiny thrust sent shards of white-hot pleasure through her clit. Each slide of his penis over desperately hungry internal muscles starved her for more. Their connection was so intense, so profound, that he became everything that mattered to her. And with a cry, orgasm ripped from the deepest part of her. A place that had never responded to another man like it responded to Ukiah. A place sealed closed until he came into her life.

Ukiah held her to him. The clenching and unclenching of her sheath on his penis exquisite agony as he savored the gift she was giving him, tried to make it last. Succeeded until she went limp in his arms, rung out from her pleasure, her channel snug and hot and wet, issuing an invitation he could no longer ignore. A siren's call that roared through him, making him pant and thrust and fill her womb with his seed.

He carried her back to the other room, laughing when she said, "Despite your having to carry me here when you found me, I can walk now," her voice light, happy.

"I enjoy carrying you," he said, placing her on the furs so she was seated with her back to the fire, then taking a moment to get a comb before kneeling behind her.

Marisa gave a low moan of pleasure when Ukiah began working with her hair, gently untangling it, the teeth of the comb lightly scraping over her back. "How close are we to where I fell?"

"If your handhold hadn't given way you might have seen the cave once you traveled several yards further. But you wouldn't have been able to get to it from where you started climbing."

"You were here?"

"No. But I arrived shortly after you must have fallen."

34

A tremor went through her as she remembered. "It was storming."

"It's still storming outside."

She cocked her head but heard nothing. "Was I unconscious when you got to me?"

He hesitated, a barely imperceptible pause. "Yes."

Marisa almost lost her nerve then chided herself as he leaned forward and one of his braids brushed against her arm. "Before I blacked out I imagined a thunderbird swooping down on me. He had eyes like yours." She reached over and stroked a bright feather with its bands of red, white and black, its subtle splashes of blue and yellow. "He had feathers that looked like this one."

Ukiah stopped combing her hair and leaned forward to rub his cheek against her hair and nuzzle her ear, to suck the lobe into his mouth. "You are on Thunderbird land."

Marisa smiled, letting herself be distracted by thoughts of the totem poles she'd passed. Accepting that it didn't matter whether she'd seen Ukiah and imposed a thunderbird form on him, or whether she'd been hallucinating.

"Do you know anything about the totem poles?"

Ukiah sucked her earlobe again and made her breath catch. His free hand went around to cup and fondle her breast, sending a rush of arousal to coat her inner thighs. "The poles near the *No Trespassing* signs?" he teased.

She found she could laugh. "Yes, those."

"I made them."

She gasped and tried to turn, but his hand at her breast made it impossible. "They're beautiful. Are you a sculptor?" She laughed again. "Silly question. I mean, is that what you do for a living? Though of course, art is so much more. I'd still create even if no one bought a single one of my paintings."

He nibbled the side of her neck before pressing a kiss to her skin and shifting to resume combing her hair. "I carve in the winter, as a hobby, though my family members manage to sneak some of my work from the lodge and offer it for sale in town."

Marisa's turned her head, yipping when the comb snagged and pulled her hair. "How in the world do they sneak away with totem poles?"

He laughed. "Most of my carvings are animals. Miniatures that can be easily concealed in a purse or jacket pocket."

"I'd like to see them," she said, tensing involuntarily, suddenly feeling awkward about the situation. About reality outside the cave. Outside this emergency dictated interlude.

"Marisa." His voice was a caress as he set the comb down and pulled her back to his front. Kissed along her shoulder, the hand which had been holding the comb going to her belly, burning through to her womb in a gesture of possessiveness and assurance. "I found you and I intend to keep you."

His hand dipped lower, cupping her mound, his fingers sliding into her slit. His palm pressing against her clit, moving in slow circles so that she whimpered and moaned. Soaked him with her arousal as she responded to his touch.

He made a guttural sound and leaned into her, used his weight against her back to force her forward onto her hands and knees. And then onto her elbows and knees with her buttocks raised, her thighs spread to reveal swollen, wet, woman's flesh.

She shivered at how vulnerable the position made her feel. The very awareness of her vulnerability making her labia grow more flushed. Making her clit strain, erect and full, the hood pulled back, desperate for his attention.

"You are beautiful, Marisa," Ukiah whispered, kissing the base of her spine, his fingers gliding over her slick folds, circling her clit and making her cry out.

She pressed into his hand, rubbed herself on his tormenting fingers, her breath coming in short pants accompanied by low moans. "Please," she begged, "please." And even though she couldn't see him, she could feel the impact of her words on him in the way his touch became more dominant, more aggressive. In the way the tension seemed to fill the cave, a primal energy that made her feel as though a huge presence loomed behind her.

Marisa jerked when he entered her. His cock slamming home in one rough thrust of ownership. His hands going to her hips to hold her in position as he began thrusting. The force of him plunging in and out of her driving the breath from her lungs in screams that signaled a mix of pleasure and pain, an exquisite, all-consuming acceptance of what he was to her.

Tears formed in her eyes and the shadows dancing on the wall in front of her blurred and blended, took the shape of a thunderbird with its wings outspread, flapping in time to each thrust of Ukiah's cock, its chest swelling as if with pleasure. The image was so real that she tried to turn her head, only to be stopped by his harsh "no", by his fingers tangling in her hair and preventing her from moving as he pumped even harder into her. The rhythm of his claiming becoming a nearly unbearable ecstasy until orgasm rolled over her, extreme and powerful, filling her as completely as his hot release filled her channel, rushing toward her like the giant shadow of the thunderbird and taking her with it into the primordial darkness.

For long moments Ukiah panted and shivered above Marisa's limp form, his cock still buried in her heated depths, his body weak even as the thunderbird's triumphant exaltation roared through him.

She was pregnant now. With his child. With the thunderbird's.

If they'd met under different circumstances Ukiah would have waited. Would have married her first and moved her into the lodge which served as both his house and his source of income. Would have let her accustom herself to her new life slowly — though he had no fear she would accept and embrace the changes, that she would thrill at what it would mean for her art.

But the choice hadn't been his to make. He walked in the spirit world now. This body a magical manifestation restricted to the cave, a duplicate to house the thunderbird's essence while Ukiah's true physical form lay miles away on a pallet in a sweat building behind his home.

He pulled from Marisa's folds. A masculine smile of satisfaction forming on his lips when she mumbled in protest and immediately moved to press her skin to his. He gathered her hair, wove it into a thick braid before lying down next to her, covering them with a fur and giving in to sleep, her back to his chest, his arms holding her to him. Possessive and protective at the same time.

Chapter Four

ဢ

Marisa woke smiling, achy in a good way — except for her bladder's insistence that it was time to find some relief. And then as if the acknowledgement of one basic need was enough to rouse others, her stomach growled.

Not very romantic, she thought, laughing softly as she disentangled herself from both Ukiah's arms and the fur. She lingered for a moment afterward to look at him, to assure herself he was real and not a fantasy she'd conjured up in a hallucination.

Reluctantly she forced herself to her feet and over to where her clothes hung on a wooden peg. She wondered briefly where Ukiah's were. Not that she wouldn't forever savor the first sight of him wearing nothing but a loincloth, but it *was* cold outside and she didn't think he'd been out hiking in only a strip of suede.

She grimaced as she pulled on clothes stiff with dried mud and blood. Their dryness making her glance at the fire.

It amazed her that something so small could put out so much light and heat and last so long. But then again, what did she actually *know* about campfires? Until this trip she'd had zero experience with actual camping — as in the kind that doesn't involve an RV or a cozy cabin at the end of a day of hiking to places where she could draw or paint.

She slipped her feet into her shoes and tied the dirt-encrusted laces. Then tried to get her bearings, seeing at first only the opening which led to the sunken pool.

It was the lack of smoke that made her look more carefully at the darkened recess behind the campfire. And almost immediately the flames flickered and she could feel a damp, cool breeze.

With one last glance at Ukiah, Marisa moved to where she thought the exit was and slipped into the shadows. The sudden presence of light—even if it was greatly muted in what served as a shallow anteroom to the cave—made Marisa close her eyes in reaction.

When she opened them she experienced a moment of confusion and disorientation. Her mind scrambling to know what time of day it was, to grasp how long she'd been in the cave with Ukiah.

Marisa stepped to the mouth of the cave and took in the deep gray clouds. She shivered as cold, wet air hit her face— the force and sting of it making her want to retreat. But embarrassment over the prospect of relieving herself in the cave, with Ukiah nearby, made her reach for an exposed root and place her foot on a small cluster of rock.

She climbed, keeping her mind from reliving her earlier fall by grumbling about how Ukiah had it easy. *She* had to go halfway up the mountain in order to find a handy place to squat while he only had to find a ledge and whip his cock out.

Marisa stilled in the act of reaching for another handhold, heat suffusing her body. A different kind of urge burned in her lower regions at thoughts of Ukiah with his fingers wrapped around his penis.

She couldn't safely begin climbing again until she banished the images and the needs that came with them. But this time as she slowly moved toward flatter ground, she wondered how Ukiah had gotten her to the cave at all.

The going was steep and perilous. Nearly impossible even without the added weight of an unconscious person. And yet he'd managed it during a furious storm.

When she finally got to the top the muscles in her arms were burning. For long moments she struggled to regain both her strength and her composure. As she sat at the edge and looked down the face of the mountain she was completely overwhelmed by the miracle that she'd been given. Not just her life. But Ukiah's presence in it.

Finally she stood and turned, seeing the small animal path that wove through low scrub growth and merged with the trail she'd been running on before making the decision to try and hide when she heard the rumble of a motorcycle's engine. Marisa's heart raced, the memories overlaying reality until she took several deep breaths and forced them away.

She walked a short distance, found shelter from the brisk wind so she could relieve the pressure on her bladder. And then like a fatal attraction, Marisa followed the path, returned to the spot where Kaitlyn had stopped the bike.

A shudder racked Marisa's body in a visceral reaction as she looked at the place where she'd come to rest when she tumbled down the side of the mountain. Where she'd been so sure she would die.

She wrapped her arms around herself, sorry now that she hadn't woken Ukiah and suggested they both leave the cave. Realizing as she looked down that her confidence had deserted her and she wouldn't be able to climb back to him.

The wind picked up, the sky darkening and roiling as though attuned to her fear and distress. The gray clouds churned, became charcoal black as thunder sounded in an ominous warning.

She retreated to the wider path and saw the number of motorcycle tracks there. Her heart skipped and beat erratically at the sight, only resuming its normal rhythm when she reminded herself that Ethan had probably veered off to check another trail and then caught up with Kaitlyn. That's why there were so many tracks.

Marisa rubbed her arms. Fought off the chill working its way under her clothing.

It was only a matter of time before Ukiah woke and noticed she was missing. He'd come looking for her. Of that she was certain. But in the meantime she knew she needed to find some semblance of shelter and the grove of trees in the distance was her best hope.

A rumble of thunder greeted her decision and she glanced at the sky. Shivered at how angry it now looked. Its dark violence filled her mind and made her hurry so that at first she wasn't paying attention to how the motorcycle tracks continued in the direction of the trees rather than upward toward the place she and Ethan and Kaitlyn had camped.

Marisa slowed. Her mind raced. Tried to make sense of why there would be tracks. Then remembered Ukiah's mention of Hohoq, the way he referred to it implying it was within hiking distance.

Uneasiness rippled through Marisa, timed to another roll of thunder. What if the tracks weren't old? What if Ethan and Kaitlyn had returned to make sure she was dead before claiming to have just found her body?

She had no idea how long she'd been in the cave with Ukiah. Or when the worst of the storm had ended though it looked like a new one was getting ready to arrive. She stopped abruptly, suddenly more afraid of continuing on than of braving the elements until Ukiah woke up.

A crack of thunder made her flinch. Lightning flickered across the sky just as two people emerged from the strand of trees she'd been heading for.

"Marisa!" Ethan called, his words whipping past her, carried by the wind.

She turned and ran, glanced over her shoulder and was relieved when she saw they weren't chasing her. But a few minutes later the sound of a motorcycle engine told her they'd returned for their bikes.

Within seconds her side was hurting and her lungs were burning. Fear nearly choked her. Not just at the prospect of them catching her, but of them killing Ukiah too.

She stumbled and went to her knees, but before she could scramble to her feet the wind grew in intensity, making it impossible for her to stand. The dark clouds in front of her became a boiling, angry mass, spitting rain as lightning strikes sizzled through the air, so close to her that she felt their energy across her skin.

A scream sounded behind her. High and feminine. Abruptly ended. And then a man's tortured shout. Followed by another bolt of lightning. Splitting into two as Marisa watched.

She gasped when the thunderbird emerged from the cloud, her rational mind and knowing heart in juxtaposition, awe and disbelief warring with her soul's certainty that the mythical creature in front of her was Ukiah.

He swooped toward her and she felt only a rush of pleasure, an answering cry in her chest, a desire to join him in flight. For a split second she thought he would pick her up with talons as black as his eyes, but at the last minute he swung upward.

She turned so she could watch him, her breath catching in her throat at the sight of the two motorcycles lying bent and twisted and smoldering on the path, two bodies next to them.

Hesitantly she began walking toward them. Her emotions volatile, ever changing. Dread and relief mixed with utter sadness.

She got to Kaitlyn first. Shuddered when she saw dead eyes staring vacantly at the sky, the charred place where a lightning bolt had struck.

Marisa moved to Ethan and knelt, tears in her eyes despite everything. She jumped when he moaned, forced herself to feel for a pulse in case the moan was only air escaping. And felt a moment's happiness that he was alive.

She wouldn't forgive him or allow him into her life again. She wouldn't let him get away with what he'd done. But he was her brother and she was glad he wasn't dead.

She stood and looked around, expecting to see Ukiah. But instead there was only the sense that he was watching from deep in the clouds, hovering close but unseen to ensure her safety.

The wind pushed against her, almost as if it was urging her to leave, to move on, toward the grove of trees and down the mountain. The motorcycles were useless and there was nothing she could do for Ethan other than to seek help. So once again she started running. Pacing herself this time. The wind against her back aiding her.

It felt like she ran for hours, though she had no idea how long it took to get to Hohoq. It seemed like a lifetime ago when she and Ethan and Kaitlyn had stopped there for lunch. Sat at the table, lingering, enjoying themselves the way people do when they're on vacation. Laughing and teasing so that others smiled with them.

Marisa closed the door on those memories. Forced herself instead to walk into town and into the first place she came to. *Hohoq General Store*. The thunderbird over the town name now resonating in her with the knowledge that it was one of the thunderbird's names.

She entered the store and noticed the carvings first. Small, delicately carved birds and animals. Then she noticed the man behind the counter, a silver-haired version of Ukiah though this man's hair was short.

His eyes widened with surprise when they met hers. "Which one of the boys do you belong to?"

"Let me handle this, Father," another man said, stepping from behind a row of shelves and making Marisa's heart rush to her throat even as she hurled herself into his arms and hugged him tight, his gentle pats to her back telling her instantly that he wasn't Ukiah. "My brother misplace you?" he asked, allowing her to pull away from him.

She noticed the sheriff's star on his chest then. The wrinkles at the corners of his eyes that told her he was older than Ukiah.

Words tumbled from her. Parts of her story probably incoherent. But he got the gist of it. As did his father, who moved around from behind the counter and flipped the "open" sign in the store's window to "closed".

When Marisa fell silent, Ukiah's brother said, "I'll take a crew up the trail. My father will take you to Ukiah."

Marisa nodded and let herself be led to a battered black Jeep with streaks of mud sprayed along its side. Her thoughts were in chaos. Wanting answers and yet the silence of the man driving reinforced the feeling that it was up to Ukiah to explain.

She laughed out loud when they passed a beautiful handcrafted sign. *Thunderbird Lodge.*

Ukiah's father spoke for the first time since leaving the store. "Sometimes it is easiest to hide out in the open."

Before she could respond the lodge came into view. A magnificent wood structure that would be a welcome sight to any vacationer. A charming design that spoke of comfort and camaraderie. Of nights spent talking and swapping tales.

The front door opened and Ukiah stepped out onto the porch, dressed in jeans and a flannel shirt. He crossed his arms over his chest. His stiff body posture and emotionless face chasing away Marisa's joy at seeing him.

"Go now," his father said, reaching over and clasping Marisa's hand, giving it a gentle squeeze. "Whatever differences exist between the two of you, they will work themselves out. You're the wife of his soul."

"Thank you," Marisa said, tightening her grip on his hand before letting go and climbing out of the car. Feeling insecure now. Uncertain. Ukiah's reaction to her presence confusing her. Hurting her.

Chapter Five

ഓ

He remained on the porch. Stoic and unmoving. Making her close the distance between them.

"Why did you leave me?" he asked, the question so unexpected, the pain she saw flicker briefly across his face so shocking that for an instant she remained mute.

But then she hurtled herself at him just as she'd done to his brother. Trusting that his reflexes would do the rest. And they did. His arms went around her just as hers did to him. "I didn't leave you!" she said. Heat rushing to her cheeks as she added, "Nature called. Then I was too scared to climb back down to the cave!"

A kaleidoscope of emotions played over his face. From chagrin to happiness to grim resolve.

"I didn't think Ethan and Kaitlyn would be anywhere close," she rushed to assure him, guessing at the path his thoughts had taken. "The truth is, I didn't even think about them at all until it was almost too late."

She hugged Ukiah more tightly. "You saved me—again. Just like you did before. You *were* the thunderbird. I wasn't hallucinating."

Ukiah relaxed his grip so he could cup Marisa's face. When he'd woken to find her gone he'd feared the worst. That she'd run after seeing the thunderbird's shadow when he'd taken her on her hands and knees. That she'd finally guessed the truth—not only guessed it, but had been terrified by it, preferring to risk death again rather than to stay with him.

He had never known such pain. And then when his spirit had shed the temporary form and he'd taken to the air, seen her once again under attack— Only the knowledge that it might make matters worse if he killed her brother had enabled him to rein in the thunderbird's fierce desire not only to protect its mate and unborn offspring, but to destroy any who threatened them.

"Marisa," he said against her lips. The word holding all the tenderness he felt for her.

He licked along the seam of her mouth and she opened for him, readily accepted the thrust of his tongue. Greeted him with joy and passion and need.

Ukiah swooped her up in his arms and she laughed, disengaging from the kiss long enough to remind him. "I can walk."

"But I enjoy carrying you."

She thought he'd do something romantic like carry her over the threshold but instead he left the porch. Stopping every several steps to kiss her. Long, sensuous assaults that left her aching and needy. Wet. Swollen. Weakened so she wasn't sure she could actually do as she'd boasted and walk if he set her down.

He took her a short distance into the woods, to a tiny building surrounded by totem poles. "Is this a ceremonial sweat lodge?"

"No. Those who stay here during the months the lodge is open enjoy it as a sauna."

He placed her on her feet. His hands going immediately to her clothing, unzipping the torn, bloody jacket and removing it, then dropping it to the ground. He was unbuttoning her shirt when the full impact of his words hit her.

Marisa grabbed his hands, stilling them, her nipples going tight as the heat from where they rested on her breasts reached her skin. She glanced around then and saw several cabins discreetly positioned among the trees. "I can't strip here!"

Ukiah laughed, enjoying her reaction. The way she grew flustered at the thought of someone other than him seeing her without clothing.

Complete satisfaction followed his amusement. Utter masculine contentment as he remembered how she'd been with him in the cave. How freely she'd given him access to her body, let him touch and kiss every inch of it. Let him keep her naked.

His cock pressed urgently against the front of his jeans. The throb of his heartbeat pounding through his shaft.

He leaned in and kissed her, nibbled on her lips because he couldn't stop himself. "There's no one here but us. The lodge is closed for the winter now."

She loosened her grip on his hands and he finished removing her clothing, ushered her into the lodge before she grew chilled. Marisa laughed and tugged at one of his braids, sending a jolt of pure happiness straight to his heart. "I notice *you* didn't strip where someone might see you," she teased.

He kissed her again, found that having her naked while he was fully clothed satisfied something deeply primal in him. "That's because my clothing isn't covered in dried blood and mud."

Marisa's hand went to the buttons at the front of his shirt, slipping them. Stroking his bared chest, her fingers teasing over his nipple and making his cock jerk and leak in reaction. "Should I help you get undressed like you helped me," she asked, her voice husky and aroused, curling around his erection and making him groan.

He let her play for long moments as his mouth reclaimed hers, his tongue thrusting and twining with hers as she toyed with his nipple and sent shards of ice-hot pleasure straight to his penis. He let her drive him to the point where it was painful to remain clothed before hastily getting undressed.

"A quick rinse and we'll go into the main room," he said and Marisa forced her attention away from him long enough to take in her surroundings, to realize they were in a small tastefully done room which served as a place to shower. "This is the men's entrance," he said, leading her to where the floor was tiled, lifting the hand-held shower wand from its wall mount before turning the water on and adjusting the temperature. "The women's entrance is on the other side." He rinsed himself first, then turned the spray on her.

Marisa tried to take the shower wand from him, her face heating with memories of him bathing her in the cave. "I can take care of myself," she said, wishing her voice didn't sound quite so breathless, but Ukiah's hand had swept down her body and now hovered directly over her cunt, sending a stream of water pounding against her clit and with it delicious waves of need up her spine.

"But I like to take care of you." He closed the distance between the showerhead and her swollen flesh, intensifying the effect of the water. When she would have moved away, he crowded her against the wall, holding her there with the force of his will and the pleasure he was giving her. "Spread your legs wider," he commanded and she had no thought to resist.

Ukiah's hand dropped to his cock, encircling it. He hadn't meant to linger in this room but whenever she was naked he lost his concentration.

Her gaze followed his hand to his penis and his balls pulled tight in reaction. In warning.

He was already so full, so tight, that he very nearly came when her tongue peeked out of her mouth and he remembered the feel of those lips on his cock. When her hand joined his, covering it, brushing over the exposed head of him with her thumb, a quick pass and then a lingering rub against the slit, Ukiah's buttocks clenched and he began pumping into their joined hands.

She'd bested him and they both knew it. Just as they both knew that if they didn't stop now he'd spew his seed on naked flesh before he could drive her to orgasm with the shower wand.

With a groan he put the wand away and turned off the water. Nearly lost control completely when Marisa started to go to her knees.

"No," he gasped, forcing his hand away from his cock, and with it, hers. Pulling her against his chest and holding her there.

She gave him a mischievous look through lowered eyelashes. "Turnabout is fair play, Ukiah. What's good for you, is good for me too."

"Marisa," he groaned, wavering for a moment. Hot need and the desire to feel her mouth on his cock very nearly overwhelming him. But he tightened his grip when she would have slid down his body. "Later," he promised. "You can do anything you want to me later, when we get back to the lodge."

"Promise," she teased, turning her head and licking over a rigid male nipple.

"Promise," he said, his voice the breathless one this time as he led her into the main chamber, afraid to delay any longer.

Marisa's breath caught in her throat when they stopped next to the fur-covered pallet and she saw the restraints, two strips of leather attached to the floor at the upper corners of the mat. "I don't think this is standard equipment for a sauna," she managed to say, even as something darkly erotic uncoiled in her womb and spread outward.

Ukiah cupped her face in his and forced her to meet his eyes. The dark, dark eyes of the thunderbird. "You are mine," he said, and she felt the words all the way to her soul. Felt them echoing from the past and had a fleeting image of standing naked, her wrists bound in front of her as these same words were once spoken in a language she didn't know. Their meaning translated by the way her captor's gaze roamed possessively over her body.

"I'm yours," she whispered, feeling arousal trickle down the inside of her thighs.

She allowed him to guide her to the bedding, to tether her wrists and make her helpless. A symbolic gesture because bound or freed, she trusted him completely and would never willingly leave him.

Ukiah knelt above her, his balls huge, heavy weights underneath a thick, flushed erection. Her beauty, inside and out, nearly undid him. And even though Marisa was the one in restraints, he knew he was equally helpless when it came to her.

He lowered himself, groaned as his sac settled on her warm belly. His mouth covered hers, captured, claimed, lingered before moving to her ear, her neck, and finally to her breast.

She began whimpering and writhing when he took her nipple between his teeth. Bit down on it, flicked it with his tongue. Sucked it. Her movements beneath him, her rubbing against his cock and testicles sending bursts of near painful ecstasy through him.

Liquid heat escaped, coating the head of his penis, marking her in the places where their bodies touched. It was primitive, raw. And Ukiah had to fight the urge to take himself in hand, to bring himself to orgasm and cover her cunt and abdomen with his seed.

"Please," she cried out, arching into him, driving all thought from his mind so that for long moments he suckled hungrily. Aware of only her breast. The wild beat of her heart. Her slick skin and fevered pleas.

It was the heady scent of her arousal that finally drew him away from her nipple. Had him kissing and biting and laving his way downward, parting her thighs and holding her open so he could look at her, taste her, drive her to orgasm by swirling his tongue over her clit, plunging it into her slit.

Over and over again he took her. Made her cry out in release. Her pleas turning to screams. Her body bowing, arms fighting the restraints until finally she went lax. And even then Ukiah couldn't get enough of her.

He nuzzled her swollen folds, sucked on them. Dragged his tongue along her creamy opening until she was whimpering again, her hips undulating. His name a ragged whisper on her lips.

Only the demands of the thunderbird gave him the strength to lift his face from her cunt and move to position himself above her, his hands going to hers, fingers entwining though he didn't free her wrists. He impaled her with a single hard thrust, forced open a channel that still seemed barely able to contain him.

Thunder rumbled as she wrapped her legs around him. Welcomed him completely. Held him deep in her body as if she would never let him go. "Fly with me," he said, his coal-black eyes mesmerizing as their bodies began moving in a timeless rhythm. An ancient dance.

There was no fire in this room as there had been in the cave, but at the corner of Marisa's vision shadows formed and flickered on the walls. Blending and merging in time to Ukiah's thrusts, to the drums and chants edging into her consciousness, filling her, building in intensity when Ukiah became more forceful, more frenzied as another orgasm built. This one a tidal wave compared the others. Arriving in a great sparkling wash of red and black and white with hints of blue and yellow. Crashing over and through her, taking her with it as the chants and drums reached a crescendo.

There was a wrenching sensation, followed by gray cold nothingness, and then by awareness. Of immense energy and power gathering and rolling through a body that was huge, feathered. The wings outstretched, riding the thermals.

She faltered and immediately felt talons on her back, a gentle grasp meant to reassure and guide her. Ukiah. She flapped the magnificent wings to communicate that she was okay and felt him lift away from her.

She flapped again, more forcefully this time. Reveling in the increased speed, the feel of the air against her as she mentally explored every inch of the thunderbird. Found the spark of life in her womb and nearly dropped from the sky. But once again Ukiah's talons on her back steadied her focus.

With a fleeting thought she was aware of her human form in the building below. Her wrists freed, her back curled against Ukiah's chest, their breathing synchronized and deep as their spirits flew free.

Emotion surged through her. Raw and fierce. Rumbling out in front of her as thunder. A shout of triumph. Of joy. Of love. Of two souls united again.

SPIRITS SHARED

෯

Trademarks Acknowledgement

ॐ

The author acknowledges the trademarked status and trademark owners of the following wordmarks mentioned in this work of fiction:

Boy Scout: Boy Scouts Of America Corporation

Scrabble: Hasbro, Inc.

Chapter One

☙

Could she really accept this? Jessica North wondered as she looked through the window of the diner. Could she really share Clay with another man?

She twisted her engagement ring around and around on her finger.

Did she want to?

A crack of thunder followed by a flash of lightning punctuated her anguished questions. Outside the diner the wind became more aggressive. Dried leaves whipped down the street. Old-fashioned wooden signs jerked against the chains holding them in place.

Hohoq. Population...three? And that was assuming someone was actually manning the general store across the street where Clay had gone.

Jessica glanced over at the mom and pop who were operating the diner. Their features were Native American but she found it impossible to guess their ages. Sixties? Maybe even seventies.

The woman interpreted Jessica's glance as an indication that she was ready to order. She walked over to the booth and surprised Jessica by saying, "Your man will be here in a minute."

Jessica glanced down at the engagement ring. *Was he really her man? Would he still be if they became a threesome instead of a twosome?*

A comforting hand settled on her shoulder. Jessica looked up into eyes that seemed like they could see all the way down to her soul. "Things have a way of working out if you let them."

Tears formed at the corner of Jessica's eyes. "Am I that obvious?"

The woman chuckled. "When you get to be my age and have raised as many children as I have, then had grandchildren come along to cry on your shoulder and tell you about their troubles with the opposite sex—well, not much gets past you, especially when it comes to matters of the heart." She gave Jessica's shoulder a pat. "Here comes your man now. By the look of him I'd say a double cheeseburger cooked well done with a side of fries." She glanced down at Jessica with twinkling dark eyes. "You're probably a grilled cheese sandwich with tomatoes and you prefer your pickles on the side with your French fries."

Jessica laughed. She felt her spirits lift for the first time since *The Revelation*. "No tomatoes on the grilled cheese, otherwise it's perfect."

The door opened. A blast of cold air barreled into the diner. Clay hurried to get the door closed behind him, then slipped his jacket off his shoulders as he moved toward the booth.

Jessica's breath caught in her throat. Her body tightened as it always did when she saw him. She'd thought he might be too good to be true the very first time she met him.

With his blond looks and fit body he could have been a cover model. Instead he was an outdoorsman who owned his own business. He put together group trips, mainly for companies who wanted their executives to "bond" while whitewater rafting or fly-fishing or mountain climbing, though sometimes he arranged trips for groups of friends who wanted adventure instead of total relaxation when they vacationed.

Clay slid onto the seat opposite her own. "Did you already order?"

Jessica shared a smile with the waitress who most likely was also one of the owners of the diner. "I think we've got it covered."

The woman chuckled. "Except for the drinks." She cocked her head. "Diet coke for you. Bottled water for your man, though I'd recommend drinking what the house serves. The water we've got in Hohoq is straight from the Creator."

Clay laughed. Jessica's heart turned over at the sound of it and the way his blue eyes danced with humor. He could be intense and serious when he had to be, when he was on the job and people's lives depended on it, but he was quick to laugh and to make others laugh with him. It was one of the things she loved about him.

Her eyes watered. She looked away. She was a mess right now but she didn't want to advertise it.

Clay and their waitress continued to talk. Their conversation was a background noise Jessica couldn't seem to concentrate on. In the scope of a day her entire reality had shifted and her confidence had suffered a blow she'd never seen coming.

She twisted the ring and thought about the quiet wedding they'd agreed on. They'd tentatively planned to have it in two months but they hadn't chosen an exact date yet because Clay's father had been sick and they wanted to make sure he'd be well enough to travel.

It was going to be a small gathering of their families and their closest friends, all people who'd been looking forward to the day as much as they...no, as much as *she* had. Right now she shouldn't assume anything about what Clay felt.

She'd thought he was as happy and content as she was. She'd thought he was as excited about finally getting married as she was. Not that it would change their day-to-day lives. They already lived together. But it was a first step toward one day having a family. They were both traditional in that they wanted to be married before they had children.

59

Maybe deep down she'd known she didn't satisfy him completely. Maybe that's why it had taken her a while to say yes to marriage and then a while longer before she'd committed to a foreseeable date. Maybe deep down she'd sensed the truth. He was enough for her, but she wasn't enough for him.

Pain moved through her. For long moments she concentrated on breathing, on the simple mechanics of inhaling and exhaling air through a throat that felt sealed up. A masculine hand covered hers where it rested on the battle-scarred tabletop. Jessica sucked in a deep breath and tried to ignore the burn in her chest and eyes.

"We can call the trip off, Jess," Clay said, his voice husky with pain. "We can turn around and go back to the apartment. We can see where we stand from there." He rubbed his palm over her engagement ring. "I don't want to hurt you any more than I already have."

She wiped the tears from the corner of her eyes before facing him again. She covered his hand with hers. In her heart she knew they would be over if they went back to their everyday life now. "Let's just keep going, okay?"

"Okay."

Their food arrived and they began eating in silence. *The Revelation* kept looping through Jessica's thoughts.

Clay's heart ached. Guilt shredded his guts. He hadn't been with another man or another woman since he'd stumbled into a bookstore and fallen head over heels in love—or at least deeply in lust—with the soft-spoken blonde who was reading a book to a group of kids in the children's section.

They'd meshed right from the start and he'd known that Jess was the one he wanted to share his life with. He loved her. Period. End of story.

You wish it were the end of the story.

Clay stabbed a fry into a pool of catsup. He fought the fear that had been threatening to suffocate him since "coming out" while he was driving. Christ! How stupid had that been?

He glanced up from his plate to find her looking out the window again. It hurt to see her like this. It'd kill him if she started crying.

His eyes went to the ring on her finger. At least she hadn't hurtled it back at him. She hadn't screamed or cursed or called him names. Not that he would have blamed her, though if she had he probably would have wrecked the car.

Her looks might have caught his attention in the first place but it was everything else about her, especially her innate gentleness, that had completely hooked him. She could take care of herself but he found he *liked* taking care of her. She could be tough when she needed to be, but she wasn't afraid to be utterly feminine with him.

Fuck. Maybe they could settle this in bed. Maybe he should find out if there was a hotel in this seven-building town and take Jessica there. He could reassure her with his body that he loved and desired her. Hell, not just loved and desired, but desperately needed her in his life.

Clay rubbed his chest in an effort to erase some of the tightness there. Christ, *need* was too tame a word, especially when it came to sex with Jessica.

He craved it like an addict who was always looking for the next fix. He could be whitewater rafting on rough water and he'd still get hard just thinking about the way she yielded and went submissive when he required that from her. Fuck, more than once when he'd been rock climbing he'd gotten a boner he could have used as a chisel when his mind had strayed to how she'd accepted the rougher aspects of his sexuality — not that he'd ever, ever hurt her.

Yeah right, asshole. Look at her and tell yourself she's one happy camper at the moment.

61

Clay risked another glance and wished he knew what she was thinking. What a fucking mess. They'd been engaged for three months. They'd dated for nine before that. He'd have proposed on the first date, that's how sure he was that she was the right *woman* for him. But she was more cautious by nature, a little less quick to grab for the brass ring than he was, so he'd taken the time she needed.

In retrospect he realized he'd also been testing himself. By the time he'd finally popped the question he'd convinced himself that he was mainly hetero. Yeah, he noticed guys and sometimes he fantasized, but mostly he wanted to fuck Jess.

The last group trip he'd led ripped that false sense of security away like it was toilet paper. He'd been tempted, tempted to the point where only his old ironclad rule to never get involved with paying clients or client employees had kept him from doing something stupid.

Clay's heart thundered in his chest just thinking about how close he'd come on his last trip to trashing any hope for a future with Jess. If he betrayed her with either a man or a woman, she would never forgive him. He'd be out of her life permanently.

It'd been a wake-up call, not just for the present but for the future. He broke into a cold sweat whenever he imagined what might happen down the road. It was easy to envision a situation where she was home with their kids and he was on a trip where there were guys who weren't clients. It would happen in a weak moment, maybe after the rush of conquering some span of water or mountain or maybe just because he'd gone years without being with another man.

Christ, he would lose everything that mattered to him. Everything. Her. Their kids. His self-respect. Everything.

It'd be easy if he could see a shrink and get "cured" or take a pill and bingo, no more urge for gay sex. For Jess, he'd do either of those things—he'd give up an inherent part of himself. But one, those options weren't available. And two, she'd never ask it of him anyway.

He knew Jessica had no problem with someone being gay or bi. Hell, that's what had led to his confession in the car.

He'd intended to wait until they'd gotten to the cabin and settled in for the week. He'd imagined himself telling her after they'd made love in front of a roaring fire. But then she'd started talking to him about a book she was thinking of writing, a teen "coming out" book and *he'd* come out. Christ. Seeing her hurt was tearing him up. Somehow he had to convince her they could work this out.

He didn't want an open marriage where they both screwed around like they were dogs with an itch that could be scratched by anyone. It'd kill him to be with her and wonder if she'd been with someone else earlier.

There'd been a time in his life when he'd been quick to fuck anyone who caught his eye. But even before he'd met Jess, he'd slowed down on the casual sex. Not that he'd been a saint, but deep down he was already waiting for the right person — the right woman. He'd never pictured himself setting up house with another guy. He'd never thought much about what it would mean to be bi and married.

The truth was, he'd never been one to overplan the future. Yeah, he was meticulous about the adventure trips because lives were on the line. But when it came to the big picture of his personal life he trusted that he'd see the brass ring and be ready to grab it when it came along.

He'd seen Jessica and he'd known she was the one. Now he had to hang on to her. The trouble was, the only way he could see that happening was if they were a threesome instead of a twosome.

Clay decided against a hotel room. He'd screwed up by rushing things but he'd have a week alone with Jess to make it right.

Outside the wind gusted even harder than it'd been when he fought his way over from the general store. He knew they'd be better off if they could get ahead of the storm and get to the cabin before the dirt roads leading to it got slick and the danger of mudslides increased. He finished the last of his fries and glanced at Jess's empty plate. "Ready?"

"As soon as I stop by the ladies room."

They both stood. Clay left a tip tucked under the plate then walked to the counter where their waitress stood behind an old-fashioned cash register. Jessica disappeared into the bathroom.

"I'll tell you the same thing I told her," the woman surprised him by saying. "Things have a way of working out if you let them." She took the money he offered and gave him change. Her hand cupped his. "Let the Thunderbird into your lives and you will find happiness."

They left under a sky that continued to darken with gray and black clouds. Thunder pealed in short bursts, the sound moving toward them instead of away. The rain started a short time later.

In the intimacy created by the storm Jessica placed her hand on Clay's thigh and whispered, "I love you."

His hand covered hers. "I love you too." He smoothed his fingers over her engagement ring. "I don't want to lose you, Jess. You're the best thing that's ever happened to me."

Her hand slid upward and found his jeans-covered erection. Clay managed a shaky laugh. "He loves you too. He thinks about you constantly."

When she didn't laugh or make an appreciative comment about his cock as she usually did when he professed its love for her, Clay's chest tightened. He struggled for something else to say, something that would turn back the clock so things were back to normal between them, but there was nothing he could say.

Silence filled the car. He stroked her fingers with his thumb and looked for the turn they were supposed to make.

They were on a dirt road climbing upward before she spoke again. "How many have there been?"

"Male lovers?"

"Yes."

"Not many. Do you really want a number, Jess?" He didn't think she did. Other than a few uncomfortable moments when they'd first started dating and needed to assure themselves they were sexually safe, they'd left previous partners in the past.

She closed her fingers into a fist beneath his hand and rubbed her knuckles against his thigh. "No. I guess what I want to know is if you ever loved any of them."

"Not like I love you. But you're the first woman I've ever felt this way about. The rest were either crushes or fun fucks." Clay gianced at her face but couldn't read her eyes. He struggled with whether or not to let the conversation fade. Finally he said, "I'm done with casual, Jess."

She stayed quiet for long moments before finally whispering, "Somebody could get hurt."

Clay heard the fear that it would be *her* who got hurt. "We'd take it slow, Jess."

Jessica wanted him to say he'd always love her and nothing would change that. She wanted him to promise a threesome would lead only to incredible pleasure and not to unbearable pain. That's what her heart wanted even though her mind knew he couldn't guarantee those things. No one could.

She forced her fingers to unclench and settle back on Clay's thigh. She wasn't sure she could really go through with becoming a threesome. She wasn't sure her heart could handle it. But she wasn't a hypocrite. She'd had fantasies of being with two men at once. She wasn't turned off by the idea of gay sex. In fact, she suspected she'd be turned on watching it if she loved the men involved.

"How would we even find a third person?" she asked and felt the pulse in his leg jump.

Clay's hand nudged hers up and over so she was cupping and rubbing his erection. "I've been so torn up over telling you..." his voice broke. "Christ, I've been so worried about losing you that I haven't gotten past the part where I convince you to keep wearing the engagement ring."

"I'm not sure I can go through with it." This time it was her voice that broke. "I don't want to get hurt."

He glanced over and saw the tears glittering against her cheeks. His throat clogged and burned. "We'll take it slow. Maybe just knowing you accept the need will be enough to keep it manageable. I'd rather cut my dick off than hurt you."

She sniffled and gave a tiny laugh. "I'd rather you not do that. It's one of your best parts and most redeeming features."

Joy surged through Clay at being back on familiar ground. He arched his hips slightly to press his cock into her cupped hand. "He's a big fan of yours too."

Jessica gave Clay's jean-protected penis a little squeeze. "He can show me just how big a fan he is when we get to the cabin."

Clay slowed as they got to a turnoff guarded by totem poles. In the rainy grayness the poles looked surreal, like a moment out of the past.

Jessica could almost hear ancient drums beating. She could almost feel the spirit and promise of the Thunderbirds perched on top of the poles, their wings outstretched as they claimed everything they could see.

"They're beautiful," she said.

"Yeah, they are." Clay's voice contained the awe she felt. He rubbed his thumb against her hand. "We can hike back tomorrow and get a closer look. This turn leads to the local sheriff's house. The next one will take us to our cabin. It's about ten miles from that point." He squeezed her hand before removing his and putting it back on the steering wheel. Jessica missed the contact immediately but compensated by curling her hand around his thigh as she often did when he needed both of his to drive. He chuckled and closed his legs, trapping her fingers there. "I love you, Jess."

"I love you too."

The atmosphere in the car grew tenser as the fury of the storm finally caught up with them. The windshield wipers swiped at water in a frantic pace. The car edged forward at a crawl.

Jessica had the fleeting thought that the storm intended to force them to turn around and retreat from their destination. She jerked in her seat when a crack of thunder was followed by a flash of lightning right above them. A rumbling vibration shook the car and sent instinctive fear rushing through Jessica an instant before Clay hit the gas and they lurched forward.

Something slammed into them and they spun off the road and careened down a steep incline. Jessica screamed as their movement was stopped abruptly and the airbags exploded open then immediately collapsed.

Pure terror filled her when she saw Clay slumped in his seat and not moving. She released her shoulder harness and seat belt and turned into him. She calmed when she saw he was breathing.

Jessica forced the panic from her mind but her hands shook violently as she lightly explored his scalp. There was a knot already forming on the side. He was scraped and the driver side window was a spider-web of cracks where he'd hit it. But none of his bones were at awkward angles and there was only a little bit of blood on the side of his face.

He moaned and the sound lanced through her. His eyes flickered open and she glimpsed uneven pupils before he closed them. She thought *concussion* but her throat tightened and her stomach churned with dread that there might be other injuries she couldn't see.

Clay's hand twitched as though he intended to reach for his seat belt. "Jess?" It came out slurred.

She covered his hand with hers. There was a measure of comfort in the sound of his steady breathing. "I'm right here."

Jessica found her purse and retrieved her cell phone but there was no signal. For a moment she sat perfectly still as her mind raced. She agonized over whether to stay with him a little longer or to go for help.

Clay opened his eyes again and said, "Jess?" His voice was still slurred and confused. She took a deep steadying breath and decided to go for help. The fear he would get worse if she didn't outweighed the fear of leaving him alone.

Jessica found the small tablet of paper she carried in her purse. She left a note in case his confusion cleared, but also in case someone discovered the car while she was gone. She argued with herself about whether to leave him where he was or to try and reposition him on the seat so his head and neck were supported. She cursed herself for not making time to sign up for the first aid class she'd planned on taking when she started going on trips with Clay.

In the end she was afraid she'd do more damage by trying to move him than by leaving him where he was. It almost killed her to get out of the car and walk away from him.

Chapter Two

ဆာ

The totem poles were magnificent up close. They were like great lightning rods serving as both guards and as the focus for a power that sprang from the earth and wind and water. Thunder rumbled as Jessica jogged past the animal faces carved into the wood. The rain eased and she had the oddest sensation that the land itself was aware of her presence.

Her throat tightened as she remembered how often Clay had smiled over her flights of fancy and claimed they were what fed her creativity. "Please let him be okay. Please let me find help," she whispered and the wind picked up as though it was carrying her words away.

Jessica slowed her pace when the stitch in her side returned. She didn't stop moving as she checked her cell phone then put it back in her jacket pocket after seeing only a single bar.

The rain returned in a fierce downpour. It drove against her back as if the storm was targeting her.

Lightning flashed with increasing frequency. Thunder made it hard to hear even the pounding of her own heart.

A cluster of dark clouds twisted and roiled and hurried across the sky in a beautiful, powerful display. The existence of the totem poles and the pureness of her surroundings touched Jessica's artistic soul. For an instant she imagined herself in another life, when survival was a hard struggle and the forces of nature were both a friend and a foe, when a mass of clouds could be a Thunderbird or a spirit guide.

Jessica ducked her head and started jogging again. The stitch was there immediately but she could tolerate it for a little while. The wind against her back made it feel as though she were moving faster. Or maybe it was because the road was slanted and heading into a valley.

She passed a stand of junipers and their scent reminded her of Christmas with Clay and how they'd spent most of the day making love. The tears came without warning. She wiped at them and tried to regain control.

The rain and the tears nearly blinded her. The storm deafened her. She had no warning that a car was approaching until it swung around a corner and captured her in its headlights.

Tekoa knew he'd find her on the road. The land had called to his spirit and brought it back to his body when she'd passed the totem poles. He'd caught a glimpse of her in passing but the hood of her jacket and his own speed had made it impossible to see her face. Now his heart filled with joy, then uncertainty, and finally alarm.

He eased the car to a stop and opened the door. Every instinct demanded that he take her in his arms and tell her everything was fine. Instead he forced himself into his role of sheriff. He forced himself to show no reaction beyond concern and professionalism though every cell in his body tightened when she told him about her injured fiancé.

Tekoa motioned for her to get in the car. He welcomed the darkness of the interior. It was impossible not to think about what it might mean that she already had another man in her life.

He had yet to get a good look at her but he already knew she was his. As a man he wouldn't have known it, but when his spirit had passed over her in the Thunderbird's form it had recognized her as his mate. As *one* of his mates, Tekoa prayed, hoping that pleasure lay ahead for all three of them, though he feared what they would find when they got to the crash site.

His heart was in turmoil and his gut tense. He was afraid that if the Creator had not chosen both Jessica and Clay as mates for him, then Jessica would endure the grief and pain of losing someone she loved before she found happiness again.

The rain eased as they got to the totem poles. Tekoa could feel her worry and see it in the rigid line of her back as she stared out the passenger window.

"It's just a little further," Jessica said. She was so focused on where the edge of the road dropped and sloped downward, that she didn't see Clay's collapsed form until Tekoa stopped the car and her gaze jerked forward. She had the door open in an instant.

Clay was breathing. That was the first thing she checked. She touched his face and shivered at how cold he was. Somehow he'd managed to get out of the car and climb the mud-slick bank back to the road, but with no jacket on, he was completely soaked.

"Let's get him to the car," Tekoa said. "Go open the back doors."

His authoritative voice was a lifeline. It calmed the chaos of her thoughts. Jessica got to her feet and hurried to the car.

Clay's eyes fluttered open when she returned. "Jess?"

Her stomach lurched with the realization that he was still confused. She took a deep breath and tried to convince herself that his being conscious at all was positive, especially after he'd gotten out of the car and climbed up to the road before collapsing. "I'm here. The sheriff's here." She stroked Clay's cheek.

His hand lifted to cover hers. "What happened?"

"A tree got struck by lightning. Part of it fell and hit the car. We went over the bank." She glanced up at the sheriff.

Tekoa leaned over Clay. "Do you remember your name?"

"Clay." His eyelids started to droop but his lips still curled in a smile. "Think I might have a concussion. Had one before."

71

Tekoa lightly tapped Clay's cheek and the eyelids lifted. "Do you hurt anywhere?"

Clay didn't answer right away. Jessica leaned down and kissed his forehead. "Clay?"

"I'm okay. Just my head. And cold." He started shivering as if saying the word had suddenly made him feel it.

"Let's get him to the car," Tekoa said.

"I can walk," Clay said and made a failed effort to sit.

They used a two-person carry to get him to the car.

"How far is it to the hospital?" Jessica asked as she buckled her seat belt then turned to look at Clay's shivering figure stretched out on the backseat.

"Mudslides have several roads blocked right now. Detouring around them would take hours. Some of the roads we'd have to take are extremely rough. Traveling over them could make him worse. It'd be better to get him to my cabin and out of his wet clothes."

Tekoa couldn't stop himself from reaching over and taking her hand. His heart raced when Jessica's fingers curled around his. The feel of her engagement ring against his palm made heat unfurl in his gut. He forced thoughts of what might be from his mind in order to concentrate on getting them back to the cabin safely.

They got Clay inside and laid him on a thick handwoven rug in front of a grated fireplace. "Start getting him out of his wet clothes. I'll get the fire going again," Tekoa said.

He turned toward the fireplace and gasped when he saw the two half-full cups balanced on the Thunderbird his younger brother Ukiah had carved into the mantel. The presence of the cups and, more importantly, the drink they contained meant the union of his spirit with Clay's and Jessica's had been blessed by the Creator. Without such a blessing it was impossible to fully join with someone not of The People.

The presence of the cups also meant he didn't need to worry about any injuries Clay and Jessica might have sustained in the crash. The Creator's gift and the sing he would do for them would heal them.

Tekoa offered a silent song of thanks before kneeling and opening the fireplace grate. While his spirit had become Thunderbird, his human shell had rested on the mat where Clay lay. When he'd been called back and seen Jessica on the road as he traveled overhead, he'd taken only long enough to dress and bank the fire before racing out in the night to claim her. Now the flames came readily to life.

Tekoa kept his back to them. He centered himself as he heard Jessica removing Clay's clothing. They might be the lovers who would share his bed and his life, but at the moment they were strangers who needed his help.

"Do you have a washer?" Jessica asked, her voice curling around Tekoa's cock.

"Yes." He steeled himself against showing any reaction to Clay's nakedness. But when he turned around he nearly pitched forward in sudden lightheadedness at his first true look at Jessica.

With her jacket and sweatshirt off he could see not only the gold of her hair but the feminine curves, and delicate vulnerability of her face, Everything about her was exquisite, soft and gentle and heartwrenchingly beautiful.

It took an extreme effort of will to keep from taking her in his arms and molding her against him. He wanted to bury his face in her hair and feel every line of her.

A blush stole into her cheeks and she looked away in sudden discomfort. He cursed himself for what she must have seen in his face. She was engaged and beyond that, Clay lay at their feet in need of care.

Tekoa stood. "I'll take the wet clothes. We can run them through the washer and dryer in the morning. The cabin uses stored energy. It'll drain the batteries to use the machines now."

He reached for the dripping clothing. She released it without meeting his eyes. Tekoa gave a soft sigh and cursed himself again. She'd removed her shoes and socks, but her jeans were soaked and muddy. "You should get out of anything wet too."

Jessica knew he was right, but other than the clothes she'd been wearing, everything else was still in Clay's car. She wanted to argue that her things would dry quickly. Already tendrils of steam were lifting from the fabric due to the fire in the fireplace, but there was still the mud to consider. She couldn't repay his kindness by coating his furniture with dirt.

He was a sheriff even if he was a man. He wasn't going to think of her as anything but a traveler who needed help. She cleared her throat of the nervousness that had formed a knot there. She started to point out that she didn't have any other clothes with her then thought better of it. His solution would be to offer her something of his and that would be too intimate.

"Okay," she said, though it was more of a croak than a word. She didn't want to leave Clay's side long enough to strip in the bathroom so she ducked her head and fumbled with the wet fabric, unbuttoning and unzipping and finally sliding the jeans down her legs. She couldn't bring herself to remove her panties and hand them to a stranger so she left them.

Jessica retrieved her wet socks from where she'd stuffed them in her shoes. She forced herself to meet the sheriff's gaze as she gave him the bundle of wet things. "Thanks."

"You're welcome." His face reflected nothing but professionalism and she relaxed.

Jessica returned to Clay's side as the sheriff left the room. In the glow of the firelight she thought Clay looked battered but otherwise fine. He'd stopped shivering and actually seemed to be resting peacefully.

Pain ripped through Jessica. If she'd lost him...

She placed her hand on his chest and took comfort in the steady beat of his heart. He mumbled something but didn't open his eyes.

The sheriff returned and knelt on the other side of Clay. "When one of my people is sick or injured we perform a healing ceremony for them. If you'd allow it, I would do one for your fiancé."

Jessica's eyes widened with surprise. For the first time she allowed herself to really look at the man across from her. She'd registered that he was Native American, and on some level she'd acknowledged that his features were strong and handsome. But with all her focus on Clay, she hadn't truly *seen* him.

Now that she was looking, she felt nervous and uncertain and guilty. He sent heat curling through her womb and her breasts in a way usually reserved for Clay.

She ducked her head to cover the sudden confusion of emotion. She blurted out the first thing that came to mind. "Is it like one of the ceremonies in the Tony Hillerman stories?"

The sheriff laughed. "No. I'm not like Officer Chee. Nor am I one of the Dineh, the Navajo."

Jessica glanced up and smiled in response to the sheriff's smile. "What are you then?"

"The name wouldn't be familiar to you. But in English you would call us the People of the Thunderbird." He placed his hand over hers where it rested above Clay's heart. "And you would call me Tekoa. Will you allow me to do a healing for him?"

"Yes," Jessica said, unable to look away from where her hand was trapped between Clay's skin and Tekoa's. There was rightness about it, as though it was somehow symbolic.

When Tekoa finally lifted his hand from hers she lifted her eyes to meet his. "Can I watch?"

Her innocent question sent a tremor through Tekoa but he quickly closed his mind to the carnal images it evoked. "You can stay in the room but I'll ask you to close your eyes." He couldn't stop himself from resting his hand on her shoulder when she frowned. It was killing him to go so slowly, to have so little information about Jessica and Clay. "There will be nothing to see, only to hear."

"Okay. Where do you want me?"

Tekoa glanced away, afraid she might read the answer in his eyes and know he wanted her in bed but he'd take her anywhere. "You're fine where you are. When I begin you won't be able to touch him." He rose to his feet. "I want to change into more traditional clothing. It'll take me a few minutes."

Jessica watched him as he walked to the far end of the cabin and opened a dresser next to the bed. He moved with the same easy confidence that Clay did, like he was a man comfortable in his skin.

Tekoa found the clothing he wanted and crossed to the bathroom. Their eyes met and held until she looked away. He slipped inside and closed the door behind him.

Jessica looked down and caught herself unconsciously rubbing her fingertip over Clay's tiny male nipple. She stilled. Emotion blocked her throat. So much had happened in such a short period of time. "Clay," she whispered, suddenly needing reassurance that he was going to be okay, that *they* were going to be okay.

His eyelids fluttered open. The pupils were still uneven but she didn't think they were worse than they had been.

Jessica leaned over and brushed a kiss against his lips. "How do you feel?"

"Sleepy." He blinked rapidly. "Concussion, right?"

"Yes."

He closed his eyes. She thought he'd gone back to sleep until he mumbled, "Didn't mean to get off to such a bad start."

"We'll be back on track soon." She kissed him lightly again but when he didn't stir Jessica straightened and studied their surroundings.

Tekoa's home was essentially a single large room, though two short walls extended out to form an alcove for a small office, and a counter separated the rest of the cabin from the kitchen. There were several closed doors beside the one leading to the bathroom, but since his bed was visible, she assumed the other doors led to closets.

Even without the warmth of the fire she thought his home would always feel cozy and welcoming. The furniture was chosen for comfort and the room was adorned with some astonishingly beautiful nature photographs as well as a mix of Native American art and crafts.

There were carved animal figures tucked away in the bookcases and on various other surfaces, including a collection on the kitchen counter. A pair of totem poles stood guard on either side of the door they'd come through when they arrived. She smiled when she saw them and wondered if Tekoa had made them. It would explain why he had so many figurines, unless he collected them, or had a girlfriend who carved them.

Jessica glanced to the bathroom and the door opened. Her breath caught in her throat when Tekoa came out. It was like seeing a warrior step from of the past. The jeans and flannel shirt he'd been wearing were gone, as was the single braid his hair had been confined to.

Now he wore only a loincloth. His hair fell in thick black waves over his shoulders and back. On either side of his face, feathers and beads had been woven into a thin braid. He was man stripped of civilization and returned to his raw, powerful essence.

Despite the wrongness of it, Jessica felt herself respond physically. Her womb fluttered and her cunt lips grew swollen and wet. Her breasts grew heavy and achy the way they did in those first seconds when she saw Clay after being separated from him for more than a few hours.

Their eyes met and held as they'd done earlier. In her imagination there was possessiveness and determination in Tekoa's gaze. She shivered in response.

Unbidden, a picture flashed in her thoughts. She saw herself naked and waiting on a blanket for him to come to her. Her heart rate sped up and Jessica forced the image away in guilt and confusion.

She lowered her gaze but despite a heart that was loyal to Clay and a conscience that demanded she close her eyes, she found herself staring at Tekoa's loincloth and noticing the erection straining against the soft material. She couldn't look away as he closed the distance between them.

Shame and embarrassment swamped her when he said, "If you'll shut your eyes, I'll start now." Added heat rushed to Jessica's face when she realized she'd been stroking Clay's abdomen the entire time she'd been looking at Tekoa. She put her hands in her lap and closed her eyes.

Tekoa's voiced filled the cabin. It started low and slow but grew louder and faster. The words were foreign and unrecognizable, yet they resonated through Jessica, their rhythm timeless, like a chord that linked her soul to not only the past, but to the power that was earth and wind and water and fire.

He hadn't been holding a drum when he knelt on the other side of Clay. But in her mind she could hear one and its beat was a heart growing stronger, louder, returning to health.

Tears rolled down her cheeks in a purging of emotion, called from her as if the song and the drum were reaching into the place left raw by Clay's confession, and trying to heal her. She wiped at the tears without opening her eyes. She willed herself to gain some control over her chaotic emotions.

Tekoa's voice grew low and slow again. It touched her soul and she turned her face away, afraid that even without seeing her eyes he would glimpse her terrible fear of losing Clay and ending up hurt and alone.

The song built and gathered power. It blended and merged with the phantom drum as they raced to a thundering crescendo that left Jessica gasping and opening her eyes.

She looked down at Clay first and found him smiling at her. It took her a second to notice the evenness of his pupils. "You're okay?" she whispered.

"Yeah, I'm okay now. I remember driving past the totem poles, but beyond that, things get fuzzy." He took her hand in his and squeezed.

Jessica knew the exact moment Clay became aware of Tekoa at his other side. He turned his head slightly. She saw him blink in surprise before his hand loosened on hers as if suddenly he'd forgotten she was there.

Clay took in all of Tekoa. His gaze settled for an instant on the loincloth-covered erection and Jessica saw the burning sexual interest in Clay's eyes. He masked it quickly but his cock told the truth by hardening.

She glanced at Tekoa and found his gaze now locked on Clay's as though they were assessing each other as potential lovers. The uncertainty and fear and confusion she'd been battling since Clay's revelation struck in a painful jolt and she knew she couldn't deal with anything more. Not now anyway. She was emotionally and physically drained.

Jessica pulled her hand from Clay's and stood. "I'll be back. I need some fresh air. I'm going to step outside for a few minutes."

Tekoa stood as well. Cop instinct and the ability to read a situation took over where a second before he'd been healer and Thunderbird spirit. His hand grasped Jessica's arm and kept her from escaping the room. He'd let her go in a minute. But even without a discussion between them he knew Clay was bisexual and she was aware of it. He also knew she was physically attracted to him though she was fighting it.

It was a start. But like cracking a witness for a case, he knew if he gave her time to shore up her defenses and rewrite her memories then any progress that might have been made in the short time they'd been together would be lost.

It was a gut read and he didn't stop to question himself. He didn't stop to question whether it was his little head doing the thinking or his big one. He just reacted. The three of them were meant to be together and he wanted to get it out in the open now.

Tekoa tangled his free hand in her hair and leaned in. Her eyes widened but by the time she tried to pull away his lips were on hers.

He didn't force his tongue into her mouth. He didn't coax or tease or try to get her to open for him. He bit and sucked and took control in a possessive kiss that didn't allow her a chance to run away or deny her physical response to him.

Tekoa could feel her hardened nipples through her shirt and bra. He could feel her body yield and knew in a heartbeat that she liked a dominant lover.

A searing wave of lust burned through his cock. He wanted her. Here. Now. With Clay watching.

She shivered as her barriers dropped. She whimpered as she parted her lips under the onslaught of his. It took every ounce of control for him to keep from plunging into the wet heat of her mouth and mimicking what he wanted to do to her with his cock.

He didn't want to push Jessica too far, too fast. He didn't want to back her into an emotional corner where running or fighting became her only options.

Tekoa gentled the kiss. His tongue breached the seam of her lips but only long enough to rub and slide against hers in several slow passes before he lifted his mouth and let her go.

Panic, confusion, desire, guilt, fear. Her emotions were easy for him to read in the seconds before she turned away and escaped to the porch.

Chapter Three

Clay's heart thundered in his chest as he got to his feet. His hands balled into fists only he didn't know who deserved the punch, him for responding physically to another man in front of Jess, or the other man for coming on to Jess.

Fuck.

Clay's cock jerked in reaction to the word. Christ. He couldn't help it. One minute he'd been completely out of it. The next minute there'd been this incredible warmth. It'd been like a hand stroking over and through his body.

He'd slowly become aware of the singing, and beyond that a drum beating, controlling the rhythm of his heart. As the heat spread in his veins there'd been a sense of coming home, of rightness.

On some level he'd known there was a man there with Jess. Fuck. He'd been half aroused even before he opened his eyes. Then when he did he'd felt trapped in a dream state where it was impossible to lie.

Tekoa. He is the one you were hoping to find. The words had whispered through Clay's mind. His cock had hardened as he looked at Tekoa and saw the answering desire in the other man's eyes. He couldn't have turned away in those first few seconds if he'd wanted too. Only Jessica pulling her hand from his had brought reality crashing down on him.

Clay speared his fingers through his hair in frustration and agony. His heart demanded that he go to Jessica even if it meant standing bare-assed naked out in the cold, but his head—the big one that was actually doing the thinking despite what his dick was saying—told him she needed some space.

Clay turned his attention to the man standing less than an arm's distance away. "I owe you, but... Fuck. I don't want Jess hurt. It was a tough day *before* the car went off the road. So lay off. Okay? Don't push her." Christ, he couldn't believe he was still hard. But he couldn't seem to shake the rightness of it. He couldn't seem to fight the feeling that somehow everything that had happened, starting in the car with Jessica's first mention of writing a teen coming-out book and his subsequent confession about being bi, had led to this place, this man, this moment.

"Fuck," he repeated and was startled into a laugh when Tekoa said, "We'll get to that. But at the moment you need some clothes." He glanced toward the door Jessica had escaped through. "And she's probably ready for some reassurance."

Tekoa reached over and casually picked up a wooden cup from the mantel above the fireplace. He handed it to Clay. "Drink this."

Clay shuddered as the honey-warm liquid slid down his throat. It was so much like what he'd experienced earlier that he had to shut his eyes against the pleasure.

Intense need spiraled through him and he wanted to reach for his cock. He wanted to reach for Tekoa's as well. Instead Clay balled one hand into a fist while the other clenched the mug. Some of the heat faded but the edgy awareness and need remained. "Christ, you just drugged me."

Tekoa's laughed. "Hardly. My constituents wouldn't be happy with me if I did that."

Clay opened his eyes and leaned over to put the empty cup back on the mantel. For a moment he was mesmerized by the Thunderbird carved into the rich wood. "Constituents?"

"I'm sheriff here."

Clay's attention jerked back to Tekoa. His gaze traveled down the hard, tanned body wearing nothing but a loincloth.

It took all his control not to linger on the erection pressed against the front of the material. "And healer?"

"Not usually. But for you and Jessica, yes." Tekoa's hand settled on Clay's shoulder. "The land brought the two of you here, but we can take it slow."

Another erotic shudder passed through Clay at hearing both his own thoughts and his earlier words to Jessica come from Tekoa's lips. His cock jerked in warning and this time Clay couldn't keep from taking it in hand to appease the ache. He gritted his teeth and forced himself not to stroke upward over the pulsing, leaking tip. He was afraid of what might happen if he did.

Tekoa's hand fell away. Clay wanted to protest the loss, but didn't. Jess had to come first, literally and figuratively. If she accepted Tekoa on her side of the bed then she would accept Tekoa on *his* side as well.

"I've got some sweats you can wear," Tekoa said, moving to the dresser. His rapid escape made Clay smile. He might be naked and hard but at least he wasn't suffering alone.

He glanced down at where his hand encircled his penis. Yeah, he'd always been one to grab for the brass ring when it presented itself, but right now he felt like he was wearing a cock ring. Christ. It took concentration and willpower. And even then he felt like he was prying his hand away from his dick one finger at a time.

He managed it. Barely.

Tekoa tossed Clay the sweats from several feet away. Clay slipped the pants on and felt his cock leak against the soft fabric. His breath caught as lust surged through him. He'd worn borrowed clothes before but this was intimate, unbearably erotic. A T-shirt followed. "You can take my jacket if you want," Tekoa said, nodding toward where it hung on a peg next to the door. "Jessica didn't stop for hers. She might be ready to come in now." He closed the distance between them and took a second cup from the mantel. "Get her to drink this.

She was hurt too, but I could only do so much to heal her during the sing. I'll be dressed when you get back in with her. Maybe we can play cards or something, spend some time getting to know each other."

Clay took the cup. His eyes met Tekoa's and he could read the need there, the same aching desire to feel another man's touch that had Clay's chest and balls and cock burning. But he also saw something else there, the willingness to wait, to take it slow, because it wasn't just about the two of them, it was about Jessica too.

"Yeah, that's a good idea. Jess likes to play cards." Clay took a deep breath. "She didn't know until today. She's trying to find a way to handle it. And she's still wearing the engagement ring. That's something." His hand tightened on the cup. His gut echoed the words that had come to him earlier, that Tekoa was the one, but his conscience and his love for Jessica wouldn't allow him to move forward without saying, "She's fragile right now. I won't let you near her if you're just looking to fuck a couple of stranded tourists until they head back home."

Tekoa's eyes narrowed. Clay imagined he saw a dark, turbulent sky with flashes of lightning in them but he stood his ground. It'd turned him on to see Jessica's body go soft and yielding as another man took her lips, but it'd pissed him off too. Jess wasn't a casual conquest and he wouldn't share her easily.

The storm in Tekoa's eyes settled. He put his hand on Clay's shoulder again. "You're home now. I'm not looking for a quick meaningless fuck."

Clay exhaled and gave a nod. He felt the truth in Tekoa's words even though he didn't intend to explore the metaphysical stuff that swirled around them like a dense fog. He'd leave that to Jess. Going with his gut instinct had always worked for him. "I'll go check on Jess."

"Give her the cup." Tekoa's eyes bored into his. "It's important that she drink what's in it."

"Sure. First thing."

Clay turned away before he could give in to the urge to lean forward and kiss Tekoa. Christ, he was hard.

Jessica glanced up when he stepped out onto the porch. It was still raining though the storm seemed to have calmed somewhat.

She shivered from the cold and he wished he'd grabbed Tekoa's jacket so he could put it around her. "Drink this, it'll warm you up," he said, passing the cup and watching as she drained the contents.

His cock pulsed when she gave a soft moan as heat spread across her cheeks. "What was that?" she asked and he nearly panted at the husky timbre of her voice.

"Don't know. Something to go with the healing. That was pretty cool, wasn't it? Shades of Tony Hillerman. Maybe you can work it into the next story you write."

Clay took the cup from her hand and placed it on the porch banister. "Jess," he whispered, slowly putting his hands on her sides and pulling her to him so that their bodies were flush.

She stiffened when she felt his erection. Clay was ready for that. He rubbed his cock against her mound. "If I weren't afraid of him catching pneumonia after all he's been through today, I'd pull these sweats down so he could greet you properly." He felt her smile through the thin T-shirt a second before her body relaxed against his with a cold shiver. Clay hugged her more tightly. "Let's go inside, baby, and get to know each other." He paused for a heartbeat before adding, "Or if it'd make you feel better, we could ask Tekoa to take us to the nearest town with a hotel. Hell, maybe there's a place to rent rooms in Hohoq."

Jessica slid her arms around his waist. "You don't really want to leave."

Clay rubbed his cheek against her rain-dampened hair. "No." He nuzzled until he found her ear. She whimpered when he licked into the sensitive canal. "You're attracted to him, Jess. I'm attracted to him. Why not see where it goes and how we feel about it? There's no rush. We're safe, we're dry. It doesn't make sense to try and do anything about the car until tomorrow." He recaptured her earlobe and sucked until her hands pushed up under the T-shirt he was wearing. "And besides that, I feel right about being here." Clay pulled back so he could study at her face. "Do you feel it too?"

When Jessica tried to look away he speared his fingers through her hair and kept her from avoiding the question. "No hiding from the truth, Jess. No secrets. That's the only way it could work. So I'll go first. It turned me on to see him kissing you. It made me even harder seeing you go soft and submissive the same way you do for me when I need that from you." His free hand fondled her breast. His palm rubbed over the hard point of her shirt-covered nipple. "At least admit you're attracted to him."

Jessica's heart thundered and her cunt clenched as more arousal escaped to coat her swollen labia. Despite the coldness of the air her womb burned and fluttered and ached with a need that was so primal she wanted to push her panties down and beg him to fill her with his cock.

It would be easy to claim it was nothing more than her body's way of handling the fear of losing him. It would be tempting to claim something in the drink he'd given her had heightened the need. Both would be true, but they weren't the only reason she felt so needy, so desperate for Clay to make love to her and reassure her with his body.

She was scared by just how right being here felt and how quickly it had happened. She was nervous and unsettled by the intensity of her response to Tekoa and how easy it was to imagine herself spreading her thighs and letting him push his cock deep inside her.

"Admit it, Jess," Clay whispered. "Admit you're attracted to him."

She shuddered and gave up the battle. "I admit it."

Clay leaned forward and took her mouth in a soft, reassuring kiss. "Good. Now let's get inside before Tekoa has to do another healing ceremony."

Jessica turned slightly, intending to pick up the cup but it was no longer on the railing. Clay grunted and leaned over to peer at the ground. "Must have fallen off and rolled somewhere. I don't see it. Let's get you inside, Jess, then I'll look for it."

They stepped into the cabin. The sheer bliss of the warmth coming from the fireplace made Jessica moan softly as it sank into her and joined the liquid heat that spiraled through her from the drink.

Clay flipped a light switch and turned to go back out. "What's up?" Tekoa asked.

"The cup fell off the porch and rolled. I couldn't see where it went."

"Don't worry about it. Just crash in front of the fire. You guys want something to eat? It's bachelor cooking but I haven't died of food poisoning or killed anyone else with it yet."

Jessica laughed and despite the tightness of her nipples and the fluttering in her cunt she found herself relaxing. "Let me help."

Tekoa made a sweeping gesture toward the kitchen area. "It's all yours."

Clay followed her as far as the counter separating the kitchen from the rest of the cabin. He pulled out one of the bar stools and settled on it.

Tekoa moved to her side. "Canned goods here. Next one over is baking stuff. There's meat in the freezer, and some ground beef in the fridge. I've also got some fresh vegetables in the fridge. I think there's still a loaf of homemade bread in box next to Clay's elbow." Tekoa leaned against the counter. "If there's something else you think you might need, just ask."

Jessica's pussy clenched as her eyes settled on his jeans-covered erection. She licked her lips nervously and his cock flexed against the material. For a second she wondered if he'd meant something else by his offer to give her anything else she might need, but when her gaze lifted to Tekoa's, his expression didn't give even a hint of his thoughts.

A blush worked itself across her cheeks. She reached for several of the cans and was pleased at how steady her hands were despite the barrage of emotions that seemed to flare up with only the slightest provocation. It made her remember her first date with Clay. She'd been hopeful and afraid and horny, unsettled then too. Jessica's lips curved upward. She glanced at Clay. She'd also felt deliciously alive and extremely desirable. It was something she still felt whenever she was with him.

His eyelids lowered and his face tightened. They knew each other so well he'd probably guessed what she was thinking and why she'd been thinking it.

Jessica shivered under his regard. He never bothered to hide what he felt for her. Right now his look said he wanted to strip her out of the shirt and panties and make love to her.

She turned away. This time there was a small tremor in her hand when she reached for another can. She wondered what she'd do if he ordered her to take her remaining clothes off and brace her hands against the counter. Part of her wished Clay would take the decision away from her and simply make her accept Tekoa as a lover. But the part of her that loved and trusted him completely was glad he'd never do something like that. He could be a thoroughly dominating lover, but he was also a sensitive, caring man who treated her as an equal and yet still made her feel incredibly treasured.

"Pots and pan?" she asked and was amazed at how calm her voice sounded.

Tekoa pushed away from the counter. "What do you need?"

"One of each. How does chili with a salad and the homemade bread sound to you guys?"

Tekoa's stomach answered with a grumble before either man could speak. Jessica laughed and threw herself into the refuge of cooking. By the time it was done and the meal eaten, she felt as though the three of them had known each other for years.

"I'll take care of the dirty dishes since the two of you worked on the meal," Clay said, sliding out of his chair and moving to stand behind Jessica's.

Tekoa pushed his chair back but didn't stand. "There's no dishwasher. Uses too much power."

Clay grinned. "I'm used to doing it the old-fashioned way. There never seems to be a dishwasher handy when I'm camping." He leaned down and nuzzled Jessica. "And there's almost never such an edible cook."

His hand settled on her belly and Jessica's nipples tightened. Clay's mouth nibbled around to catch her gasp as his fingers glanced over her clit underneath the table.

Desperate lust flashed through her as if it'd been simmering below the surface and all it took was a single touch to ignite it. She closed her legs in fear that his fingers would discover the slick arousal coating her inner thighs. If he did he'd never be able to resist the urge to slip his hand underneath the elastic of her panties and play with her.

She couldn't afford to let him touch her so intimately. She was already riding a thin emotional edge, already needy and so close to orgasm that his experienced touches would make her lose control.

Clay's tongue forged into Jessica's mouth and rubbed against hers in retaliation for her denying him access to her cunt. Christ, he hadn't meant to start this. Yeah, he had a raging hard-on, but when he leaned down he'd only planned to torture himself with a quick touch of her skin against his.

He'd been thrilled beyond words with how things had gone since he and Jess came inside. She might not realize it yet, but she and Tekoa had slipped into the same easy kitchen routine that the two of them shared at home, with her directing the action, pointing at cans to be opened or onions to be chopped, while he served as assistant. And dinner...Clay didn't see how it could have gone any better. He didn't see how there could ever be a better third for them. The conversation was free flowing, light and serious and everything in between. There were so many points of common interest. There were so many ways they were a good fit. The sexual tension shimmering underneath only amplified that fact.

Clay wanted to force Jess's thighs apart and slide his hand into her panties. He wanted to cup her mound and feel her wet heat. He wanted to fuck her with his fingers and swallow her scream.

She'd come for him if he wanted it. Here. Now. With Tekoa watching. Clay had never had a woman respond to him the way Jess did. When she'd given her heart and her body to him, she'd given him everything, including her complete trust.

He made himself end the kiss. "I'd better get to the dishes. Why don't you two decide what we're going to play? I'm fine with anything, but Tekoa mentioned cards earlier."

Tekoa rose from the table as if he didn't notice Clay's erection or Jessica's flushed features and beaded nipples. It took her several seconds before she followed him to where he stood in front of an opened cabinet next to the television set.

Despite her heightened awareness and aching arousal she marveled at how well Tekoa used what space he had in the cabin. The shelves were built into the wall and housed an impressive collection of board games as well as a rack of poker chips and several decks of cards, both opened and unopened.

She glanced sideways and found him watching her. "What's your preference?"

His smile reached into her chest and stroked her heart. "Lady's choice."

"Don't let her choose Scrabble," Clay said from his position in front of the sink. "Being a writer gives her an unfair advantage. The last time I beat her was six months ago, after she'd been drinking."

Jessica laughed and reached into the cabinet. She picked up a poker chip and studied it. Not all of them were created equal. By the weight and feel of the one in her hand she knew Tekoa wasn't a casual player.

"My purse is still in Clay's car. In all the panic to get help and then to get him taken care of, I forgot about it."

"We can keep the stakes low. I'm sure you're good for the money." Tekoa reached over and pushed a stray tendril of hair away from her face. It was a casual, intimate gesture that made Jessica's heart race and her womb flutter. She had a sudden vision of the three of them playing strip poker.

"Poker it is," she said, turning away before he could read what she was thinking in her eyes.

Tekoa grinned and took the opportunity to boldly survey the long, tanned legs left bare below the shirt he'd loaned her when she'd showered while the chili was cooking. He was making progress with her. Jessica's sudden retreat and the unconscious way she was rubbing the poker chip told him that.

His body tightened with thoughts of how it would feel to have those same fingers stroking his flesh, exploring his sac and his cock. A moan nearly escaped as he thought about having those beautiful legs wrapped around his waist as she clung to him in passion.

Tekoa picked up the chip rack in one hand and the cards in the other in order to keep both hands busy. She was killing him, turning him into one huge erotic ache.

He glanced at the mantel above the fireplace. His heart and cock swelled with sweet emotion and carnal anticipation.

The cups had been offered and the contents accepted by Clay and Jessica. Now it was up to the three of them to find their way to intimacy.

They played until well past midnight, only stopping when all the chips were stacked in colorful towers in front of a grinning Clay. "Same time, same place tomorrow?"

"I'm in," Tekoa said. He rose and stretched. His gaze went to the bed. He longed to be at the point where all three of them would settle there and find the ultimate peace of ending one day and beginning the next in each other's arms. If he couldn't have that, then he would at least have the satisfaction of knowing Clay and Jessica were in his bed. "Since there are two of you and only one of me, you take the bed. I'll crash on the sofa."

Jessica made a small sound of protest but before she could verbalize it Clay's arm went around her shoulders. "Sounds good to me," he said. His eyebrows lifted and fell several times in a parody of lasciviousness. "Maybe we can find a way for you to pay off your chip debt, babe."

Jessica's cheeks flushed. Her eyes flashed to Tekoa then back to Clay. In a heartbeat sexual tension replaced the friendly competitiveness that had masked it while they played cards.

For an instant Tekoa was afraid Clay's comment would erase the progress they'd made and cause Jessica to retreat. She surprised him by recovering first.

Jessica slapped Clay's thigh and said, "You were more endearing when you had a concussion."

Clay leaned in and nuzzled her. He started to tell her he was more than willing to lie down and pretend he was helpless again while she kissed him back to health.

He didn't even care where her lips started, as long as they ended up on his cock. His penis jerked. A bead of arousal escaped to wet the tip along with the soft cotton of Tekoa's sweatpants.

Clay closed his eyes and breathed deeply. Jessica's scent was overlaid with the smell of Tekoa's soap and shampoo.

Christ, he wanted them both.

Clay burrowed through her silky hair until his mouth found her earlobe. She shivered and tried to pull away but his arm across her chest prevented it.

From the first moment he'd seen her it'd been like this between them. A look, a touch, sometimes only a single word, and the heat swamped them, the need overpowered them.

He fought against the intense desire to suck her earlobe, to trace the delicate shell of her ear and then slide his tongue into the sensitive canal. Jess would go up in flames if he did that.

She'd spread her legs and welcome his hand between her thighs. She'd whimper as his fingers slipped underneath her panties and glided over her clit before pressing into her hot sheath.

She'd be wet. So, so wet.

He could finger-fuck her until she was begging for his cock. He'd done it often enough since they first became intimate to be completely confident about her response. And once he got her that far she wouldn't fight him if he pulled her panties off and placed her on the table.

She'd take his cock. She'd take Tekoa's cock.

But it wouldn't really be her choice. It wouldn't be the way it needed to be. It wouldn't be taking it slow, like he'd promised they'd do.

"Let's go to bed, Jess," Clay whispered. His voice was husky and hoarse with need. He didn't try to hide his intentions. He was going to fuck her. And even though she would try to be quiet so her moans and whimpers didn't fill the dark cabin, she'd know Tekoa was nearby. She'd know Tekoa was aware of what they were doing and was imagining himself on the bed with them. She'd wonder if Tekoa's fingers were locked around his own cock, gliding up and down in time to the sounds of Clay's body pounding into hers.

"Bed," Clay said, stepping away from her. He took her arm and helped her stand. Victory rushed through him at the way her nipples pressed hard and tight against the front of Tekoa's shirt, at the way her head was tilted so her hair shielded her face.

He let her go so she could hit the bathroom before climbing into bed. As she walked away his attention stayed on her, lingered on the curve of her ass and her long, sleek legs before she disappeared behind a closed door.

Clay turned and found Tekoa near the fireplace. Their eyes met, held, then traveled downward, each noting the muscled firmness and aroused state of the other. When Clay's gaze returned to Tekoa's face, Tekoa's mouth curved upward in a wry smile. "Enjoy the bed. I have a feeling the couch is going to be sheer torture."

Clay moved to stand near Tekoa. They didn't touch though the need radiated off them both.

"I was afraid this would be harder," Clay said. He felt as if a hot wire was leading right from Tekoa's dick to his own.

Tekoa laughed. "If it gets any harder you'll be taking what's left of me to the emergency room. But I know what you mean, despite the painful choice of words."

Another round of cock-jerking lust seared through Clay. He wanted Jess with an intensity that would have become an obsession if she'd left him. But he wanted this too. He wanted to feel masculine hands, masculine lips on his body. He wanted to feel Tekoa's cock penetrating him just as he wanted to thoroughly explore Tekoa's body before sliding into his tight back entrance.

It'd been so long. He craved it. And yet it was more than just the need for sex. Thanks to what he had with Jess, he'd experienced the ultimate and unparalleled pleasure of being intimate with someone he loved completely. The love would come with Tekoa, Clay didn't doubt that for a moment. The respect and friendship were already there. The shared purpose and sexual attraction made it seem like they already *were* together in the most meaningful sense.

Clay knew that once he and Tekoa were lovers, once they were a threesome with Jess, he'd never be tempted again like he'd been on his last trip. He'd never have to live through the gut-wrenching fear of one day losing everything because in a weak moment he'd cheated with another man.

"I'll find a way to leave the two of you alone tomorrow," Clay said.

Tekoa's smile was slow and sensual and made Clay want to slide his hand beneath the borrowed sweatpants in order to take his cock in hand. Or better yet, push the pants off his hips and let Tekoa do it.

The bathroom door began to open. Tekoa's eyes reflected hunger. "I'll turn off the lights once you two are settled. But I'm not in a hurry to get to sleep."

Clay shivered with dark anticipation and primal awareness. Tekoa meant to do more than just listen to what was about to take place on the bed, he intended to watch as well.

Chapter Four

Clay laughed softly as he eased between the sheets. Jessica was still wearing the flannel shirt even though they both knew he wouldn't allow it to stay on for very long.

Even the ultra-sexy nightgowns and teddies she paraded around in at home didn't last once they got to the bedroom. He liked her naked and she liked being that way for him.

Clay rolled up on to one elbow and kicked the sheets and blankets down past their feet. The fire made any kind of covering completely unnecessary. But then he knew that wasn't why she'd pulled them up to begin with.

He didn't intend to let her hide.

"I love you," he said, keeping his voice to a whisper.

His fingers went to the front of her shirt. She made a small murmur of protest. He silenced it by covering her lips with his and forging into the wet heat of her mouth with his tongue.

It took only seconds to dispense with the buttons and push the shirt aside. His hand stroked over her belly and found the elastic of her panties. He jerked them down roughly and tossed them away from the bed in a gesture that said the shirt had been pushing it but the panties were an outrage.

She wasn't going to deny him. They both knew that. She needed him as desperately as he needed her.

For an instant he flashed back to the moment the car had started to slide off the road. Christ, he could have lost her to a rockslide or a tree, or a hundred other things that could have gone wrong. Instead everything had turned out all right, better than all right.

Clay cupped her mound and she whimpered. Her clit stabbed his palm. It was a tight, hard knob that he knew how to handle.

He rubbed over it and she bucked. He did it again and she opened her thighs.

She was wet. So, so wet. Just like he knew she would be.

He fucked her mouth with his tongue. He fucked her cunt with his fingers.

Her soft whimpers always filled him with intense satisfaction. She could never be completely quiet when they made love.

If he lifted his lips from hers she'd say his name. She'd ask him prettily to make love to her. Or she'd beg him to fuck her if that's what he wanted.

Christ. Tekoa didn't have to worry about it being over too soon. Once was never enough with Jess.

Clay's cock pulsed. He could feel Tekoa watching, getting off on the sight of them making love. It turned Clay on, just as he knew that watching Tekoa fuck Jess would have him jacking off and panting and coming all over himself when they came.

Tekoa's hand moved in time to Clay's. The glide of rough palm over soft foreskin was exquisite and at the same time unbearable. The steady pull on his cock, the rhythm as he matched Clay's movements kept Tekoa both in his body and hovering above it in a spirit-place where he was neither fully man nor completely Thunderbird.

Erotic lightning burned in his veins and flickered through his penis. Clouds of lust massed in his chest and crashed together in violent, rapid peels of thunder that served as his heartbeat.

Tomorrow he would mate with her. Tomorrow it would be him eating at her lips as his cock filled her and his hips jerked in a timeless dance of procreation. Tomorrow he would be the one to swallow her sounds of pleasure, to hear his name whispered in a husky voice.

Tekoa panted. He arched and struggled to avoid coming as his spirit-eyes watched Clay's mouth leave Jessica's and move downward.

Her breasts were perfect, as beautiful as the rest of her. He moaned when Clay's mouth captured one dusky nipple. He wanted to capture the other.

It was easy to imagine both of them pleasuring her in perfect sync with one another, suckling at her breasts then moving to her cunt. Their lips and tongues touching, sharing the taste and texture, the wonderful feminine mystery and finding utter ecstasy with each other at the same time they loved Jessica.

Tekoa's balls pulled tight. White-hot shards of sensation spiked through his cock in warning.

Sweat coated his body and he knew that if Jessica and Clay weren't already lost to passion they'd hear his breathing. They'd hear the creaking of the sofa and know by the tempo that he was close to spewing his seed across his abdomen.

There was no way he could look away. Clay's face was above Jessica's pussy. Clay's hands were on her thighs, holding her splayed, open, so it was easy to see her swollen, parted cunt lips. They were bare beneath a tiny triangle of golden pubic hair, flushed, glistening with arousal, so tempting that Tekoa didn't know how Clay withstood the urge to press his mouth against her sweet, wet flesh and consume her.

"Grab the headboard," Clay growled and she obeyed him immediately.

Tekoa tightened his fingers on his cock. He imagined securing her wrists and ankles to the bedframe. He imagined having her love, and with it the complete trust that Clay already possessed.

Clay glanced at the sofa, as though he could sense Tekoa watching. His eyebrows drew together in puzzlement. It lasted only a second, until Jessica's whispered *please* had him lowering his face.

Jessica gasped as Clay's tongue swirled over her knob. She bucked when his lips formed a seal around it and he began sucking. She needed to stay quiet. She fought to stay quiet and yet at the same time it was darkly erotic to know they weren't alone.

Clay's tongue stroked and rubbed aggressively. He growled against her flesh and sucked hungrily.

A cry escaped. Then another.

She was panting. Whimpering.

Jessica tried to get it under control but he wouldn't let her. He never did. He wouldn't stop until she came. *Fair's fair, babe,* he'd told her more than once. *You know how much I like it when you suck my cock.*

She did. When he wasn't away on a trip she'd take him into her mouth almost every day, sometimes twice or three times a day. It was an incredible high knowing she could give him so much pleasure. It made her feel powerful and feminine, adored and completely loved. Clay always gave as good as he got.

Jessica's hips jerked as his tongue flicked back and forth over the bare head of her clit. It was like a small penis, something she'd thought before but never dwelled on. It hadn't seemed important then. But now...

Unbidden pictures came to mind. Of Clay and Tekoa touching each other's cocks. Of Tekoa standing behind Clay and holding Clay's cock in his hand while she sucked and licked until Clay was completely helpless between them, of Clay doing the same as she pleasured Tekoa.

Jessica shuddered under an onslaught of need. "No," she whispered, but her cunt clenched viciously and her hips lifted off the mattress.

Jory Strong

Clay became savage, as if he sensed what she'd been thinking and wanted to sear the erotic images into her mind. She fought against orgasm but she'd long ago relinquished control of her body to him. It wouldn't be denied. He wouldn't be denied.

Scream after scream filled the cabin as she came. Arousal soaked into the sheet of Tekoa's bed. Jessica trembled, wrung out from pleasure, but the need was like a banked fire ready to explode, waiting only for the correct accelerant. Clay.

He crawled up her body and took her hands in his. He wove their fingers together before pressing the backs of hers to the mattress. "Christ, Jess. I love you so much it hurts."

With a quick, hard thrust, he penetrated her.

That's all it took to make her desperate, needy, ready for him all over again.

She locked her legs around his waist and he grunted.

"I love you too," she said. "It'd kill me to lose you."

"I'm here, baby. You know I'd never willingly leave you."

Clay covered her mouth with his. He couldn't hold back now. Lust and need clawed at him, drove his cock in and out of her tight channel in an unrelenting pistoning of hips.

The bed shook under the force of it. She whimpered and tightened her legs around him as though she was afraid he'd somehow leave the hot wet fist of muscles that made his life worth living. Not a chance. He wasn't going to stop fucking her until he passed out and even then he'd pin her lower body to the bed with his and stay inside her.

"Come for me, Jess," he gasped, lifting his mouth from hers only to turn his head slightly and find her ear. He ensured her obedience by thrusting his tongue into the sensitive ear canal and assaulting it with hot, wet breath and loving strokes.

Fire raced up his spine. He panted and groaned and fought against orgasm until finally she sobbed underneath him.

100

Her inner walls clamped down on him and it freed him from all restraint. With a shout he poured his seed into her as wave after wave of fiery ecstasy pulsed through his shaft.

Clay thought he heard an echoing shout from Tekoa, but he couldn't turn his head away from Jess. He couldn't do anything other than revel in the exquisite pleasure. He couldn't do anything but rejoice as he worshipped with his body.

They were safe. They were together. They were so close to having it all.

He took her repeatedly through the night. He took her until one final orgasm pushed her into an exhausted sleep. Only then did Clay reach down and pull the sheet over them. He did it for her sake, not for his. Jess would have enough to face in the morning. She was comfortable with her body, at least around him. But he knew she'd feel awkward, embarrassed if she woke up naked and exposed with Tekoa in the room.

Clay rubbed his cheek against her hair. One of the things he loved about Jess was her innate honesty, not just with other people but with herself. She wouldn't claim he'd seduced her or caught her in a weak moment. She wouldn't scream or rage or blame him for taking her when there was another man present to witness it. She wouldn't pretend it hadn't happened or that it didn't change anything.

She was strong enough that if she hadn't wanted and accepted what was going to happen, she wouldn't have gotten into bed. She'd have curled up on a chair or crashed on the floor in front of the fireplace.

Yeah, she'd probably be a little shy around Tekoa in the morning. But that was going to be *his* problem and Clay was a hundred percent positive Tekoa could handle it.

Christ, he knew he had to leave in order to give Tekoa some operating room. That'd make it go a lot smoother and faster with Jessica. But, damn he wished he could stick around and watch as Tekoa made love to her.

Clay pressed a kiss to her forehead and snuggled against her. Tomorrow was going to change things permanently for all of them. There'd be no going back for any of them.

It didn't mean they were home free. He and Tekoa would have to be careful not to do anything Jess wasn't ready for. They'd have to make sure she never, ever thought they were fucking her so they could do each other. He and Tekoa might even have to wait until Jess said or did something to let them know she *wanted* to watch them together sexually.

Clay grinned. Yeah, he could see Jess doing that. Or at least, he could imagine her asking why he and Tekoa weren't intimate, especially since she knew how much he wanted sex with another man.

Jess wasn't afraid of the hard questions and he wasn't afraid to tell her the truth. Hell, now that the brass ring was in their hands, he and Tekoa could even put off kissing if that's what it took for Jess to feel completely secure. She was worth suffering for because life without her would be bleak.

"I love you, baby," Clay whispered before finally allowing sleep to claim him.

Tekoa rose from the couch and padded softly to the bathroom. He slipped into the shower with a wry smile. The saying about being careful what you wish for cascaded through his thoughts as the water struck his chest and abdomen and cock. He was coated with his own seed.

A soft laugh escaped. He wondered if it was the drink he'd passed on to Clay and Jessica that had given them the stamina for a long night of lovemaking, or if this was normal for them. He hoped it was the latter.

Tekoa's penis stirred and he nearly groaned out loud. *Save it for tomorrow* he told himself, smiling at how eager his cock was to recapture the ecstasy.

Jerking off in the same room with his two mates was better than anything he'd ever felt before, including intercourse. Not that he wanted to make a habit of substituting it for the real thing.

He lathered his hands with soap and made a purely functional pass along his shaft and over his balls before moving upward to his belly. *His mates.*

The wry smile returned. When Clay was unknown, unconscious, it was easy to think of him in those terms. But now the word *partner* was a better fit.

Clay's personality was too big, his attitude was too dominant to consider him anything but fully equal. Not that Tekoa thought Jessica was less, she was everything. She was the one who would hold them all together.

He had barely dared to hope that the Creator would hear his heart's deepest desire and answer by granting him two mates instead of one. He'd never known of such a thing happening, though their legends sang of the possibility.

The times he had allowed himself to hope and dream, he'd imagined himself at the center of the relationship. He was born of The People after all, not created as a gift from the Creator.

A chuckle escaped for his earlier arrogance. His reality was so much different than how he'd expected it to be when both cups appeared on the fireplace mantel.

Rather than being the center, he was the outsider who must be welcomed into the nest. Rather than being the dominant one, he found himself sharing the role with another while the gentlest and most submissive of their newly formed family controlled their happiness and pleasure.

Tekoa rinsed the soap off then left the shower to towel dry. As silently as he'd crossed to the bathroom he moved to the bed and looked down on them. Clay's chest was pressed to Jessica's back, his arm was draped possessively over her side.

In the firelight their faces were chiseled perfection. Clay's strong and noble while Jessica's was delicate and timeless.

They were both beautiful. Breathtaking. Their golden hair and skin made Tekoa think of ancient gods and goddesses from foreign lands.

He couldn't resist lightly stroking Jessica's cheek and then Clay's before returning to the couch and offering a final prayer of gratitude for their presence in his cabin and in his life.

He closed his eyes, afraid that anticipation would make it impossible to sleep. Tomorrow he would claim Jessica. He would couple with her and gain the right to always do so. Then later, when he was sure she accepted it, he and Clay would become lovers.

* * * * *

Jessica woke to the wonderful smell of coffee and the feel Clay's warm chest plastered against her back. Both of them made her smile.

It was still raining. She could hear it pounding against the roof in a steady beat.

For a moment she was tempted by work. She loved to write or read to the music of raindrops.

Thunder rolled across the sky and brought memories of the previous day and night with it, along with the realization that they weren't at the apartment or even at the rental cabin. They were in Tekoa's home.

Heat rushed to Jessica's face. She opened her eyes just enough to see Tekoa. He was standing in front of the space that served as his office, apparently engrossed in something either on his computer or on his desk.

Even in profile he stirred her, called to her with his innate strength of character and body. He was a man who could be trusted, counted on. He was a man whose protective nature and sense of duty had led him to become a sheriff. He was a man whose wife and children could count on him to care for them and see to their needs.

Her womb fluttered at the thought of being this man's wife and one day having his children. Her labia became flushed and the liquid evidence of her arousal trickled from her slit.

Jessica closed her eyes but couldn't keep them shut. The temptation to study him while he was unaware of her was too great.

Like the day before he was wearing jeans and a flannel shirt, this one hunter green with black stripes. They made him look rugged, competent.

He was barefoot today. His feet dark against the pale blue of the small area rug he was standing on.

His hair was braided again. It was impossible for her to see it and not imagine undoing the braid and combing her fingers through the long black tresses.

She shivered as more sensual images invaded her mind. Images of his hair draped over her thighs as he explored her hot folds with his tongue and lips. Images of his hair falling on either side of her face and enclosing them in a private world as he kissed her. She pushed the images away only to have the memories of what had happened with Clay assail her.

Next to her Clay stirred and woke. She tried to relax so he'd think she was still sleeping but she was too late.

"Love you," he said, leaning over and kissing the spot where her neck and shoulder met before he left the bed.

Jessica watched from beneath her eyelashes as Tekoa turned. His gaze flickered over Clay's nakedness as though it was an everyday sight for him. "Coffee's ready. I've got cereal and fresh fruit if you like your breakfast light. Most days I have eggs and sausage, either with toast or on biscuits. What's your preference?"

"Real food. Cereal and fruit doesn't cut it for me."

Tekoa laughed. "I'll start cooking then."

Clay glanced at the floor. Alarm rippled through Jessica as she followed his action. Yesterday's borrowed clothes were nowhere in sight.

"Sorry," Tekoa said, "living in such a small place has made me a neat freak. Either that or it comes with being a law-and-order type. I put some clothes for you and Jessica in the bathroom. I figured you'd both want to hit the shower first."

Clay's laugh was utterly masculine and full of carnal satisfaction. "Yeah, you got that right."

He headed for the bathroom, so comfortable and casual with his lack of clothing that Jessica felt like an uptight virgin in comparison. She knew he wasn't doing it as a come-on, though Tekoa didn't look away or head for the kitchen until Clay had disappeared into the bathroom.

Jessica closed her eyes and listened to the sounds both inside and outside the cabin. She couldn't hide in bed all day. She didn't even want to though she'd be doing great just to meet Tekoa's eyes this morning.

Silky desire coiled in her belly. Need pulsed through her clit. She'd known what would happen when she climbed into bed last night. She'd known what she was agreeing to, that she and Clay would make love with Tekoa only a short distance away.

In the dark it had been easy to lose herself in the passion once the decision was made. In the light of day she wasn't sorry any of it had happened but that didn't mean she was ready to parade around the cabin naked. She'd never been as quick to adapt, to grab for the brass ring, as Clay was.

He stepped out of the bathroom wearing sweats and a T-shirt again. As he walked to the bed he finished toweling his hair dry.

"Here you go, baby, I thought you might want this," he said as he stretched the towel between his two hands so she could slide from beneath the sheets and into the protection it afforded.

It was damp but she was grateful to have something to wear. "Thanks," she whispered.

He nuzzled her overly warm cheek with his. "You okay with what happened?"

She nodded.

"Good. After breakfast I'm going to see if Tekoa will lend me his car. I'm pretty sure with the rain and the mud that mine is a lost cause right now, but I want to get our luggage."

"I'll go with you. I need my purse."

"No." He tempered the refusal by sucking her earlobe into his mouth and stroking down her bare spine until he reached the edge of the towel. "Stay here with Tekoa, Jess. Give him a chance. Except for finding you on the road, which doesn't count, he's had zero time to be alone with you." Clay traced up her spine and along her shoulder. "I want whatever happens between the two of you to be your choice. I want you to go as fast or as slow as you want without me being here to interfere or make it awkward."

She buried her face in the crook of his neck and shivered. She wanted to deny that anything *would* happen, but her stiff clit and the wetness coating her inner thighs would expose her as a liar.

How could one day make such a difference? How could she go from being terrified of ending up hurt and alone to confident that she could share her life with these two men and accept that they loved each other as well?

Fear twisted through her chest along with the image of Clay in those first seconds after the car crash when she hadn't known whether he was dead or alive. That's how.

"I'll stay," she whispered, nervous and anxious and aroused at the same time. She wasn't sure she was ready to go all the way with Tekoa, but she *was* ready for more. She *did* want the door to intimacy to open and even though she didn't think she was brave enough to do it herself, she didn't doubt that Tekoa was.

Jessica kissed Clay's collarbone and pulled away. "I'd better hurry up and take my shower."

Clay watched her disappear into the bathroom. Pride and love and so many other emotions held him in place until he heard the shower turn on. A grin formed. Tekoa was a man after his own heart. He'd left Jessica a shirt to put on, but nothing else.

Clay joined Tekoa in the kitchen area and between them they got the breakfast prepared and on the table so it was waiting there when Jessica emerged from the bathroom. The telephone rang just as they were sitting down. Tekoa made an unhappy sound and told them to go ahead and start breakfast without him as he reached for a portable phone resting on the counter.

Whoever was calling talked for several minutes before Tekoa said, "They're here with me now. I found them last night. Their car went off the road. I was going to call in and tell you I'm on vacation until further notice."

Jessica heard masculine laughter and risked a glance at Tekoa. He looked like a man talking to a nosy relative.

The laughter on the other end of the phone faded. The caller said something that had Tekoa frowning as his body posture went from relaxed to tense. "You've contacted the others?"

"Good. I'll be here if the situation changes. Don't assume I'm watching TV." There was a burst of laughter through the receiver. Tekoa let it run its course before saying. "Call me if there are important updates."

He hung up a minute later and joined them at the table. Clay said, "Work?"

"One of my deputies. The bad weather caused a bus carrying convicts to crash. The driver and guard were taken to the hospital. Two of the convicts stuck around. The other ten are missing. Most of them are doing time for nonviolent crimes. But a couple of them are considered extremely dangerous and most likely armed by now."

Chapter Five

ဢ

Jessica rubbed her arms and glanced at Clay. "I'll be fine," he said. "We're a long way from where they're loose."

Clay turned his attention to Tekoa. "Is it okay if I borrow your car and see about retrieving our luggage?" He grinned. "Looks like you're stuck with us for a while."

"Sure. I can't let you have the cruiser, but I've got an old truck parked behind the cabin. It's got a police radio in it if you run into trouble." Tekoa reached over and tucked Jessica's hair back behind her ear. The touch went all the way to her cunt. "By trouble I'm talking about getting stuck in the mud."

She nodded but couldn't quite meet his eyes yet.

Then all too soon breakfast was over and Clay was gone.

Jessica felt like she was plugged into an erotic current. Every nerve ending was strung tight with awareness. Every inch of her skin screamed for Tekoa's touch.

She stood near the door where she'd given Clay a kiss before he left. Her fingers toyed with the edge of the borrowed shirt. A trickle of arousal slid down her inner thigh and past the fabric hem. She wiped at it surreptitiously as additional color flooded her cheeks. She'd counted on Tekoa coming to her. She'd imagined him seducing her. Instead he'd retreated to the space carved out as an office and left the first move up to her.

Clay had been relentless when they'd first started dating. He'd made her crave his touch and want to please him sexually. He'd ruined her for any other man—until now.

Jessica's cunt clenched. Her nipples tightened to the point she wanted to unbutton the flannel shirt and play with them in order to relieve the ache, or beg Tekoa to do it.

She closed her eyes and tried to calm the too-fast beat of her heart. Instead memories of the night flooded in. Her own husky screams and hoarse pleading echoed through her thoughts.

Jessica bit her bottom lip to keep from whimpering as heat flickered in her belly like a small spark ready to flare up and become a wildfire. The sensation reminded her of what she'd experienced when she'd swallowed the contents of the cup Clay had given her on the porch.

For a brief shimmering moment she'd felt as though she was close to something so vast and powerful that it couldn't be truly understood. And yet at the same time the heat that slid through body had been sensuous and welcoming. She'd felt as though she'd found the place she was meant to be. *Home.*

It made no sense to Jessica, but Clay had felt it too. He'd told her that he felt right about being here.

She inhaled on a shaky breath. She needed to do this for them both. She needed to take the first steps toward a threesome.

Tekoa opened a cabinet and exposed a map stuck to the back of the door. It gave her an excuse to go to his side.

The scent of Jessica's arousal nearly dropped Tekoa to his knees. He was trying to be good. He was trying to keep from pouncing when every instinct demanded that he mount her.

She was his mate. She was the one who would bear his young.

Desire lashed through him with the force of a lightning bolt. The Thunderbird's spirit urged him to take her to her hands and knees and breed her.

Tekoa fought the demand though he paid a price for it. His cock burned. His sac was heavy and tight with seed. His heart thundered in his chest.

It took sheer force of will to remain standing next to her in a seemingly unaffected manner. He indicated a blue line on the map. "This is where my territory stops."

Out of the corner of his eye he saw her frown but didn't dare turn to face her. Every time she caught him looking at her she blushed and hid behind her hair or under lowered eyelashes.

She was a fascinating mix of strength and shyness, innocence and unconscious seductiveness. Even if she hadn't been given to him by the Creator she would have drawn him like a moth to fire.

"Isn't that a lot of area for a single sheriff?" Jessica asked, drawing Tekoa's attention back to the map.

Amusement rippled through him along with a small measure of chagrin at forgetting she was both beautiful *and* intelligent. He'd have to be careful until he revealed his true nature.

His finger moved toward the eastern edge of the map, to where Hohoq was marked within a smaller enclosure of jagged, roughly connected red lines. "This is my official jurisdiction. But our people are spread out and where they are I go when called." His finger left that area and settled on another spot. "This is where the bus carrying the convicts crashed. I doubt any of them will get close to us. Criminals have a habit of returning to familiar places."

She chewed at her bottom lip in a worried gesture he found endearing. Tekoa caught himself before he could lean over and chase her concern away with a kiss.

Jessica touched a dark blue line near where his fingers rested. "It's far away from your official territory, but it's close to the area you care about. Will you have to go look for the convicts if they're spotted on this side of the line?"

"There are others to do it."

She glanced at him, a quick look before she turned her head so her glorious blonde hair shielded her face. She was nervous, aroused, still shy from having him witness her passion.

Tekoa's heart turned over. A small measure of his resolve to wait melted. She'd made the first step by coming to his side. He wouldn't insist she do anything more, at least for the moment.

Tekoa turned toward her and cupped her cheek. "Jessica," he whispered, letting her hear the longing in his heart as he gently tipped her face so their eyes met. "Having you and Clay here is the answer to a prayer I barely dared to make for fear of being disappointed. Last night was beyond any ecstasy I've ever known." He brushed his lips across hers. "I loved every sound of pleasure you made. The only thing better would have been for me to join you and Clay in bed."

He didn't give her time to retreat. His mouth lowered to capture hers. His tongue glided past soft feminine lips and found hers.

She whimpered and pressed against him. He wrapped his arm around her waist and pulled her tighter. The feel of her soft curves was exquisite. The scent of her was beyond compare.

Tekoa deepened the kiss. His tongue went from gentle exploration and greeting to that of an aroused male offering a taste of what she would experience once his cock was sheathed inside her.

Jessica melted in his arms. She was so softly submissive that he had to fight against freeing his cock and impaling her where they stood.

With a groan he swept her up in his arms and carried her to the thick pile of woven rugs in front of the fireplace. He stretched her out on them as Clay had been stretched out the previous day, only this time Tekoa lay down too.

He'd thought he couldn't get any harder but he'd been wrong. When he was finally able to shed his jeans he'd find the veins on the underside of his cock pulsing savagely. He'd find his foreskin pulled back and the head of his penis nearly purple with the need to slip inside Jessica's wet slit.

"Jessica," he whispered on a tortured breath when his lungs demanded that he pull his mouth from hers.

She made a small whimpering sound and lifted her head in order to initiate another kiss. He moaned and answered her sweet siren call.

Her body lured his on top of it. Her legs wrapped around his waist. Tekoa knew it was madness to torture himself like this, to lie between her thighs fully clothed. And yet at the same time it heightened the pleasure and the anticipation. It recaptured the wild, heady rush of teenage lust and first love, only those feelings were intensified by experience and maturity. They were made profound by the knowledge that the woman underneath him was his wife, his mate, the female who would be his even after the Creator called their spirits for a final time.

"You're testing my control, Jessica," he said when their mouths parted again.

"I don't want you to have any control."

He rewarded her honesty with a soft kiss, by sucking at her bottom lip before he forced himself onto his side. He knew she was telling the truth. She wanted him to lose control of himself but take control of her.

He ached to give her what she was asking for. His cock screamed for him to let go and pound into her until they both cried out in release. But he wanted more.

This was their mating day. He wanted to savor her full surrender, not because he'd taken the control but because she'd willingly shared her body, her heart, her soul with him.

His mouth returned to hers. His tongue rubbed and twined and danced with hers. His hand cupped her cheek for a long moment in a gesture of protective desire before trailing down her neck and over the flannel material of the shirt to settle on her bare thigh. He caressed the silken skin with his palm but was careful not to trespass beyond the shirt's boundary, not to touch anything not willingly exposed.

Spasm after spasm rippled through Jessica's cunt. Her fingers unbraided Tekoa's hair as she ate at his mouth. She needed him to touch her. She needed him to fill the horrible aching emptiness between her thighs.

Clay was the only other man who'd ever been capable of doing this to her. Until now he'd been the only one who could make her hunger desperately and reduce her vocabulary to a single word. "Please," she begged, sliding one of her hands down Tekoa's arm until her fingers found his. "Please," she whispered, drawing his hand beneath the shirt and taking it to the hot, wet core of her.

Tekoa groaned and covered her lips with his again. Tension vibrated through every part of him as his fingers explored her slick folds.

In a heartbeat she knew this was what he'd been waiting for. She knew he wouldn't take complete control until she'd consciously shared every part of herself with him.

Jessica shuddered when he found her erect clit. Her hips arched off the thick handmade rugs as his fingers slid back and forth over the tiny, sensitive head. She couldn't contain the whimpers, the tremors, the jerking movements of her body as each one of his touches sent exquisite pleasure burning through her swollen knob and upward to her nipples, her heart.

"No," Jessica cried out when his fingers left her aroused flesh just as she was on the precipice of orgasm. "Please don't stop."

He pressed his fingers into her slit in answer. Her inner muscles clamped down, rippled over them, but it wasn't enough.

His mouth found the delicate shell of her ear. He was struggling for breath just as she was. "I don't want to rush with you, Jessica."

He explored her ear with his tongue. He took the earlobe between his teeth before sucking it in time to the rhythmic thrust and retreat of his fingers in her channel.

Jessica clamped her legs together in an effort to trap his palm against her clit so she could press into it and gain a small release. Tekoa laughed, a purely masculine sound that stroked down her spine and flooded her channel with additional moisture.

"If this wasn't our first time together I might punish you for trying that," he whispered. He bit down on her earlobe in warning. "You know I don't want you to come yet."

His mouth returned to hover above hers. Their eyes met and held. His palm rubbed over the head of her clit in tiny circles that had her hips jerking and her breath coming in small, sharp pants. "You're so incredibly beautiful and desirable, I bet Clay has to punish you sometimes just to remind you who you belong to and who's in charge. Doesn't he, Jessica?"

"Yes." It came out shaky.

"Do you like it when he punishes you?"

"Yes."

"Good, because sometimes I'm going to punish you too."

Her thighs tightened on his hand. Her cunt gripped his fingers as her hips canted and moved. She rubbed her clit against his palm in blatant defiance and temptation. "But not today?" she said.

His smile was dark and very nearly feral. His unbound hair fell on either side of her face as it had done in her fantasy. "Not today. Open your legs, Jessica."

She obeyed immediately, then whimpered when his hand retreated to her inner thigh and left her feeling anxious and bereft. She put her hand on his chest and tentatively undid one of the buttons. His face tightened and the familiar rush of feminine power coiled in her belly and spread through her cunt and breasts. She slowly bared his chest.

116

"You're incredibly beautiful and desirable to me," she said, repeating the compliment he'd given her.

"I'm glad."

Jessica stroked the smooth bronzed skin of his chest and abdomen. She explored the tiny, dark nipples and reveled in the way he held himself completely still though she knew it cost him not to lose control while she was touching him.

She leaned in and nuzzled a nipple, then lapped it. His breath caught in his throat. The muscles in his arms became rigid. She suckled.

Tekoa's hand went to his erection and squeezed through the denim of his pants. Lust roared through him. His reality telescoped down to the thunderous pounding that made it feel as though his heart now resided in his cock.

Jessica nudged him over and he rolled to his back. When she positioned herself on top of him and he felt the wet heat of her pussy against the back of his hand, Tekoa realized the flaw in his plan.

He'd forbidden himself from taking control because he wanted her to come to him willingly, but that didn't mean she wouldn't turn the tables on him. He should have factored in her relationship with Clay. He should have suspected that she might know exactly how to retaliate and bring a man to his knees—or put him on his back when she wanted to. He should have remembered how intelligent she was and questioned the wisdom of eliminating the threat of punishment.

Her teeth clamped down on his nipple and he bucked as an arc of erotic pain shot straight to his penis. "Jessica." It was a plea and a command, a helpless acknowledgment that she had him at her mercy.

She released the tortured nipple and smiled against his skin before slowly rising so she was straddling him, drenching his hand further as gravity pulled her arousal over the swollen cunt lips now holding his hand to his erection. Nothing could have made him look away as her fingers freed the buttons on the borrowed shirt. His spirit eyes had seen her breasts the night before but now it was his human eyes that were riveted to the beautiful globes with their dusky, pouting tips.

Jessica tossed the shirt aside and gave him a smile that kicked through his gut and made his cock scream for mercy. "Does showing them to you mean you'll touch them?" she teased. "Or do I have to put your hand on them like I had to do with my pussy?"

"Jessica," he warned. But without the threat of punishment to back it up Tekoa saw only feminine amusement in her eyes.

She cupped her breasts as if weighing them to determine their value. Her thumbs brushed over the tips and he groaned. He wondered if she'd lick them, then had to tighten his grip on his penis so that pain chased away the overwhelming urge to come.

"Does Clay like to see you touching your breasts?" Tekoa asked, deciding to fight for control with words since he'd already forfeited the use of his body.

She shuddered in response and he knew he'd won a small victory when he felt her cunt lips contract and release against the back of his hand. But the victory was short-lived.

"Yes, he likes it," she whispered, taking the nipples between her fingers and squeezing them before leaning over so that they were just inches away from his mouth. "But he'd rather touch them himself. Do I have to ask you to touch them? Or is this good enough?" There was a wealth of feminine satisfaction in her voice when she added, "I know you don't want to rush into anything."

Lust flashed through Tekoa. With a growl he pulled her to him and then rolled so that she was underneath him. His hands went to her wrists and pinned them at her sides. His mouth took hers in a savage, punishing kiss before he moved to her breasts.

Jessica arched in pleasure as Tekoa began suckling with hard, hungry pulls. He ravaged her nipples as though he was starving and wanted to nurse. Her womb pulsed with heat as she imagined coming to bed after feeding their son and having Tekoa demonstrate the difference between a child's needs and a man's needs.

"Take your pants off," she begged as she ground her clit against the hard ridge of his jeans-covered erection.

Tekoa slowly lifted his face. Masculine satisfaction was written on every line. "Only if you promise to behave."

"Because you don't want to rush," she said, this time through lowered eyelashes in a show of submission.

His laugh was husky. "Because I want to savor every moment of our first time together, Jessica." He turned his head and captured her other nipple. He pulled on it with the same hungry intensity he'd applied to its twin.

Jessica closed her eyes and gave herself up to the sensation. She loved to be suckled, just as she loved to have a man's mouth between her thighs. Some afternoons she and Clay spent hours kissing and touching each other, loving each other physically.

She shivered as an imagine of having both Clay and Tekoa at her breasts rose in her thoughts, followed by one with Clay thrusting his tongue into her slit as Tekoa alternated his attention between kissing her and sucking her nipples. "Let me touch you," she whispered, tugging against his hands where they still held her wrists shackled to the floor.

Tekoa gave her nipple a final, hard pull then rolled to his side before standing. Jessica couldn't look away as he stripped out of his shirt and jeans.

His cock jutted out, hard and proud. It was darker than Clay's but no less impressive. He was uncircumcised but she'd expected him to be. Clay was the same. She liked it. It satisfied something primitive inside her.

Jessica rose to her knees and put her hands on Tekoa's hips. His penis jerked at the proximity of her mouth.

She looked up at Tekoa through her eyelashes as she slowly leaned forward. His nostrils flared. His body tensed under her hands. The tip of his penis gleamed as additional moisture escaped through the small slit.

"Stop."

Jessica obeyed though a small smile played over her mouth as his cock demonstrated it had a mind of its own by bobbing just enough to brush against her parted lips.

Tekoa speared his hands through her silky hair. Emotion and instinct rioted inside him. He'd never had a female enthrall him so completely. He'd never had one capture him so thoroughly or claim every part of him as Jessica did.

He'd known it would be like this. But intellectual knowledge was nothing against the raw, primitive needs coursing through him.

He wouldn't last once she put her mouth on him. He'd come as quick as a schoolboy with his first girl.

His fingers tightened in her hair. His chest burned as he tried to control his breathing and keep from panting. His buttocks clenched with the effort to keep from thrusting as his cock repeatedly closed the infinitesimal distance between it and Jessica's mouth.

Need and reason merged. He wondered why he was fighting so desperately not to come. Last night had demonstrated just how many times his penis could fill when she served as the inspiration.

Erotic images filtered through the haze of lust. Only instead of Clay's face between her thighs it was his. He already knew how responsive Jessica was. He'd already promised himself that he would press his mouth to her lower lips and explore the sweet feminine mystery of her.

"Lie down," he ordered and experienced a dark thrill when she obeyed him immediately. Before Jessica he'd always kept this part of his nature out of his sex life. He'd never thought to question it and now he didn't have to. He'd been waiting for her.

This was something to experience only with a mate because dominance was a two-edged sword. He would crave her submission while at the same time feel the intense need to protect and care for her.

Tekoa knelt near Jessica's head. His gaze traveled from her lips to her cunt before returning to her face. Her eyes were filled with carnal knowledge. Instinctively he knew that she'd taken Clay's cock in her mouth as Clay had feasted on her cunt.

He leaned down and traced the shell of her ear with his tongue. "You belong to me now."

"And Clay."

"And Clay," Tekoa agreed before leaving her ear and trailing kisses to her breast.

He grunted when Jessica's hand found one of his nipples. A bolt of ice-hot lust shot from his nipples to his cock when her mouth found the other one and her bites and sucks mimicked his own.

He worshiped her breasts for as long as he dared, then moved downward, hyperaware of her lips and tongue as they trailed over his chest and then his abdomen. His mouth found her wet folds and stiff clit just as hers found his cock.

Tekoa's hips bucked in warning but it was too late. He was lost to exquisite sensation and ravenous hunger. There was no separating what he was doing from what was being done to him.

Moans and whimpers blended with grunts and sighs. Bodies writhed to get closer as hands clutched and explored while lips and tongues gave pleasure beyond all measure.

Tekoa came with a shout as the walls of Jessica's pussy clutched at his tongue in orgasm. He rolled them to their sides so that he could nuzzle her mound as she lapped his cock.

Utter happiness and contentment filled him along with the overwhelming urge to care for her. His tongue darted out, capturing the taste of her even as he began thoroughly cleaning the arousal from her heated, swollen flesh.

His cock filled again. His heart rate sped up. At the edge of his consciousness a drum began beating and ancient voices rose from the mists of the past in a prayer for fertility.

Jessica stilled as though she could hear the song. Tekoa fought to deny the primal call.

Her tongue flicked into the slit of his cock head and lust poured into him with the force of a violent storm. He wrenched away from her body and rose to his knees as he tried to stay in control.

He was in a fever to mate with her. Tender. Rough. It no longer mattered as long as he claimed her.

She came to him and wrapped her arms around his neck. There was uncertainty in her expression, fear, a shadow of pain. "Tekoa?"

His arms pulled her tightly against him. "This is permanent, Jessica. Once I come inside you, we'll be considered married among my people. Do you accept that?"

Her eyes widened in surprise. "You've never come inside a woman before?"

He laughed despite the song's rising urgency. "Not under these circumstances."

"What about Clay? I'm engaged to him, Tekoa. I'm going to marry him."

"He will be accepted as both your husband and my lover." She shivered and Tekoa kissed her in reassurance. "It will be a permanent bond with him as well."

He kissed her again and felt her acceptance. She was so soft and submissive now, so totally enchanting that it almost hurt to look at her.

He, didn't need her formal words to forge the bond between them and make it permanent. It had already been forged when she drank from the cup.

Tekoa turned her so she was facing the fire. As soon as his lips touched her spine, Jessica went to her elbows and knees. Her thighs were open, her folds parted and glistening with slick invitation.

He gave himself up to the song then. He pierced her with his cock and the Thunderbird's spirit rose within him.

It expanded beyond the limits of his flesh so that a smaller version of its true form enveloped his mortal body and shimmered around him in red and white splendor with splashes of blue woven into phantom feathers.

Its wings were spread in victory and possessiveness. Its energy and magic vibrated through Tekoa so that each stroke of his penis into Jessica's welcoming channel was a profound act of devotion and love, a sharing of everything he was.

Chapter Six

Incredible pleasure knifed through Jessica as Tekoa's cock entered her. She'd thought his cock would feel like Clay's, but now that it was inside her, it felt thicker, longer, as though it had grown beyond what she'd seen with her eyes.

She whimpered and clutched at the rug. Tekoa's hands slid up her back and then around to cup her breasts possessively. "You are my mate."

Jessica heard it with her ears but the message echoed through her mind and lodged in her soul as if another voice was speaking a truth that could never be denied. "Yes," she whispered, acknowledging that truth.

Tekoa's hands left her breasts to glide over her sides and settle on her hips. His cock retreated and she cried out in protest, pushing backward, needing the feel of it inside her.

With a groan, his grip on her hips tightened. He held her where he wanted her as her cunt fisted and unfisted, clutched desperately at his penis as it slid almost completely out, then plunged home.

He retreated again. Filled her again. He did it over and over and over until she was shaking with need. Until reality became a sensual haze.

At the edge of her consciousness she heard a drum. Its beat matched Tekoa's thrusting, slow at first, but gaining in power and speed as his cock filled her, stretched her, became all that mattered to her.

The fire in the fireplace roared and flickered as if feeding on the wild emotion and sexual pleasure taking place in front of it. The flames rose and flared, became so hot they forced

Jessica to look away. Up. To the Thunderbird carved into the mantel.

It seemed to hover above her, a real presence that filled the room with ancient, unknowable power. Tekoa's thrusts became more aggressive. Her moans and cries joined the drum. Her voice was added to his.

Lightning flashed in the dark, dark eyes of the Thunderbird. Ecstasy shimmered within her grasp. "Please," she heard herself beg as the drum and song grew in intensity.

Tekoa's hand left her hip and found her mound. "You are my wife now," he said as his fingers caressed her clit.

Orgasm thundered through her and she screamed. Her channel spasmed violently, milking Tekoa's cock and filling with his hot seed. It went on and on and on until she became boneless, weak, completely sated. And yet she still whimpered in protest when he pulled from her body.

Tekoa's spirit felt as though it might take wing. Love filled him along with happiness.

He lay down on his side and pulled Jessica against him, wanting nothing more than to cuddle with her for a few minutes. Clay would be home soon.

Tekoa smiled at the thought and nuzzled Jessica's hair. His hand moved to her breast and she murmured in contentment.

They'd been here less than a day and yet Tekoa knew the cabin would feel empty without them. He'd feel empty without them.

His hand left her breast and settled on her abdomen. He'd prefer to wait but the choice wouldn't necessarily be his to make. She might well be pregnant by the springtime, her womb a welcome nest for two Thunderbird children, Clay's and his.

He rubbed her belly in small circles before slipping lower to feel the wet heat and soft down of her cunt. He wanted to tell Jessica that he loved her but he knew it was too soon. Instead he said, "How'd you meet Clay?"

She laughed and rolled to her back, then to her side so she was facing him. "I was at a local bookstore reading one of my books during story time. The audience was mostly children with a couple of interested moms. He came in, sat right down in the front and I lost my place in the story and started blushing. The kids were old enough to catch on. Some of them giggled and one romantically inclined little girl asked if he was my husband."

Tekoa took her left hand in his and rubbed his thumb over the engagement ring. "What'd you say?"

"Before I could say anything, Clay said, 'Not yet, but I'm going to be'."

Tekoa chuckled. He could easily imagine Clay doing just that. "How long ago was that?"

"A year," she whispered, hiding her expression and thoughts by ducking her head.

Tekoa's fingers played with the engagement ring. He sensed he was on unstable ground which only meant he'd tread more carefully, not abandon it.

"Jessica," he said, placing her hand on his chest so he could cup her cheek and force her to look at him.

His lips covered hers. His tongue pushed into her mouth. There was a tiny resistance, a tiny hesitation, but then she softened in acceptance.

He kept the kiss gentle, reassuring. He already understood her well enough to know she was much more cautious than either he or Clay.

He suspected Clay would have rushed her to Vegas shortly after meeting her, but a year later he probably considered it a victory that she wore his ring and belonged to him in all the ways that mattered, save for a legal document.

When she gave her heart she gave it completely. It was a testament to her love for Clay that she'd allowed another man to touch her. Claim her.

Tekoa's cock filled but it was only an outward show of the desperate need coursing through him, not just for the right to her body, but for everything she had to offer a man. He wanted what Clay had.

With a low moan he pushed Jessica to her back and settled between her open thighs. He lifted his mouth from hers only long enough to say, "Put me inside you."

Fire raced up his spine when her hand found him and guided him to her slick, welcoming heat. It might be too soon to tell her how he felt about her but he showed her with tender touches and long slow strokes.

He worshipped her.

He gave himself to her.

He swallowed her cries of pleasure and release until finally he couldn't hold back any longer. And then he poured his love into her with lava-hot jets of semen and whispered words in his native language.

"What did you say just then?" she asked as they clung to each other afterward.

You hold my heart within you, he wanted to say. Instead he laughed and teased, "Maybe if you beat me at poker I'll tell you."

The phone rang and she tensed.

"I'd better get that. It might be one of my deputies calling with an update on the missing convicts." Tekoa pressed a kiss to her forehead before getting to his feet and moving to his office space to answer the phone.

Jessica followed, but moved away from him after he paused from his conversation to tell her it was a citizen calling on another matter. He grinned when she retrieved the discarded shirt before disappearing into the bathroom. Now that he'd gotten her naked he had no intention of letting her hide her beautiful body, especially not with *his* shirt.

The hot water cascading over her skin reminded Jessica of Tekoa's hands and lips. It reminded her of the fluid play of his muscles and the heat that radiated off him.

Her mind was trying to process the reality of what had just taken place with Tekoa. Her heart felt as though she'd stood on the edge of a cliff and jumped, only instead of plunging downward, she was soaring.

This is permanent, Jessica. Once I come inside you we'll be considered married among my people. Do you accept that?

She'd never said *I do* and yet she'd answered him all the same. She'd given herself to him and reveled in every moment.

The diamond in her ring glittered accusingly. Uncertainty returned with a vengeance.

Unlike Clay's push-the-limits, grab-for-the-brass ring approach to life, she'd always been more introspective, more cautious, though in her mind the end result was the same. No regrets.

No regrets.

Jessica took a deep breath and used the words as a mantra to shore up her confidence. If she'd met and dated Tekoa first, she would have fallen in love with him first. He had the qualities that were important to her in a man—honesty, strength, tenderness, intelligence, and that was just a small sampling of what she'd discovered in him since he found her on the road. Add those to a body that was mouth-wateringly gorgeous and she knew she'd never find a better man to share with Clay.

Her heart rate jumped at the thought. Images crowded in. She wondered if they'd want her to leave for a while. The uncertainty tried to return. Jessica resolutely pushed it away.

Clay and Tekoa might want each other but they also wanted her. She knew that with every fiber of her being. If they needed some "alone time" for their first sexual encounter then she'd go into town. Before Tekoa, she'd felt threatened by the intimacy Clay would have with another man. She'd been so afraid that she'd end up hurt and alone. She wasn't going to worry about that any more.

"Just because you've always been cautious doesn't mean you have to *always* be cautious," Jessica said as she turned off the water and left the shower. "This is a threesome now. They can do what they want with each other. And you can do whatever you want with *either* of them or *both* of them."

Heat coiled in her belly. She toweled off then reached for the hair dryer. Thanks to Clay she knew some very wicked games. She could hold her own either *with* them or *against* them.

Jessica half expected to find Clay and Tekoa engaged in sexual activity when she stepped out of the bathroom. But Tekoa was on the phone and there was no sign that Clay had gotten back with their luggage.

Flames flickered invitingly in the fireplace. Her womb fluttered with a flashback of how wonderful it had felt when Tekoa made love to her on the rug.

Her attention went to the Thunderbird carved into the mantel. It was magnificent, and yet as she looked at it, it seemed to be just an extremely beautiful piece of functional art. There was none of the otherworldly power she'd felt as she'd neared climax.

A small laugh escaped. Of course, she wasn't hearing a drum or an ancient song right now either.

Her gaze shifted away from the Thunderbird and found Tekoa instead. He'd pulled on a pair of sweatpants but hadn't bothered with a shirt. His black hair was still unbound and flowing over his shoulders. Healer. Lover. Warrior. Was it any wonder that sex with him had been a nearly mystical experience?

She crossed the room and slipped her arms around his bared waist. Contentment filled her when his arm immediately encircled her and pulled her more tightly against him as he continued talking on the phone.

She rested her cheek on his chest and studied the books in his bookcase. There were police-type books, texts about forensic science and criminal profiling, but there was also a surprising amount of fiction. He favored mysteries and true crime, though she recognized some of the wilderness survival books that Clay enjoyed.

The feeling of rightness wrapped more securely around Jessica. Though she and Clay didn't share the exact same tastes when it came to books, it was important to her that he was a reader like she was. It made her feel closer to him, and on nights when there was nothing they wanted to watch on TV, she loved cuddling up next to him or lying with her head on his lap while they both read. It made her happy to know she could do the same thing with the other important man in her life.

"That was a long conversation," she said when Tekoa hung up the phone.

He chuckled and rubbed his cheek against her hair. "No, you were just in the bathroom for a long time. That's my fifth phone call."

"Everything okay?"

"As of a few minutes ago, seven of the ten convicts have been recaptured."

"That's good."

Jessica nuzzled a tiny male nipple and reveled in the way his body tightened. She licked over the hard nub and smiled when he gasped. Liquid lust coated her swollen cunt lips and slid down her thighs. It was such a heady rush to have him respond to her. She couldn't stop herself from tormenting him.

Tekoa slipped his hands under the shirt and cupped her buttocks. "I'll never get enough of you, Jessica," he whispered as he found her ear with his mouth.

"No fair," she moaned.

"You started this."

His hands moved up and down, palming the globes of her ass. His tongue traced the shell of her ear before flicking into the sensitive canal.

Jessica cried out. Her nipples tightened to hard aching points. "Tekoa," she whimpered, helpless under the onslaught of his tongue.

With easy strength he lifted her and placed her on the edge of his desk. Jessica's thighs splayed automatically and his fingers discovered the wetness between them.

Tekoa's cock filled in a rush that left him lightheaded. She was so sweetly responsive that he was already addicted to her.

He'd planned to cuddle with her on the couch and talk when she finished with her shower, but as soon as she initiated the lovemaking he was lost. His hands left Jessica long enough to push his sweatpants down before going to her hips. He was mesmerized by the sight of her pussy peeking out from beneath the flannel material of the shirt she was wearing.

"I want my shirt back," he said.

"Now?" Her voice was sultry and feminine and tinged with amusement.

"Now," he said, somehow managing to tear his gaze away from her cunt and sound as though he meant the command.

Jessica licked her lips and his penis jerked. Her feline smile told him she'd noticed her effect on his cock.

"Take the shirt off, Jessica."

He knew he should temper his orders or *he'd* be the one paying the price. He didn't doubt for a moment that she remembered his promise not to punish her today. But he couldn't seem to stop himself. She was beyond anything he had ever imagined having in a mate.

The temptation to push him flashed through her eyes in a small hint of defiance. But his promise was a two-edged sword.

He saw the instant when she realized it.

She was smart enough to know he'd retaliate. She was clever enough to guess that his method of teaching her a lesson might leave her hot little pussy empty and her body screaming for his touch.

Jessica unbuttoned the shirt and handed it to him. He tossed it onto the chair then rewarded her obedience by licking over her nipple before slowly sucking it into his mouth.

She arched her back and made a little mewing sound that had his foreskin pulling back in readiness. He covered the other nipple with his palm. Her heart thundered in time to his. The scent of shampoo and arousal swirled off her body and surrounded him. He wanted to kiss downward until he could once again bury his face between her thighs and know the sweet, erotic taste of her. He wanted to hear her scream and feel her sheath spasm against his tongue. He wanted to take her clit in his mouth like a tiny penis and torture it with pleasure.

His cock pulsed in warning. The connection forged by the Creator's drink allowed him to sense Clay's location and know Clay was on the way back to the cabin. His first time alone with Jessica was nearing an end.

Tekoa forced himself away from her breast. "Lean back and brace yourself."

Jessica's eyelids lowered as she obeyed. She tilted her head and her golden hair spilled over the wood of his desk like a silky curtain.

"Watch while I take you," he growled, closing the distance and slowly entering her hot channel.

The command had been for her but Tekoa couldn't take his eyes off the place where their bodies joined, where his darker, harder flesh slid into her dusky, delicate folds. She was so wet, so slick. And yet her sheath clung to him, gripped him.

She whimpered each time he slowly retreated. She moaned each time he pressed all the way in.

It was intoxicating to see her skin flush and her body arch with pleasure. It was exhilarating to hear the sounds of her enjoyment. It was completely and utterly satisfying to know she belonged to him.

For long moments he tortured them both with his slow fucking in and out of her channel. But when her hips began lifting in need with each inward stroke, when she began begging him to come inside her, Tekoa knew he'd never be able to deny her anything.

"You're perfect for me, Jessica," he said, bracing his hands on the desk and anchoring himself so he could give them both what they wanted. It only took one hard, deep thrust for him to need another, and another, and another.

His world became the hot, tight, sheath of his mate, his wife.

His worth became measured by how thoroughly he could pleasure her, by how much of his seed he could give her.

When they both collapsed, panting and covered in a thin sheen of sweat, Tekoa labeled himself an extremely rich man.

They rinsed off together in the shower before returning to the office area. Jessica reached for the shirt but he stopped her with a hand on her wrist. "No," he said, tempering the command by kissing her.

"Fair's fair, then," Jessica said, her womb fluttering as she recognized this particular game. It always made her feel both extremely vulnerable and deeply desired, though she'd never played it with any man other than Clay. "If I've got to stay naked then so do you."

Tekoa only chuckled and pulled her to him. He was still without a shirt but the sweatpants were back on. "You're beautiful, Jessica. I want to look at you. Stay naked for me."

His hand went to her breast and she couldn't hide the shiver of pleasure. She liked to be touched. She liked to be admired and petted and loved. Clay had taught her to enjoy this game though it always took some coaxing to get her to play it.

"Just until Clay gets back," she said.

Tekoa laughed. His eyebrows rose in disbelief. "Are you telling me that Clay's going to want you to put your clothes on just because he's home?"

Jessica tried to imagine Clay's reaction to walking in and finding her naked while Tekoa wasn't. He'd know right away how thoroughly Tekoa had made love to her.

Heat flushed through Jessica's body. Her heart rate sped up and her cunt lips grew more swollen. She snuggled into Tekoa and buried her face in the crook of his neck. She wanted to hide but she whispered, "Okay."

His arms went around her waist. He nuzzled her cheek before sucking her earlobe into his mouth. It felt so good to be in his arms, so natural. Intellectually she knew they were still strangers in so many ways but that didn't stop her from feeling deeply connected to him.

She'd always believed that for the most part people's choices dictated what their lives were like. But she also believed there were intangibles, luck, fate, higher powers that interceded for reasons of their own. Standing in Tekoa's arms it was easy to believe that one or all of the intangibles had something to do with their coming together.

A small smile played over her lips with thoughts of coming together. He was hard again.

She couldn't resist the temptation of finding a tiny male nipple and rubbing her tongue over it. The sweatpants didn't hide his response. His cock jerked against her belly. His arms tightened around her. "Clay will be here in a few minutes. I have no problem with him walking in and seeing us making love, Jessica."

She stilled. It was raining outside but she thought she heard the sound of an engine. Instinctively she reached for the shirt.

Tekoa captured her wrist again. "No." This time his voice demanded obedience.

The engine noise grew louder. The cautious part of Jessica wanted to cling to Tekoa and avoid seeing Clay's initial expression when he walked in and was confronted with the reality of her accepting another lover. But the part of her that had firmed with resolve and accepted the reality of being in a threesome insisted that she tackle this head-on.

She pressed a kiss to Tekoa's chest then stepped away from him. She moved to the window and watched as the truck drove in.

Clay got out and her heart sang in welcome. She suspected that even when she was eighty she'd still be reacting the same way to the sight him.

He disappeared from view once he got to the porch but she was already turning to greet him as the cabin door opened and he stepped inside. It took him only an instant to take in the situation.

Christ. Clay wasn't sure what he'd expected but it hadn't been this. In the space of a heartbeat every drop of blood had gone straight to his cock. He was surprised his brain could function at all.

His eyes flicked from Jess to Tekoa then back to Jess. There was a little spasm in his chest that *might* have been pain though he didn't allow himself to contemplate it.

Christ. He'd wanted this. He still wanted this. But the reality was a little overwhelming.

Jess had been well and truly fucked. And not only had she given her body, she'd given a piece of her heart as well. Otherwise she'd never play *any* sexual game with Tekoa.

The big head knew this turn of events was a good thing. The little head, where his heart seemed to have lodged, was screaming *mine, mine, mine, mine, mine* and wanting him to prove it with a caveman stunt like tossing her over his shoulder and carrying her away.

Uncertainty settled on Jessica's face, a vulnerability that made Clay's heart and brain and cock finally reach an agreement. When she started to fold her arms over her breasts in order to shield herself, he said, "Oh, no you don't, baby, I'm all for this. I vote that you greet Tekoa and me this way every time we come home. Now come here."

Chapter Seven

ଧ

Clay waited for Jess to come to him. Then when she was standing in front of him he took a moment just to look at her and let her see how deeply she affected him.

"I love you so much," he whispered, kissing her thoroughly. She was everything he'd ever wanted in a woman.

The ache in his chest was back. He wished a woman's touch was all he'd ever need.

His cock had gotten over the feelings of possessiveness. It was gung ho about having Jess naked. It was primed and ready for sex, any kind of sex as long as it involved Jess or Tekoa.

His heart was having a harder time with it. He knew he was on the verge of screwing this up big-time. Jess was on shaky emotional ground and there was only one way he could give her the solid reassurance she needed. He had to pay the full cost of being a threesome, that meant sharing *all* of Jessica — not just her body.

Clay pulled her tight against him. His tongue rubbed and tangled and caressed hers as he got his emotions under control. He would not screw this up.

Clay took her hand and carried it to his cloth-covered erection. "He's been all alone and out in the cold. He's suffering. He needs you."

Jessica massaged his penis with her thumb. Her nipples were hard points against his chest, her skin flushed and hot.

"He knows I'll always take care of him," she said and Clay was tempted to push the sweatpants down and tangle his fingers in her hair so he could guide her mouth to his cock.

Tekoa shifted position and Clay caught the expression of longing on his face. His heart stuttered as he realized how easily he and Jess had slipped into a familiar intimacy that excluded Tekoa.

Clay gave her a quick kiss then gently set her aside. His gaze met Tekoa's. "Great minds think alike. I left the luggage in the car because I didn't want Jess making things difficult with lots of layers of clothing."

Tekoa smiled and Clay's heart responded to it. He felt the rightness and sense of being home settle back into place.

"Just as I was about to cut the engine there was an announcement on the radio that they'd caught the eighth convict," Clay said. He moved into the space that served as Tekoa's office and regretted it almost immediately. Tekoa was too close, too much of a temptation.

He'd told himself he wouldn't act on the attraction right away. He'd give Jess time to get used to it. But Christ, it seemed like the most natural thing in the world to come home and kiss both Jess and Tekoa. He was having a hard time fighting it. It had been so long since he'd known the press of another man's lips, the feel of another man's hands and cock.

Jessica's fingers trailed down Clay's back and his penis jerked in response. "If you'll bring the suitcases in so I have something to wear, I'll go to the grocery store and pick up something special to cook for dinner."

Clay looked at Jess. Her color was still high but her gaze was steady, accepting when it met his. She was willing to give him the same thing he'd given her, time alone with Tekoa.

Tenderness and love flooded his heart. He pulled her back into his arms and showed her with his kisses just how much he adored her.

Tekoa laughed silently as he remembered those first heady moments when he'd known the Creator had given him two mates. Had he really thought it would be easy from there on? Had he truly thought their coming together would be without an awkwardness that would take effort to overcome? He stepped into their embrace so that his chest touched Jessica's bare back.

Her body shivered in greeting and he responded by brushing her hair to one side so he could kiss her neck and shoulders. Her hips jerked and Clay was the beneficiary as her cunt connected with his cock. His moan made Tekoa smile in anticipation.

Tekoa ran his hands up Jessica's sides, then slid them between her chest and Clay's so he was cupping her breasts, rubbing, squeezing. Her nipples stabbed his palms. Clay's tiny shirt-covered ones stabbed the back of his hands.

Jessica whimpered and Clay panted. Both of them pressed against Tekoa's hands and sent fire straight to his cock.

The heat rose between them, coating the air with the scent of hot arousal. Tekoa crowded closer so his cock was tight against Jessica's buttocks. He fought the urge to push his sweatpants down. There'd be time for that later, when he could afford a threat to his control. He nearly laughed at the thought. He wasn't sure anymore just how much control he had.

Jessica was shivering with need. The small tremors were so erotically intoxicating that he wanted to bite and suck and kiss every inch of her. Visions of the three of them moving over to the bed or to the rug in front of the fireplace tempted him almost beyond bearing.

She'd be so wet. So responsive. She'd welcome both of their touches. She'd let them take her as many times as their cocks could fill to do it.

He lifted his face to suggest they move just as Clay's mouth left Jessica's. Their eyes met. Clarity returned to Tekoa's thoughts. Understanding passed unspoken between them. This was their chance to break through the initial awkwardness of being intimate in front of Jessica.

Clay reclaimed Jessica's mouth as Tekoa's hand slid downward, over her naked belly and between her thighs. She bucked when he found her clit. She whimpered when his fingers filled her channel.

He pumped in and out, the motion rubbing his palm over her swollen knob at the same time the back of his hand glanced over Clay's erection. Clay's hips pumped, letting her know what was happening and how good it felt. His hands moved from Jessica's sides to Tekoa's.

Tekoa whispered, "Free his cock, Jessica. Take it in your hand."

They gave her enough room to obey and she did it willingly. She pushed Clay's sweats down then wrapped the fingers of one hand around his penis while the other hand cupped and stroked his balls.

Clay's eyes closed. His head went back on a moan.

"That's right. Let him know how happy we are that he's home," Tekoa said, brushing a kiss over Jessica's shoulder as his palm rewarded her obedience with slow, hard circles against her engorged clit.

"Please," she whispered, abandoning Clay's balls in order to cover Tekoa's hand and hold it more tightly against her knob in an effort to gain release.

Clay groaned and Tekoa chuckled. "That's bad, Jessica, leaving him to suffer while you do something you know is going to get you in trouble."

It nearly killed Tekoa to do it, but he forced his hand away from her hot, wet flesh and stiffened clit. "Remember what I said earlier about trying to rush?"

"Yes," she said, but her fingers settled on her clit.

A bolt of lust went through Tekoa. He felt an answering shudder go through Clay.

"We can play it that way if you want to, Jessica," Tekoa said, using the same tone he'd use on a hardened criminal.

"Get down on your knees. If you want to come then you can do it while you're sucking Clay's cock."

Tekoa's hand chased hers away from Clay's erection. Clay's cock jerked in greeting and Tekoa felt an answering burst of pleasure in his penis.

Jessica made a little sound that might have been protest but Tekoa didn't relent. "I'm not going to tell you twice, Jessica. I said I wouldn't punish you today, but I'm sure Clay would be happy to do it."

She hesitated for only a second before slowly sinking to her knees. Her hand curled around Clay's thigh for support. Her tongue darted out in quick licks but her mouth remained closed when she brushed it against Clay's swollen, throbbing cock.

Tekoa was mesmerized by the sight of her. He loved the way she obeyed and yet still managed a little bit of defiance.

"Jess," Clay growled in warning.

She took him into her mouth, stopping only when her lips touched Tekoa's hand. Then she pulled back, leaving Clay's cock glistening as her lips enclosed only the very tip of him.

It was the most erotic thing Tekoa had ever witnessed.

Clay thrust through Tekoa's closed fingers in an effort to forge all the way back into Jessica's mouth.

"You're going to get a spanking instead of a fucking," Clay said and Tekoa felt Jessica's body tighten with temptation then soften in complete surrender.

She began sucking Clay's cock as her fingers played in the wet, slick place between her thighs. Tekoa groaned. He promised himself that sometime soon he'd put Jessica on the bed or the rug in front of the fireplace and order her to touch herself until she came.

He slid his free hand into his sweats and gripped his penis. Clay's hands slid downward, pushing the sweatpants out of the way.

Tekoa groaned when Clay cupped his balls. He leaned forward and Clay met him.

There was no tentative exploration, no dance of dominance and submission in their first kiss. They ate hungrily at each other's mouths, dueled aggressively with their tongues.

Clay's hand took possession of Tekoa's cock. Tekoa's fingers tangled in Jessica's hair.

One kiss led to another, and another, and another. They parted only for breath, only to shudder and fight against orgasm.

Jessica's sucking controlled the rhythm and neither man could fight it. Her soft hums blended with their moans and pants.

At the edge of his consciousness Tekoa heard a drum begin beating in preparation for the ancient, mystical sing that would bind Clay and him together. He wanted it desperately and yet the feel of Jessica's silky hair made him realize he couldn't open himself fully to the Thunderbird's spirit while she was there.

He'd taken her on her hands and knees so she wouldn't see, wouldn't know all that he was. He'd have to take Clay the same way.

Later he would teach them, help them embrace the Thunderbird's spirit and merge with the storm as both messenger and protector. It was too soon to do it now. Their relationship was new and not completely defined.

The drum grew louder, the song began. Tekoa's hand tightened in Jessica's hair. "Hurry," he said, knowing that only the hot rush of seed through his cock would halt the song.

Jessica obeyed. She used her knowledge of Clay's body to make him come even as Tekoa felt her shudder in release.

Tekoa let go of his control. His cock jerked and spasmed against Clay's fingers. Hot splashes of semen struck his abdomen and chest, reminding him of the night before, only this time the pleasure was shared instead of separate.

They clung to each other afterward, all three of them struggling for breath as their heartbeats slowly calmed. Clay was the first to speak. His hands went to Jessica's hair and then to her face, stroking her in a gentle caress. "Thanks, baby," he said.

Jessica kissed his inner thigh in response before standing. It surprised her how quickly it had all happened, how natural it felt to be pressed against Clay's front while Tekoa was pressed against her back. Had she really doubted that a threesome could work?

The pain of the recent past had been replaced by a happiness of greater measure. It felt so good, so right, so perfect to be with both these men.

It had turned her on to see Tekoa's hand on Clay's cock. It had turned her on when they started kissing, though she could only feel it in the way they pressed closer and their bodies tensed. She hadn't been able to see it, not with Clay's cock in her mouth. She gave a soft laugh. She'd remedy that the next time. But at the moment she felt completely sated and utterly content. She felt like cuddling on the bed or in front of the fireplace. It seemed like she'd been licked, kissed, sucked, petted and fucked since climbing into bed with Clay the night before—not that she was complaining. She wanted to spend time luxuriating in the memories of what had already happened before moving on to create new ones.

That's what she wanted. But she could feel the tension between the two men. She could feel their cocks slowly filling again with the possibility of sex with each other.

Her cunt clenched in reaction. All it took was the feel of their erections—smooth skin over steel desire—to tempt her imagination into picturing them together. She could play the voyeur. She'd *like* to play the voyeur. Or she could participate. She knew without doubt that they'd include her, or pleasure her until she passed out, if she was willing.

All of it appealed it her. And yet…her gaze was drawn to the Thunderbird carved into the fireplace mantel. She remembered the intensity of those moments when Tekoa had taken her on her hands and knees, when he'd filled her so deeply and so fully that she'd felt like the wife he claimed her to be. She'd known without doubt that she was his mate then. She had felt it in her heart and soul. It'd been incredibly intimate, mystically spiritual, a private, ceremonial moment between the two of them. She wanted the same for Clay though she had no way of knowing if it would be.

Her cheeks heated, wondering which man would be on the top and which would be on the bottom. Would there be tenderness? Or would it be a battle ending only when one of them finally yielded?

Clay liked anal sex. Until he'd come along she'd never considered it erotic. But like so many of the other things he'd taught her when it came to intimacy and pleasure, she'd come to enjoy it, to love the feel of him taking her in such a darkly carnal manner.

Jessica forced her mind away from the heated paths it seemed determined to travel. She pressed a kiss to the spot where Clay's neck met his shoulder. "I think we should go back to my original suggestion, the one where I get dressed and go to the grocery store. I'd like to celebrate tonight with a special dinner." She tilted her head back. Their eyes met and held. She willed him to read her complete acceptance as well as her desire to give him some time alone with Tekoa. "Fair's fair," she murmured.

Tekoa's cheek rubbed against her hair. His arms went around her in a hug. She thought he was going to vote against her idea. Instead he surprised her by saying, "I like the idea of us celebrating this day with a special meal."

Clay leaned in. His mouth settled on hers. His tongue slid against hers in one wet sensuous stroke after another until Tekoa's arms around her waist were the only thing that kept her from melting to the ground. "Are you sure, Jess?" Clay asked.

"Positive."

He nodded and pulled up his sweatpants before retrieving the luggage from the truck. It took her only a few minutes to clean up then kiss them goodbye.

The rain had finally stopped though the clouds remained dark and threatening. It'd been harder to leave than she'd thought it would be.

Jessica rubbed a hand over her heart. *I haven't even made it off the dirt road and I miss them already. Pathetic.*

The totem poles on either side of the road leading to Tekoa's cabin came into view. She'd promised herself she would study them and now seemed like a good time. She wasn't in a hurry to get to the grocery store. She wasn't even sure there was a grocery store in Hohoq.

Jessica stopped the truck and got out. Like the first time she'd seen them, the rain-generated mist gave the totem poles an almost eerie, from-the-past presence. And like before she could almost hear ancient drums beating. She could almost feel the spirit and promise of the Thunderbirds perched on top of the poles, their wings outstretched as they claimed everything they could see.

She looked at the wispy tendrils of gray rolling across Tekoa's road and imagined that the poles stood guard, like sentries placed on either side of a gateway leading to a mystical place. Healer. Lover. Warrior. In her mind she heard Tekoa's voice rising and falling as it had done during the sing for Clay. The words had been foreign and unrecognizable yet they'd resonated through her like a chord that linked her soul not only to the past but to the power that was earth and wind and water and fire.

She'd felt something equally primal when Tekoa had positioned her in front of the fireplace and mounted her. The sounds she'd heard with her ears had been ones of passion instead of healing but she would have sworn she heard a deeper song, an ancient voice accompanied by a drum. Then, just as ecstasy shimmered only a few heartbeats away, the Thunderbird carved into the mantel had seemed so real that she would have sworn lightning flashed in its dark eyes as it filled the room with unknowable power.

Jessica moved closer to the totem poles. They were beautiful awe-inspiring works of art. She wondered if Tekoa's brother Ukiah had also created them. She guessed that he had.

Almost reverently she reached out and traced the figure of a badger carved at shoulder height. Next to it was a raven, below it, a fox. Everywhere she looked, animal faces and birds stared out at her.

She glanced up to where the Thunderbird was poised. Its lower body blended into the wood while its wings stretched wide. The Thunderbird was a part of the traditions and beliefs of many Native American cultures. She knew for some they were deities. For others they were supernatural beings.

In some traditions they were the Creator's messengers. In others they were protectors. In a few cases they lived as men but took the form of a Thunderbird when necessary. In almost all belief systems the beat of their massive wings caused the thunder while lightning shot from their eyes.

Her earlier impression of the poles standing as sentinels returned. She remembered the lines on the map, the red marking Tekoa's official territory as sheriff while the blue designated the wider area he felt compelled to protect.

Tekoa had said his people were known as the People of the Thunderbird. She had nothing to base her assumption on but somehow she felt sure that they viewed themselves as guardians of this land, as the enemy of any evil that would find its way here.

With a self-conscious laugh at her flight of fantasy, Jessica returned to the truck. She'd always had an active imagination. That's what made writing as natural as breathing for her. And yet even as she told herself that her impressions and conclusions had stemmed from her creativity, she couldn't shake the feeling that somehow she'd touched upon a truth of Tekoa and this land.

Jessica headed for Hohoq. When she left the cabin she'd thought of going to the diner and passing some time there. But just as she got to the edge of town she decided to keep going.

She vaguely remembered a larger town not too far away. She hadn't paid much attention to it when she'd passed the exit with Clay, but the extra distance would mean more time for her guys to be alone.

Her guys. Jessica felt a burst of happiness. She was really, really starting to like the sound of that.

She grinned. Maybe she'd even buy a can of whipped cream, though the dessert she was thinking to use it on wouldn't be cake or ice cream.

Her cheeks flushed as she remembered the flavored, edible oils Clay used to bring with him early in their relationship when he was trying to coax her into giving him blowjobs.

A laugh of pure happiness escaped. Since she wasn't pressed for time, maybe a bigger town meant a sex shop she wouldn't be mortified to go into.

She bit her lip an instant later and wondered how closely Tekoa's activities were monitored by the people he served. Would it be a problem if the sheriff's wife were seen entering a sex shop?

Her eyebrows drew together. *Wife.* The word felt so natural even though it shouldn't. She looked at the engagement ring on her finger and felt anxiety begin to swirl in her chest. But as she'd done before, she pushed it away. The reality was that she and Clay and Tekoa were together. They were a threesome. The details of how they presented themselves to the outside world and how they'd find a way to live together could be worked out later.

Jessica leaned forward and switched on the radio in an effort to keep her resolve firm and any worries at bay. Almost immediately there was a news bulletin announcing that another convict had been captured. Only one remained free, a man convicted of assault, rape and murder.

Chapter Eight

❧

Clay rolled his shoulders in an effort to get the tension out of them. He felt Jess' absence in a way that made him want to tell Tekoa to get on the radio and have her turn around. Of course, that was assuming the telephone calls would ever stop. It seemed like there'd been one after another since Jess drove away.

He sighed, a long exhale that made him grimace. Christ, he was wound up. He'd probably be doing both Tekoa and himself a favor if he just disappeared into the bathroom and jerked off while he took a shower. That might help.

Clay sprawled across the sofa and closed his eyes. He placed his hand on his cloth-covered erection. The last couple of hours had been torture.

He'd imagined himself with Tekoa. He'd imagined Jess with Tekoa. He'd imagined all of them together on the bed. He must have stopped himself from hurrying back to the cabin a hundred times. But it'd been worth it.

Clay heard Tekoa end the conversation and hang up. He didn't hear footsteps but he still knew the moment Tekoa was standing over him. Clay opened his eyes but didn't bother to sit or take his hand away from his cock.

"Sorry about that," Tekoa said.

Clay shrugged. "Comes with being a sheriff. You have to go out?"

"Not yet. There are others monitoring the situation."

A spasm of fear surprised Clay. His hand left his cock in order to ease the sudden pressure in his chest. "The situation with the convicts?"

149

"Convict. All but one has been recaptured. Some of my relatives fear he may be on our lands now."

Clay sat up. "Close to here?"

Tekoa shook his head. "Unlikely." He sat down on the edge of the couch, his hip close to Clay's. "Jessica shouldn't be in any danger."

"You could get on the radio and tell her to come back," Clay said, grimacing even as the words left his mouth. Christ, he was acting like a nervous virgin who wanted a friend there for moral support when he went out on his first date.

Tekoa grinned. "I could. After enduring a night on the couch with only my hand for company while you made love to her on my bed, I've got quite a collection of fantasies I want to explore. The majority of them include her. But not all of them."

Clay's tension slid into anticipation. He smiled. "It worked though. She accepted you."

Tekoa leaned in. His mouth hovered above Clay's. "Yes, she did."

Clay closed the distance between them with a groan. Hard masculine lips pressed together. Tongues forged aggressively into the wet heat of hungry mouths. Clay's moan was echoed by Tekoa's.

Where Jessica liked to tease, to slowly explore tiny male nipples with fingers that were exquisitely feminine and gentle, Tekoa's touch was a bold sweep of rough, sure hands over flesh that craved another man's touch. He didn't linger to explore but went straight to the waistband of Clay's sweats. His hand slipped underneath the elastic and found Clay's engorged penis, its tip already flushed and wet.

Clay's hips bucked. His hand mimicked Tekoa's. His fingers closed over a shaft as hard and hot as his own.

Tongues rubbed, twined, slid against each other in the same rhythm as cocks pushed through closed fists and thumbs glided over slippery, aroused flesh.

Clay allowed himself to be pushed backward so he was once again sprawled on the couch. Tekoa followed him down, both of them feverish with need.

Chests touched. Clay's free hand went to Tekoa's shoulder. In his fantasies it had been his body covering Tekoa's. It'd been his cock finding the tight, dark, forbidden hole and pressing inside. It'd been his hips pistoning, bringing them both to the point where ropy jets of semen jerked out in nearly unbearable pleasure.

But this felt good too. This felt right. It'd been so long and now he was free to enjoy this without fear or guilt.

Clay opened his mouth wider and the kiss deepened. He couldn't contain the moan or the shiver of need.

Tekoa's hand tangled in his hair and anchored him in place. Tekoa's other hand left his cock long enough to pull Clay's sweats down.

Visions of Tekoa doing what Jess had done, sucking him to a mind-blowing orgasm, had Clay struggling to keep from coming. "Fuck," he panted when Tekoa's mouth lifted from his.

Tekoa grinned. "We will. You have my word on that."

Clay moaned in pleasure when his testicles were cupped, weighed, claimed at the same time Tekoa's fingers smoothed over the skin between his balls and his anus.

"Fuck," Clay said again, jerking, his hips rising off the sofa.

Tekoa chuckled then lowered his mouth for another kiss.

Clay's hand pushed at Tekoa's sweatpants until they were riding his dark, muscular thighs. Cocks bobbed, strained toward one another now that they were both free. Clay didn't protest when Tekoa slid more firmly on top of him, when Tekoa's fingers encircled both cocks and held them in a handmade channel.

It felt so good that Clay almost came.

Hips pumped. Breath grew even shorter.

Clay's heart thundered like a drum beat. If he'd been free of the sweatpants completely, if they'd both been free of them, he would have spread his legs and told Tekoa to fuck him.

He wanted it. He needed it.

"I'm not going to last," he warned when Tekoa's lips lifted from his own.

Satisfaction and lust whipped through Clay at Tekoa's tight features and hungry eyes. He wasn't the only one hurting, needing.

Without a word Tekoa rolled to his feet and kicked off his sweats. Clay sat and did the same. Their eyes met. Then Clay's traveled downward in a slow perusal. Christ. He'd never felt such raw lust for another man.

Yeah, he'd gotten hard-ons and been attracted, but this was different. This was intense, extreme, something that went deep, the same way what he felt for Jessica went—only different, rougher.

Another day, another time, maybe he and Tekoa would slow down, use a softer touch as they explored each other's bodies. Or maybe not. Somehow he didn't see them cuddling unless Jess was between them, gentling them.

Clay's attention settled on Tekoa's cock. It was flushed, leaking, straining. He leaned forward and grasped it, wrapped his fingers around it as his mouth hovered only inches away. A flash of heat had him clenching his buttocks and fighting not to grab himself as well. He used his free hand to cup Tekoa's balls instead.

Tekoa's head went back with a groan. Clay glanced upward. He savored the view of taut, bronzed muscles, of Tekoa's chest rising and falling in short pants, of Tekoa's balled fists as he fought to keep from begging to have his cock sucked.

Clay's mind flashed on those sublime moments when Jessica had knelt and taken him into her mouth as he and

Tekoa had kissed for the first time. "Fair's fair," he murmured and Tekoa's hands went to Clay's hair, drawing him in though Clay was already closing the distance between them.

His lips encased the heated, wet tip of Tekoa's cock. Tekoa's moan sent another jerk of lust through Clay's penis. Fuck, he needed this so badly. Clay closed his eyes and began working Tekoa's cock the same way he liked his own to be taken.

Tekoa nearly passed out from the rush of pleasure that whipped from his cock to his brain. His fingers tightened on Clay's hair. His hips bucked in an effort to drive all the way into the mouth that was tormenting him.

Somehow he'd lost control of the situation. Again.

Amusement flickered through him even as his balls pulled tightly against his body. Who was he trying to fool? He'd never been in control when it came to Jessica and Clay.

Tekoa shuddered as Clay's tongue and lips worked his cock. It wasn't something he'd experienced often, either with another man or with a woman. It wasn't something he'd ever craved before, but between Jessica and Clay that had changed.

It had been pure ecstasy to bury his face between her thighs as she took his cock in her mouth. It had been incredibly erotic to hold Clay's cock and feel it pulse with pleasure as Jessica's wet lips slid up and down the thick shaft while Tekoa's tongue battled with Clay's.

Tekoa's heart thundered but its beat was driven by human desire and not by spirit need. White-hot lust curled in his balls. He clenched his buttocks and fought against release.

It was a challenge to both himself and to Clay. It was a challenge Tekoa knew he was destined to lose.

Clay's fingers glanced over the pucker of Tekoa's anus and Tekoa's hips jerked. His chest rose and fell in rapid, shallow pants. Clay's mouth became more aggressive. His tongue became more demanding as it swirled and rubbed and explored.

Tekoa's reality became Clay's hands, Clay's mouth. He fought against closing his eyes. He fought to continue watching as his shaft slid past Clay's lips. He lasted one heartbeat, two—until Clay took his cock all the way to the back of his throat and swallowed.

Tekoa couldn't hold on any longer. His shout was a clap of thunder that heralded his release. Ecstasy ripped and splintered through him like a lightning strike in a discharge that was so raw and violent it took him to his knees and then to his back.

He ended up on the rug in front of the fireplace with Clay's body covering his, with Clay's rigid cock rubbing and sliding against his softened one. When Clay's mouth captured his in a reversal of position, Tekoa hardened again.

For the moment he was still free of the spirit drum and the song he couldn't refuse. He was still only a man in the grip of first passion with a partner who would remain his for life.

Tekoa met Clay's tongue and tasted himself. He yielded to the pressure of Clay's thighs against his own and spread his legs. They both moaned as their sacs touched more intimately.

"My turn to come," Clay said when they parted for breath. His face was taut. His body was slick with sweat, his breathing just as rushed and rough as Tekoa's.

"There's lubricant under the couch cushion at this end," Tekoa said.

Clay laughed despite an overwhelming need to fuck. "You planned ahead?"

"It pays to be prepared."

Clay levered himself to his knees and retrieved the lubricant. His penis pulsed and leaked. He wasn't even sure he needed the lube but he squeezed the bottle and made a show of covering every hard inch of his cock with it.

When he was done he leaned forward and watched with satisfaction as Tekoa's face tightened and his eyes darkened when Clay circled the pucker of Tekoa's anus with lubricant-coated fingers. Tension and resistance greeted Clay's fingers when he slipped the tips inside the dark orifice. A warning flashed in Tekoa's eyes like lightning before a wild storm.

Clay tossed the bottle aside. He'd been willing to let Tekoa take him first but this was better. This was closer to the fantasy and it set the stage for future encounters.

They were equals with Jess. They were equals in this too. He always gave as good as he got.

Clay returned to his earlier position above Tekoa, only this time the tip of his cock pressed against Tekoa's anus. "Be prepared, huh?" he said against Tekoa's lips. "Somehow you're not reminding me of a Boy Scout at the moment."

Tekoa's laugh was swallowed in a kiss that became more carnal as Clay's cock fought its way into the tight fist of hot muscle that was a torturous paradise. Clay nearly came just getting all the way in the first time.

Christ. He loved anal sex with Jess but it wasn't the same as this. It couldn't fill the need this filled.

She didn't have a cock that would rub against his abdomen and coat him with seed when he took a partner from the top. She didn't have a cock that he could slide his hand up and down until it jerked in release as he fucked a partner from behind.

Clay began thrusting. He tried to slow it down, to savor it, but it was impossible. The need was too raw. The passion too urgent. Hands and tongues and bodies strained toward release and found it. Lava-hot semen erupted in jets of sheer ecstasy that had them both grunting, shivering, collapsing in boneless satisfaction.

Clay didn't resist when Tekoa nudged him off and to the side. "Shower," he muttered but didn't have the strength to get to his feet.

"First one there controls the temperature," Tekoa said though he couldn't summon the energy to make it a race.

Next to him Clay grunted and said, "That's assuming I'll share it with you."

"You'll share Jessica but not the shower?"

Clay smiled. "With Jessica I don't have to worry about bending over to get the bar of soap if I drop it."

Tekoa chuckled. "It's a legitimate worry."

"You happen to have a hot tub?"

"No."

Thunder rumbled in the distance. Rain began hitting the cabin roof again.

"We should build one," Clay said. "We could put it under a gazebo so that even on days like this we'd be able to use it. Maybe we could even make the gazebo portable so we could move it out of the way and sit under the stars on good nights."

Warmth flowed into Tekoa. This is what he'd dreamed of, companionship to accompany the sex. "Sounds like a plan," he said, easily imagining the two of them working together on the project, then rewarding themselves with a hot soak and an equally hot woman. "Jessica like hot tubs?"

"I've never been in one with her." Clay turned his head and their eyes met. "But we've camped places where there was shallow water and privacy. I think it's safe to say she'd enjoy a hot tub and we'd enjoy having her in it with us."

Tekoa's cock stirred. His spirit reached for Jessica's and he frowned at how far away she was. She was beyond the range where he could tell her exact location, at least while he remained tied to his human form.

A shiver of uneasiness passed through him. He'd expected her to go to Hohoq and pass time at the diner owned by his great-aunt or at the general store run by his father and grandfather.

He hadn't worried when Jessica left because he knew that as soon as his relatives saw the touch of the Thunderbird on her and realized she was driving his truck they wouldn't let her out of their sight. Tekoa smiled despite his concern. The truth was they'd pump her for information and then when she mentioned her intention to make a celebratory meal, they'd fill the car with food.

He rubbed his chest and Clay picked up on his disquiet. "Something wrong?"

Tekoa shook his head. No doubt Jessica had decided to go to a larger town. In all likelihood she'd assumed that she'd find a better selection of items elsewhere and she'd known a longer trip would mean he and Clay would have more time alone together. Still, he couldn't prevent himself from rolling to his side and propping up on an elbow so he could study Clay's reaction when he asked, "You don't think Jessica would panic and bolt, do you?"

Clay's answer was instantaneous. "No. Not a chance."

The worry eased in Tekoa's chest. He leaned closer to Clay. The lust that had been satisfied only moments earlier flared between them.

Tekoa groaned when Clay's hand tangled in his hair and pulled him down so their lips met. Their kisses were less a battle and more an exploration. The rub of tongue against tongue wasn't a test for dominance and submission but the parry and thrust of two equally matched opponents.

They swallowed each other's moans of pleasure. Their hands roamed, this time seeking out tiny male nipples and sliding over muscled arms and backs.

The flames in the fireplace flickered and danced. In the recesses of Tekoa's soul he felt the ancient song poised, ready to begin. With the single beat of the drum his heart would be commanded by the spirit that was both a part of him and separate from him. With the first words there'd be no stopping until Clay and he were bound together more permanently than any human law or custom could ever dictate.

Tekoa settled more of his weight on Clay. His tongue forged deeper. Their cocks were velvet steel trapped between soft skin and hard muscle.

Clay moaned and Tekoa answered it with moan of his own. The hunger built. It became a howling spirit wind.

Primitive urges flared. The need to position Clay onto his hands and knees became too much to ignore.

Tekoa lifted his mouth from Clay's. He rose to his elbows. But before he could speak thunder filled the air and was followed by the ominous ring of the telephone.

"Fuck," Clay said.

Tekoa rolled to his feet. The sense of uneasiness returned and grew with each step toward the phone.

* * * * *

Jessica eyed the pouring rain. It didn't look as though it was going to stop anytime soon.

She glanced at the plastic bags in the grocery cart. There were seven of them, three for each arm and she could hold the seventh. As long as she had her key out she could probably get in the truck before her jeans were totally soaked.

"No time like the present," she muttered, pulling the hood of her jacket up and retrieving the car key from her pocket before lifting the bags and settling them into place.

Even in the miserable weather, the grocery store she'd found a short distance from the highway had quite a number of shoppers—enough so that she wasn't parked close. She braced herself for the sting of cold water against her face and left the protective overhang. A blast of wind whipped the hood back. A clap of thunder made her jump. The bolt of lightning that followed made her long for the cabin. She was more than ready to get back and make some hot chocolate with marshmallows. She was more than ready to snuggle up with Tekoa and Clay.

Jessica laughed despite the frigid water soaking her hair. She just hoped the guys had something left for her—two large, hot somethings that could warm her from the inside out.

She darted toward the truck. It was impossible to avoid the puddles. Water splashed up on her jeans and soaked into her socks.

Wet hair and rain in her eyes left her struggling to insert the key and unlock the car. Just as she managed to open the door, water sprayed across the back of her legs as a car pulled in next to her. She was irritated but she didn't bother turning to glare.

Jessica wrenched the door open against the wind and stepped onto the running board so she could lean in and put the dripping plastic grocery bags onto the passenger-side floor. She was only vaguely aware of the car behind. A door opened and shut. She straightened, started to sit, only to be roughly shoved onto the truck's bench seat.

* * * * *

Tekoa studied the map as his cousin, Tenino, relayed the news. A child arriving home from school had discovered his father beaten, ankles and wrists bound, his mouth taped shut. The family car was missing, as was a gun. The victim had identified his assailant as the convict who was still at large.

A short while ago the stolen car had been found abandoned just inside the boundary of Thunderbird land. An elderly man was discovered unconscious in the trunk of that car. He'd been taken to the hospital. His wife said he'd gone to the store in their now-missing-and-assumed-stolen car.

"There's no reason to think he's heading this way," Tenino said.

"But he's still on our land." Tekoa felt sure of it.

"Several of the elders say yes. The police on the scene have roadblocks in place. If he's still in the area and he stays on the asphalt they'll catch him. If he goes off-road he's likely to get stuck in mud and abandon the car. We'll find him if he takes off on foot. We've got it covered. You're better off staying where you are and taking care of what needs to be taken care of."

His cousin was right. Most likely the escaped felon would get stopped at a roadblock. If he didn't, then one of The People would find him. The storm called to them and they rode the winds in spirit form.

They weren't all that they'd once been in the days before foreign ships brought physical and spiritual and cultural death to the ones whose belief had given life to the Thunderbird. But his people could still sense evil when it walked on Thunderbird lands. They could still protect against it.

A crack of thunder drew Tekoa's attention to the window. Out of the corner of his eye he saw Clay go into the bathroom. The shower was turned on. His cock responded despite the news about the convict and despite his uneasiness that Jessica was out in the storm.

On the other end of the phone a bell chimed as a door was opened and closed. In the background someone ordered coffee.

"Keep me posted," Tekoa said.

"Will do."

Tekoa hung up the phone and followed Clay into the bathroom. Need rippled down his spine and through his cock like an erotic current as he stepped into the shower.

Chapter Nine

Water cascaded over Clay's flesh. It caressed the firm muscles and glistened on smooth tanned skin. He had an athlete's tight, hard body, shoulders that were strong, a waist that narrowed and flowed into taut lean buttocks.

Tekoa's cock ached as his gaze followed the water. He took it in hand as Clay's head tilted back to rinse the soap from his chest and genitals.

"Everything okay?" Clay asked.

"A couple of assaults but no deaths so far. The convict is now armed and jacking cars. There are roadblocks in place and we know where he was last. It's north and west of here. Jessica went south and east."

Clay turned and moved to the side so that some of the water splashed onto Tekoa's chest. His attention flicked to Tekoa's face before moving downward.

Tekoa slid his hand along the length of his penis and palmed the head when Clay's gaze stopped on that part of his anatomy. Between a night of intense masturbation and what he'd already done with both Jessica and Clay, he should be worn out. But if anything, he was even harder, even hungrier than he had been only moments ago when Clay leaned forward and took his cock into his mouth.

Clay grinned. His hand slid between Tekoa's legs and cupped his balls. "Tempting. Maybe I'll go down on my knees in here and you'll go down on your hands *and knees* out there."

Tekoa's hand found Clay's penis. "I don't think so." He stepped into Clay and crowded him against the shower wall.

Their mouths met in a kiss every bit as wet and hot as the water striking their flesh. Tekoa shifted his grip so that one hand held both of their cocks while the other fondled Clay's balls. Clay moaned and bucked.

The temperature of the water turned lukewarm in comparison to the heat they generated. Need roared through Tekoa. His mouth left Clay's and traveled downward. He'd intended to turn Clay toward the wall and fuck him but images of the first kiss they'd shared, with Jessica kneeling at Clay's feet and sucking his cock, drove Tekoa downward.

Jessica and Clay were both too good at oral sex not to do a lot of it. Tekoa wanted to share everything they enjoyed. He wanted to do everything they desired. He wanted to know them as well as they knew each other.

"Christ," Clay said, driving his cock through Tekoa's closed fist as soon as Tekoa's tongue stroked the underside of his penis.

Tekoa looked up the line of Clay's body. Dark eyes met heated blue ones. He licked again.

"Put your fucking mouth on it and keep it there," Clay said, tightening his fingers in Tekoa's hair.

Tekoa grinned and pulled back. Clay's cock jerked in protest. "It may have escaped your notice, but I'm not Jessica. I don't follow orders. I'm too used to giving them."

Clay's lips pulled back in a grimace that doubled as a snarl. "Christ. What do you want?"

Tekoa's tongue darted out and rolled over the tip of Clay's penis. He could feel Clay shudder with pleasure. "You're an addict."

"So blow me."

Tekoa chuckled. "I'm getting to that." He took the head of Clay's cock into his mouth. This time he assaulted it with his tongue as he sealed his lips around it and sucked.

Clay groaned and doubled over. "Oh yeah, like that," he panted. "But take me deeper. Fuck. Take me deeper."

Lust roared through Tekoa at the sound of Clay's neediness. He used his mouth and hands ruthlessly until Clay shouted in ecstasy then slumped against the shower wall with his eyes closed.

Tekoa stood and let the water cascade over him for a moment before redirecting the shower spray so that it struck Clay. When Clay only grunted but didn't have the strength to open his eyes, Tekoa's earlier amusement returned. He stepped into Clay so that his cock was a steel ridge against Clay's belly. "Jessica I'd carry into the other room in order to fuck. You I won't. So either turn around here and now or give me some indication that you can make it out of the bathroom."

Clay laughed. His eyes opened. "Christ, you're a hard case."

Tekoa grinned. "Tell me about it." He pressed closer, his cock an exclamation point between them.

"Fair is fair," Clay said. "Bed?"

A crack of thunder sounded. Its boom was so loud that it felt as though the walls and floor shook. Tekoa reached over and turned off the water. Rain pounded against the roof in a fury that had his spirit wanting to soar.

It was a warning that he heeded. If he was called, he'd need to take Clay with him.

There was no time for explanations or training. There'd be no time for meditation. But orgasm served as well to free the Thunderbird spirit from the body of a mate who didn't yet know the ways of The People—or so his brother Ukiah had told him. Tekoa would have to take Ukiah's word for it since he'd never tried it before himself.

"The rug in front of the fireplace," Tekoa said as he stepped from the shower and quickly toweled dry.

Clay shrugged and followed. He'd have preferred the bed but somehow the rug was fitting.

His cock stirred as he remembered coming out of the concussion and seeing Tekoa for the first time. His eyes appreciated the sight of flowing muscles and bronzed skin as Tekoa crossed the main living area of the cabin.

When Tekoa knelt on the rug in front of the fireplace and reached for the lubricant, Clay couldn't take his eyes off Tekoa's cock. Christ. His own cock began to fill again. He was starting to wonder exactly what was in the cup Tekoa had given him the night before. Not that he was complaining. And not that he couldn't fuck like a rabbit on his own, but this—this was beyond his experience.

"What, no foreplay?" Clay joked as he plopped down next to Tekoa. He stretched out on his side and watched Tekoa coat himself with the lube.

"Roll over," Tekoa bit out but Clay could hear the amusement in his voice.

Clay rolled to his hands and knees. Tekoa's hand grasped Clay's penis and he groaned.

"Okay, this works as foreplay," Clay panted, sucking in his stomach when the lubricated fingers of Tekoa's other hand circled the pucker of his anus.

Heat seared through him. He spread his thighs wider without being asked or told.

His breath caught when Tekoa's fingers pressed in. Clay had a bad feeling the only thing that was going to keep him from coming before Tekoa's cock was inside him was Tekoa's hand gripping his penis.

Clay's hips bucked and his penis began leaking when Tekoa moved behind him. He went down on his elbows when Tekoa's outer thighs touched the insides of his own. The feel of skin against skin, of Tekoa's fingers being replaced by Tekoa's cock had him moaning. He pushed backward and knew intense satisfaction when Tekoa groaned.

Christ. It had been so long. It had been years since he'd known what it was like to be fucked by another man—and that experience was a pale imitation of this one.

Thunder sounded—above the cabin or in his own head. Clay couldn't be sure. His heart was racing, its beat rapid and uncontrollable.

Sweat poured off them both as Tekoa's cock forged deeper and deeper. Clay shivered and moaned. He welcomed the pleasure and pain of being claimed in such a darkly primitive manner.

Tekoa stilled when he was all the way in. Clay gripped the rug to keep from begging in the same way he liked to make Jess beg.

A small sound—too close to a whimper—escaped when Tekoa stroked Clay's cock and fondled the wet tip. Clay clenched his jaw to keep a second sound from escaping.

"This is forever," Tekoa murmured. "You and me and Jessica. There's no changing it now."

It took a second for the words to register with Clay. When they did they only added to the sense of rightness. "That works for me."

"Good."

Tekoa began thrusting and Clay's reality narrowed to the moment, to the intense pleasure of Tekoa's hand stroking his shaft while Tekoa's cock slid in and out of his anus.

The sound of a drum edged into Clay's consciousness, accompanied by a voice. His heart and soul recognized the song even if his mind didn't. He had the fleeting worry that when he came, he'd pass out. But he couldn't hold the thought.

Tekoa became more forceful as orgasm built. Clay's balls were hard and tight and full. He couldn't fight the release building with each stroke, couldn't deny it. When hot jets of semen filled his dark orifice Clay gave himself over to incredible sensation, to an ecstasy unlike any he'd ever known.

The pleasure was followed by a wrenching sensation. By gray, cold nothingness and then by awareness, disbelief and confusion.

Stay with me! Tekoa said and his voice felt like it was piercing Clay's mind.

Immense energy rippled through Clay. Power gathered and rolled through a body that was now huge and brightly feathered, the wings outstretched, riding the thermals like a Thunderbird.

Clay's first rational thought was that he'd had a heart attack and died during sex. The idea gained purchase when the gray nothingness blurred at the edges of Clay's vision and he heard Tekoa's voice screaming in his mind. *Stay with me!*

He felt talons on his back, digging in roughly, the sharp ends painful and real. Clay moved his arms in an effort to escape, only it was a pair of wings that cut through the air in a boom of thunder.

Stay with me! Tekoa repeated. *Jessica's in trouble.*

Clay felt his heart then. He heard it pounding and racing in his chest.

The confusion returned. His mind struggled to process what was going on. In a horror-filled instant he remembered the car wreck and wondered if he was in a coma and the last day had been an intense erotic fantasy because his brain couldn't cope with reality.

The claws tightened on his back. *This is real, Clay. Accept it. Follow the bond we have with Jessica.*

Clay thought of Jessica and immediately felt her terror. That was all it took for his confusion and disbelief to disappear.

He'd deal with this weirdness later—or not. Jess was more important. He knew without doubt that she was fighting for her life. He even knew where she was—not a location he could pinpoint on a map or even a place he could envision— but a destination he could get to all the same.

Her spirit was linked to his and Tekoa's by long, honey-gold strands that made him think of the two cups Tekoa had taken from the fireplace mantel. *Do you know what's happening to her?*

No.

No?

The talons in his back loosened and then disengaged. *Focus* was all Tekoa said.

Clay felt the downward sweep of wings that were as powerful as the ones he now seemed to posses. Tekoa pulled away, leaving the clouds swirling angrily as thunder followed in his wake.

* * * * *

Jessica acted on instinct. She reached for the door handle on the passenger side of the truck. Her assailant was faster. He struck her across the face with the cold metal barrel of a gun then pressed it against her temple.

Raw terror coursed through her. She hadn't seen a picture but she knew she was looking at the escaped convict.

"One scream, one word, bitch, and you die right here, right now." He pulled the driver-side door shut.

Even if she'd been able to do it, Jessica didn't think a shout for help would be heard over the pounding rain. She remained motionless, frozen in place with her heartbeat thundering so loudly in her mind that it sent her thoughts skittering wildly, unable to focus on a way to get out of the truck alive.

She had so much to live for, Clay and Tekoa, their new life together, she couldn't die now. Not now.

Tears welled up and escaped. She didn't waste the energy trying to fight them. Instead she drew on the same strength she'd found when Clay was hurt. She'd been scared then, but she'd done what needed to be done. She'd do what needed to be done here too.

He wouldn't kill her right away. With icy clarity she knew he'd rape her first. That's what he'd gone to prison for — assault, rape, murder.

The escaped convict reached over and picked up the keys she'd dropped on the floor. His attention shifted to the police radio on the dash and he smiled. "Well, well, well. Groceries, a cunt, and an inside track to what the cops are doing. Life just got real good."

He flicked on the radio. There was a burst of static then nothing. He smiled again before turning his attention back to Jessica. Bile rose in her throat at the look in his eyes. Her fear excited him.

His smile widened. He traced the trail of tears with the tip of the gun. "Do what I say and you might even enjoy the things I'm going to do with you. Cross me and I'll hurt you real bad before we're done."

He switched the gun into his left hand long enough to get the key in the ignition and start the truck. Jessica choked back a sob of terror. She fought desperately to get herself under control. She accepted the fear. But she refused to be paralyzed by it.

She wasn't bound or restrained — yet. That meant she had a chance to fight or run.

The gun was still pointed at her, but it wasn't pressed against her forehead any longer. That gave her some room to maneuver.

"You don't look like a cop," the convict said as they left the parking lot. "But this is a cop radio. So I'm thinking that makes you a cop's pussy." He turned his head slightly and licked his lips. "Open the jacket. Real slow and real careful. If I have to shoot I won't kill you with the first bullet. As long as you're breathing and I've got a hole to fuck, I don't care whether you're bleeding or screaming."

Jessica's hands shook as she unzipped the jacket. She wanted to close her eyes and block out the sight of his hand leaving the steering wheel long enough to unzip his pants. She wished she'd taken the time to put a bra and turtleneck on before she left the cabin. She'd started to but at the last minute she'd given in to the desire to keep Tekoa's soft flannel shirt close to her skin.

The convict shifted in his seat and his cock sprung free. "Unbutton the shirt, bitch."

A whimper escaped before Jessica could stop it. She closed her eyes and he struck her in the ribs with the gun. "Open your eyes, bitch. You think because some cop shoves his dick into you that you're too good for mine?"

Jessica opened her eyes. He slammed the butt of the gun down on her mound. Pain screamed through her but she bit her lip to keep from crying out.

"Now unbutton the fucking shirt and show me your tits."

She had to get out of the car. The thought beat through her as numb fingers fumbled with the buttons.

Slowly she edged into a half-sitting, half-leaning position. The truck was an old, stripped down model without power locks.

They merged onto the main road. If there were other cars they were hidden by the grayness of the day and the sheets of water that made it impossible to see more than a few feet in front of the truck.

The barrel of the gun slammed into her ribs again. "Hurry the fuck up. I want to see some tits then you're going to crawl over here and suck my cock."

A part of her mind tried to distance itself from what was happening. Thoughts of the Thunderbird with its outstretched wings came unexpectedly to mind. Thoughts of Clay and Tekoa followed. Staying alive was the important thing. Whatever she had to do to stay alive, the three of them would deal with the fallout later.

Jessica got the last button undone but couldn't make herself spread the shirt and expose herself to him. If she could just unlock the door and get out of the truck...

He was driving fast, but not that fast. There was water on the road. It might serve as a cushion when she landed. There were ditches on either side of the road, and woods beyond them. She couldn't see any of it but she knew it from the drive into town.

The radio crackled to life. Jessica tried to position herself to unlock the door while he was distracted.

A voice announced they'd found a stolen car abandoned in the grocery store parking lot and were scrambling to set up new roadblocks while they questioned employees and customers to see if they could account for everyone who'd been in the store. The convict started cursing. He pounded the steering wheel with a fist and swung the gun so it glanced across Jessica's breasts with a painful sting. "This is your fault, bitch. Your fucking cop probably doesn't even trust you to go to the grocery store alone. Whores. You're all fucking whores that can't be trusted. The only thing you're good for is your pussies."

She cowered against the door and let him see her fear, hoping that the sight of it would keep him from noticing the subtle shifts in her position. If they cornered him, she'd become his hostage.

He slammed on the brakes and sent her crashing into the dashboard. Then he backed up and turned onto a narrow road. Several feet in there was a sign. *Private. No Trespassing. Hunt Club Members Only.*

The graveled road became a dirt road as it sloped upward. There were thick woods on either side but the convict didn't take his eyes off her as they traveled.

Jessica's breath became trapped in her throat when they rounded a corner and she saw a cabin ahead of them. It was dark, abandoned for the winter.

He'd make his stand there and while he was doing it he'd rape her repeatedly. He'd kill her or leave her for dead if he fled again.

It might take hours, possibly even days for the police to investigate the private road. She couldn't let him get her inside the cabin.

Thunder boomed overhead with a violence that seemed to shake the ground. Lightning flashed.

Now! The command screamed through her like a howling wind. She reacted impulsively, instinctively, the scene rehearsed in her mind so there was no wild scrabbling to unlock and open the door.

She landed on her knees and heard the gunfire almost simultaneously. *Missed*! her mind screamed in victory an instant before she became aware of the searing heat where the bullet had grazed her back. She scrambled into the woods, not caring whether she used her hands or her knees or her feet to get something between her and the gun.

A bullet ricocheted off a tree. A second one followed. She didn't know how many bullets he had left.

He got out of the car and screamed profanities. She darted forward, dodging the trees, her breath loud and fast.

A sane person would have let her go. But he was incensed, trapped—a man with a great capacity for violence and nothing to lose. He crashed after her, venting his rage with promises about what he'd do to her once he caught her.

She ran and slid and fought to keep from being a target. The clouds gathered and roiled above her as if they were reacting to the life and death struggle taking place beneath them.

The wind picked up. It whipped through the thinning trees, driving her forward and sideways.

Jessica stumbled. Her hands braced her. She kept going, fighting against slick leaves, barely looking up until suddenly confronted with open space. Panic filled her at the sight of the fallow field with its rutted grooves. She'd never make it across before he got close enough to shoot.

He was still behind, closing in on her even as she tried to think. There was no backtracking, no going forward. She ran along the edge of the field and tried to put as much distance as she could between them without having to dodge the trees. She prayed that she was heading in the direction of the paved road and that she'd be able to duck back into the woods before he emerged and saw her.

Lightning flashed, closer now. The air felt charged with power.

Her lungs burned. Pain stabbed through her side.

She risked a glance over her shoulder. Her foot hit a soft muddy spot and she pitched forward.

Even before she scrambled to her feet she knew she was in trouble. The ankle gave. She tried to stand again. She endured excruciating pain for several steps before going to her knees and trying to crawl into the woods.

There was a shout of triumph. A bullet struck a tree in front of her. "Stop right there, bitch, on your hands and knees where you belong." She stopped even though every instinct demanded she run. She braced herself, expecting a bullet to strike her.

Nausea rose in her throat. Sex was the only weapon she had left to fight with. She couldn't outrun him, not now, not when she could barely stand. If he thought he'd won... If she could only endure... There'd be an opportunity when he orgasmed...when he'd be weakened, unfocused...when maybe she could get the gun...

She didn't let herself think about what would happen when he got to her, how badly he'd hurt her before getting down to the business of raping her. She didn't let herself think about anything except the importance of surviving. Whatever happened she'd rather be alive than dead.

Jessica risked getting to her knees. The shirt and jacket she'd undone in the car parted and even through the pounding rain she saw him focus on her exposed breasts. His hand went to his fly though he didn't unzip his pants again.

A downdraft nearly forced her to the ground. She glanced up at the roiling blackness of the clouds as thunder exploded and lightning flashed in one furious thrust after another. It charged the air with its violence. A scream suddenly cut short had the hair standing on her arms.

Disbelief, hope, a wrenching sob, all of them crowded her chest when she saw the escaped convict lying on the ground, his body twitching as though electrical current still flowed through him. She glanced at the sky again. The dark clouds rumbled, parted, and for a moment she could swear she saw two Thunderbirds hovering in the sky, protective spirits who'd come with the storm and saved her life.

Tears flowed freely. Her heart soared, wanting to merge with them, almost feeling as if she could. Her vision blurred and when she blinked there were only dark clouds. The lingering sense of a powerful storm remained overhead even as there was also the contradictory feeling that a part of it was moving away.

Slowly Jessica got to her feet, careful not to put much weight on her damaged ankle. She was shaking. From fear, from relief, from the frigid rain striking her bare chest and from her soaked clothing. With trembling fingers she rebuttoned the flannel shirt and zipped the jacket.

Her attacker was dead. He had to be.

The body was still now, the eyes open, staring sightlessly into the sky as the rain struck his face. Jessica glanced upward again and found only clouds, and yet she still offered a prayer of thanks.

The logical part of her argued that the Thunderbirds had been a powerful hallucination brought on when two extreme emotions collided — when absolute terror gave way to overwhelming relief. But the part of her that accepted Tekoa's ability to heal Clay through a sing, the part of her that had *felt* the Thunderbird's presence both when Tekoa had made love to her on the rug in front of the fireplace and when she'd been looking at the mist-shrouded totem poles, that part of her believed that somehow, someway, when she'd accepted Tekoa as her "husband" she'd become connected to the Thunderbird's spirit.

Warmth uncoiled and slid through her, reminding her of the drink Clay had given her on Tekoa's porch when she was shivering and cold and frightened by the future. Tears choked her, happy grateful tears that she still had a future to look forward to.

Jessica took a hobbling step forward and whimpered with pain. *I can do this. I will do this.* She needed to check the body. There'd be little point in making the long, painful trip back to the abandoned truck if the keys were here. She could break the window in order to use the radio and call for help, but she'd rather not.

She wanted to go home. She wanted to take a shower and then climb into bed with Clay and Tekoa. She wanted to feel their hot bodies pressed to hers. She wanted to hear them whisper words of love and tell her everything was okay. She wanted it with an intensity that consumed her.

Jessica forced herself to take another step. This time nausea welled up along with the pain. She looked around for a stick and found one that would work as a crutch.

Thunder rumbled above her like a growled warning. A gust of wind held her in place.

She tried to press forward. This time the thunder was an angry splash of sound accompanied by more forceful winds.

Jessica glanced upward again. Her heart rate spiked. There was no mistaking the Thunderbird this time. It hovered in plain sight for timeless seconds, its gaze fixed on her in a silent command to stay put.

She obeyed.

Chapter Ten

ဆာ

Clay tried to stay in the moment, in the form that was so surreal it might just have blown his mind if Jess' well-being wasn't at stake. Fuck! Even in his wild teen years when he'd blacked-out, passed-out, and done his share of puking his guts out, he'd never even come close to something like this. Then again, back in those days his recreational drug of choice had been alcohol instead of acid or some other stupid-ass thing.

This whole experience would have rivaled a Sixties trip down psychedelic lane—except how could he argue with the sight below him and the aching, wrenching pain in his heart?

Christ. He'd died inside when he'd seen Jessica on her knees with her shirt and jacket hanging open.

Her terror and horror had been like a kick in the gut with a steel-toed boot.

It'd been over in a heartbeat. He'd watched in awe as lightning streaked from Tekoa and slammed into Jess's attacker.

From his trailing position, he hadn't seen the flashes come from Tekoa's eyes, but he knew enough about Native American myths to know that's where the lightning had come from. Fuck! Myth? He'd have to rethink that one, or better yet, let Jess do it. That kind of thing fired her creative cells.

It was all so un-fucking-believable. The thunder, the wind-blown clouds, the lightning.

Amusement rippled through Clay despite his frustration at not being able to do anything other than stand guard over Jess until help that was closer than Tekoa's cabin arrived. He could almost hear Tekoa saying, "Now don't try this at home, you two, especially when I'm not around to guide you."

Clouds filtered in between Clay and Jess. An updraft pushed him higher. The cold seeped in and he found it harder to think. At the edge of his consciousness he saw his human form lying on the rug in front of the fireplace and had the strong sense that his spirit needed to return to the flesh that usually housed it.

Grayness crowded in at the edge of his vision. He felt a tug deep inside, almost like he was a fish on a line. As soon as he thought it he remembered the golden strands he'd followed to Jessica and guessed this pull was Tekoa, reeling him in.

Clay fought the call. He used the sweep of wings to clear away some of the clouds so he could see Jess.

Two men emerged from the woods near where she was sitting with her back against a tree. From a distance one of them could have been Tekoa though Clay knew it wasn't. The second man glanced up and without being told, Clay recognized that both men were whatever the hell he'd become.

He felt the tug again, only now he was ready to follow it. He wanted to get to Jess. He wanted to hold her in his arms and make love to her.

Focus, Tekoa had said before leaving. Clay wasn't sure whether he needed to *refocus* or do the opposite of focus.

Christ. He wasn't sure he was cut out for this mystical shit.

The gray coldness began closing in on him, more tightly this time, and though he didn't have lips to grin with, inside the Thunderbird's form his spirit managed it. Hell, who was he kidding? This was the ultimate adventure—or it would be next time, when he could experience it while Jess was safe.

* * * * *

Jessica struggled to her feet when two men emerged from the woods. "Tekoa," she whispered, her heart stuttering with happiness and relief.

When the men got closer she realized it wasn't Tekoa, but even that knowledge didn't dampen her spirits. She was safe and someone was here to take her home.

"I'm Ukiah," the first man to get to her said as he swept her up in his arms.

She recognized the name, though his face told the same story. "You're Tekoa's brother."

"Yes. And this is our cousin, Tenino."

"Are you hurt?" Tenino asked.

"My ankle. I can't walk very well on it."

Ukiah crouched on the ground with her on his lap. His fingers lightly brushed the place where the bullet had grazed her back. Tenino crouched beside them and removed her shoe and sock. Heat radiated from his hands as he gently examined her bruised and swollen flesh. Ukiah's warmth seeped into her from where his cheek very nearly rested against hers. It was strangely intimate to be cocooned between two of Tekoa's very masculine relatives, and yet it was also completely nonsexual.

Jessica winced when Tenino's fingers found a tender spot. She jerked when he discovered a second one.

"You up for a sing?" he asked.

Jessica wasn't sure who he was speaking to.

Ukiah said, "What's the damage?"

"Bad sprain. It'd heal in a week or so with rest, but we'd have to carry her out of here and chances are it'd swell a lot more by the time we met up with Tekoa and Clay." He looked up then and grinned, his expression reminding her so much of Clay's playfulness that Jessica felt laughter bubble inside of her just as Tenino added, "Two men, one woman, a scare like this one—even with all the mud she's currently wearing, I'm guessing the windows of the patrol car are going to get all steamed up once we make the handoff. It might be worth some get-out-of-jail-free points if we fix her up before we turn her over to your brother."

Jessica's cheeks flamed. Her heart did an erratic hip-hop in her chest.

Better get used to everyone knowing it's a threesome, she told herself. Tekoa had told her that his people would view her as his wife and Clay as both her husband and his lover.

Ukiah gave her a little hug. "You know what we're talking about doing?"

"Yes. Clay had a concussion. Tekoa did a sing for him."

"Good," Ukiah said.

Tenino started to unzip his jacket. Jessica guessed he was planning to place it on the ground in a chivalrous gesture. She shook her head and teased, "Unless you've got to strip down to a loincloth like Tekoa did, don't bother. I'm already soaking wet. A few minutes of lying on the ground aren't going to be worse than these clothes."

Both men chuckled as Tenino did his best to clear the sticks and wet leaves from a small area. Jessica eased off Ukiah's lap and lay down. "Eyes closed?"

"Yes," Ukiah said.

She closed her eyes though almost immediately she was tempted to peek. There was no drum, yet she heard one. Her heart matched its beat. Ukiah's voice then Tenino's joined the drum in a merging of words and sound. The song blurred Jessica's thoughts even as she felt a healing, impossible heat move through her body.

* * * * *

"We getting close?" Clay asked.

Tekoa grinned and cut a look over at his companion. "That your version of 'Are we there yet?' because if it is, we're taking separate cars when we go on vacation."

Clay laughed but he didn't lean back in his seat. If anything he'd been getting more and more wound up with each mile they traveled.

Tekoa didn't blame him. Even knowing Jessica was safe, healed, and traveling by car in their direction, they were both going to be strung out until they got her home. And even after they got her back to the cabin, he wasn't sure how long it'd be before they'd let her out of their sight.

He'd been a cop long enough to have experienced some dicey, dangerous situations. But nothing had ever scared him as badly as seeing Jessica defenseless and kneeling as a would-be rapist and murderer walked toward her with a gun in his hand.

A few minutes later...maybe even a few seconds later... Tekoa took a deep breath and closed his mind against bloody, might-have-happened scenarios. She was safe and according to both his brother and cousin, she was handling what had happened well enough to say she'd drive the truck back.

There was no chance of that happening. Ukiah would take the truck to his place and stash the groceries there. Tekoa figured he and Clay and Jessica would get around to collecting them—eventually.

Technically he should go to the crime scene but with the escaped felon dead by natural causes and the carjacked victim soon to be in an even more protective custody than she was currently in, Tekoa was content to let others deal with the body.

His heart raced with anticipation when the radio chirped and Tenino's voice said, "I'm just passing the road to the old Briggs' place. Visibility is almost zero but I think I'm seeing lights. That you up ahead?"

"That's us."

* * * * *

Despite Tenino's prediction of steamy windows and wild sex in Tekoa's patrol car, Jessica was bundled in a blanket on Clay's lap with his arms a vise around her waist and Tekoa's hand enfolding hers. After the initial tears and kisses, followed by Clay's terse warning that she wouldn't be going anywhere alone for a long time, they'd settled into muted conversation and a shared longing to get back home where clothes could be shed and bodies merged.

It'd been on the tip of her tongue to tell them about the Thunderbirds, but in the confines of the car those moments seemed more like fantasy than reality. Maybe later, when they snuggled against one another in the aftermath of sex she'd be able to whisper what she'd seen, what she'd experienced, what she'd guessed. Maybe she'd ask Tekoa about the People of the Thunderbird and what it meant to be married to one of them.

She shivered when they left the paved road. A small whimper escaped as she flashed back to the moment the escaped convict had also turned off the wider road.

Clay's arms tightened on her, as did Tekoa's hand. "Almost home," Clay whispered, brushing a kiss against her forehead.

The totem poles came into view. They stood tall and stark, darkened by water and the fading daylight. Somehow they seemed fiercer than before, as though they would guard not only against real danger but any that might ride in on a nightmare.

Her heart raced in her chest. "You're safe now," Tekoa said, rubbing his thumb over her knuckles.

Clay carried her over the threshold of the cabin within a minute of Tekoa parking. When he would have taken her straight to the bathroom and placed her in the shower himself, she insisted he set her down near her luggage.

"Don't bother," he said, knowing her well enough to guess what she was planning to do, but he relented and turned away when she told him not to hover.

Jessica dug out a pale blue nightgown then escaped to the bathroom. Normally she had to force herself out of a hot shower, but this time the silky feel of the water caressing her skin didn't tempt her to linger, not when she hungered for the heated skin and firm masculine touches that were waiting for her.

She showered quickly and dried her hair. She donned the nightgown, though she doubted she'd be wearing it for long.

Clay and Tekoa were both standing just outside the bathroom. Jessica's womb fluttered at the sight of them. Her breasts tightened and need flared in a hard burst that made her pussy weep.

They'd changed from jeans back into sweatpants. They'd stripped out of their shirts and shoes and socks, but there was nothing casual in their stances.

They closed the distance in the span of heartbeat. Tekoa's mouth captured hers as he pulled her against his chest. Clay's front pressed to her back. His lips chased the strap of her nightgown off her shoulder with hungry, sucking kisses and tiny nips.

She'd expected the heat and passion, but she'd thought it'd be a slow burn instead of an explosive inferno. Clay's hand curled around her thigh. Tekoa's tugged at her nightgown, pulling it up, baring her in the seconds before Clay's fingers played in wet arousal then slipped inside her.

Jessica whimpered into Tekoa's mouth as her sheath clamped down on Clay's invading fingers. Tekoa's tongue answered by sliding and rubbing, tangling with hers, his movements echoing the thrust and retreat, the swirling of slick fingers over an erect clit.

Her fingernails dug into Tekoa's shoulders as she held onto him, desperate to remain on her feet under the onslaught of passion. His hands continued upward, the nightgown flowing over his forearms as he cupped her breasts and palmed the nipples before taking them between his fingers.

They were relentless in their touches and kisses, as if only the sound of her crying out in orgasm would assure them she was all right.

Jessica didn't fight the sweet sensation, the rising need, the soul-searing pleasure that lifted her on wings and made her soar.

She clung and cried out. She shuddered and pressed against them, unashamed to share everything she was with them and to let them know with her body that they were her world.

It was Tekoa who swung her up into his arms and carried her to the bed. The nightgown fluttered to the floor only a second before he followed her down, his chest a welcome, hot weight against her side and breast. Clay stripped off his sweatpants and joined them. This time he was the one whose lips covered hers, whose tongue rubbed against hers in a sensual dance.

Jessica moaned and arched as Tekoa kissed down to her breast. He laved the nipple, bit it, then pulled it into the wet heat of his mouth. Her hand found Clay's cock and her fingers encircled it, slid up and down in time to Tekoa's suckling.

Clay's tongue became more aggressive. His fingers found her stiffened clitoris.

She bucked under the assault. Her knees rose and her hips lifted off the bed.

Tekoa's fingers found her wet slit and filled her with rough thickness. "Please," she begged when Clay lifted his mouth and allowed her to breathe.

"Not yet."

He kissed her again, a long wet declaration of devotion. Then he left her lips to join Tekoa at her breasts.

She shivered at the feel of them both suckling. Her hands tangled in their hair. Her thighs widened even further in a silent request for them to touch everything, to love her everywhere. She couldn't control the whimpers, the breathless pleas that were more sound than words.

Tekoa's face lifted though he held her nipple until it popped free of his mouth. His eyes met hers and she saw in them the same heartfelt caring she'd seen in Clay's so many times.

Jessica didn't know how it had happened so quickly. She was cautious by nature, fearful of getting hurt emotionally, and yet he'd already claimed her heart and soul, as well as her body.

The fingers tangled in his hair tugged so that once again his mouth hovered above hers. "I love you," she whispered, suddenly needing to give him the same words she gave freely to Clay.

His smile was like the sunshine. His happiness so open and honest that it brought tears to her eyes.

"I love you too," he whispered.

He kissed her gently, tenderly, reverently, as though the kiss was an unspoken covenant. Then he kissed her again, only this time when he lifted his mouth from hers the skin around his eyes was crinkled in amusement. "Clay's going to take a little more effort, but you I already adore."

Jessica laughed but the sound quickly merged into a gasp and then a moan of pleasure as Tekoa's mouth returned to hers and Clay's found the wet, needy place between her thighs. They kissed her deeply, thoroughly. Their tongues probed and stroked, licked and rubbed as their lips ate hungrily at flesh already sensitized, primed for their touch.

She screamed as wave after wave of searing ecstasy pulsed through her. Her body shuddered with the force of her release. Grayness crowded in at the edges of her consciousness and she fought against passing out.

It took effort to open her eyes even partway. Clay's face was above hers now, his eyelids lowered, his mouth a sensual line that begged to be explored. Jessica kissed him and tasted herself. The need that had coalesced into a mind-blowing orgasm returned with a vengeance, only this time she knew she wouldn't truly be satisfied until she felt their cocks inside her.

She became aware of Tekoa's arm then, how it rested across her pelvis so the fingers of his hand could wrap around Clay's cock. Dark fantasies crowded in, images she'd explored while she'd been driving, when she'd been wondering what Clay and Tekoa were doing together.

Jessica wriggled downward and out from underneath Tekoa's arm. He didn't protest when she rose to her knees and removed his sweatpants so he'd be as naked as she and Clay were.

For a long moment she just looked at her two men. They were beyond gorgeous to her. They were everything she'd ever want.

Jessica chased Tekoa's hand away from Clay's cock and replaced it with her own. He was hot, hard steel.

Tekoa's cock pulsed against her palm when she encircled it with her hand. He didn't resist when she used her grip on his heated flesh to maneuver him onto his side and closer to Clay.

She felt their anticipation like a current traveling down her arms and straight to her cunt. They wanted their cocks to touch, they wanted her to see them touching.

She leaned down and licked the head of Clay's cock, then did the same to Tekoa's.

They panted. Their hips jerked in reaction.

She continued teasing, sucking one of them, exploring the slitted tip, then doing the same to the other until they were both straining, quivering, threatening her with punishment and hoarse promises of getting even.

Jessica rubbed the slick, swollen tips together. She loved them with her mouth and tongue, caressed and sucked as their sensitive cocks touched.

The pleasure drove them into each other's arms, into a kiss that was hard and hot and wetly passionate. When it ended their breath was shuddering in and out of their chests. Their eyes glittered with male intention.

Clay rose to his knees. His face was taut, the demand in his eyes so familiar she licked her lips to tease him further. "Suck my cock, Jess, or Tekoa's going to see you get a spanking."

Her cunt clenched in reaction. Liquid arousal leaked from flushed, parted lower lips.

Another day, another time, she'd gladly take the spanking. She wanted it now, but she wanted their cocks inside her more.

She crawled forward on her hands and knees, hyperaware as she did so that Tekoa had positioned himself behind her.

"Now, Jess," Clay said, his hips giving a small thrust toward her mouth.

She obeyed and was immediately rewarded by the feel of Tekoa's hand between her thighs, cupping her mound, pressing his palm to her clit before sliding his fingers over her opening.

"That's good, baby," Clay said, spearing his fingers in her hair as she made love to him with her mouth. "You're so good."

His praise flooded her channel with more arousal. She pressed backward, driving Tekoa's fingers deeper.

"She's so wet," Tekoa said. "She's always so wet and ready."

Jessica's mouth left Clay's hard flesh just long enough to say, "Please, Tekoa. Please put your cock in me."

His fingers retreated and she whimpered. His hands smoothed over her bare buttocks before settling on her hips.

Jessica moaned as his cock found her entrance. It was sweet torture to feel him entering her, stretching her one slow inch at a time. She tried to rush him, to impale herself on him, but his hands on her hips prevented it.

Clay's chuckle made her shiver with anticipation. His fingertips grazed over her scalp and her breast tingled. "Suck me, Jess, take me all the way back while Tekoa fucks that beautiful little pussy of yours."

Jessica couldn't have disobeyed if her life depended on it. She'd worried that Clay's coarse talk would remind her of the convict and have her shying away from his demands before she could stop herself from doing it, but love and trust kept that from happening.

She liked Clay's rough side just as much as she liked the tender side he was always willing to show her. His dominance turned her on as much as his caring did.

"That's right, baby," Clay said, tightening his grip on Jess's hair.

His head tilted back and he couldn't keep his eyes open despite the lust pouring through him at the sight of Tekoa's glistening cock powering in and out of Jess' hot slit.

Christ, she made him feel helpless and powerful at the same time.

He was addicted to her. He'd been completely lost from the first moment he'd seen her reading one of her stories to an audience of children.

"I'm not going to last much longer," he warned when his balls pulled tight and his heart thundered in his chest.

They'd agreed to take her together when they got back to the cabin, to make love to her until she was sated by multiple orgasms, then to give her both their cocks at the same time and push her over the edge of consciousness and into Thunderbird form.

It'd save a hell of a lot of explaining, which Clay was in favor of. Plus he'd be able to experience the Thunderbird again without the fear for Jess' safety.

But at the moment he was having a hard time coming up with a reason why it had to be done *now*.

Ecstasy was Jess' mouth on his cock.

He moaned and leaned forward. "Oh god, Jess, that feels so good. Don't stop. Don't stop."

White-hot shards of pleasure skittered along his backbone. He was close. Almost there.

Jessica whimpered, then he did too when her mouth left him.

Clay's eyelids flew open. He was panting. His hips were pumping, air-fucking where Jessica's mouth had just been.

Tekoa's hand landed on Clay's chest and pushed him backward. "Get on top of him, Jessica," Tekoa ordered. "Put his cock inside you."

She obeyed instantly.

Clay moaned and arched.

The tight muscles of her sheath clamped down on him, every bit as hungry and wet as her mouth had been. *Oh yeah*, he thought, driving himself deeper, *this is better*.

"I love you so much," he whispered, once again tangling his fingers in her hair, only this time he brought her face to his and melded their lips together so his tongue could mimic what his cock was doing.

Tekoa didn't bother reaching for a bottle of lubricant. His cock was wet. Her back entrance was coated with arousal.

"Easy," he whispered when she tensed at the feel of his cock against the pucker of her anus. "Let me in, Jessica. Let me share you with Clay."

She relaxed a little bit and he rewarded her with kisses to her shoulder, her neck, her ear. She whimpered when he sucked her earlobe. She widened her thighs and tilted her pelvis when his tongue explored the sensitive canal.

"Perfect," Tekoa praised, licking into her ear before leaning back.

Clay's hands swept down her spine. He palmed her buttocks then spread them.

Lust flashed thorough Tekoa, it burned him with a soul-deep need that would only be appeased one way. He placed the head of his cock at her back entrance again. He fought against the tight ring of muscles keeping him from being with both of his mates at the same time.

Inch by inch he joined with them. Ecstasy swamped him. Nothing in his life had prepared him for the feel of another man's cock against his as they were both held deep in a woman's body.

He stayed motionless for as long as he could. He savored the pulse of their shared heartbeat. He offered a prayer of thanks for both Jessica and Clay.

And then he began pumping. Slowly at first. Then faster. His cock in tandem with Clay's. His cock in counterthrust.

Between them Jessica writhed and moaned and whimpered. Her pleasure intensified theirs. Her heated flesh inflamed them, drove them to give everything.

Jessica felt full, not just from the dual penetration of their cocks, but from the emotion swamping her. It was almost too much, as though her body couldn't house the sensation coursing through her, the feeling of having them both love her so intensely at the same time.

Her heart raced and thundered in her chest. Her muscles tightened on them, as if somehow she could stop the wild rush if she could only hold their cocks still in her depths.

Tekoa's mouth found her ear. "Don't fight it, Jessica. Let go."

Clay's fingers squeezed her nipples and sent erotic pain flashing to her clit. "Come for us, baby. Come for us."

He tightened his fingers again and she lost the battle. Jessica screamed as the hot wash of their seed poured into her and an orgasm unlike any she'd ever experienced cast her into the unknown.

For a split second there was only the gray cold of a scattered mass in the moments before a cloud is born. It was followed by cognizance, a consciousness forming, then by joy as Jessica became fully aware of the Thunderbird spirit now merged with her own, of the brightly feathered body that was myth and reality at the same time.

Tekoa was above her. Clay was beneath. Exhilaration filled her as they soared together over vast tracks of forest and mountain, called by the storm and the land, the drumbeat of their combined hearts singing of spirits shared.

TWO SPIRITS

෨෮

Acknowledgement

℀

Thanks to James H. for reading this story and giving me feedback from a gay man's perspective.

Trademarks Acknowledgement

℀

The author acknowledges the trademarked status and trademark owners of the following wordmarks mentioned in this work of fiction:

Jeep: Daimler Chrysler

Jockey: Jockey International, Inc.

PlayStation: Sony Corporation

Xbox: Microsoft Corporation

Chapter One

❧

The oppressive feeling of having his life completely out of control settled around Trey Masters like a heavy fog. *Could it be any worse?*

His stomach clenched as soon as he thought it. Yeah. Yeah, it could be a hell of a lot worse. He could be in some unmarked grave or at the bottom of the ocean. The Veron family could still be ruining lives with him as an unwitting accomplice and his students or the kids he coached as victims.

Trey closed his eyes and rested his forehead against the cold window of the police cruiser. He wasn't sorry for what he'd done. There'd been no choice but to do the right thing. He was an elementary schoolteacher, for god's sake. What kind of a man would he be if he'd said no when the Feds showed up and asked him to help them bring down a powerful family making and distributing child pornography?

No, he wasn't sorry he'd helped. Even if he'd known beforehand that Patricia Veron made a deadly, vengeful enemy, he would have kept sleeping with her and kept pretending everything was okay because he'd been desperately clinging to the illusion of heterosexuality.

Bile rose in his throat as he wondered if he might eventually have asked her to marry him if the Feds hadn't stepped in. He wanted to believe the answer was no.

Old feelings of self-loathing threatened to return but Trey ruthlessly stomped them down. Pretending, yeah, he was good at that. Pretending and denial had been a part of his life since he was twelve years old and got an erection thinking about his best friend.

He'd been convinced he was going straight to hell then. He'd become certain of it when the fantasies become more detailed and erotic as he grew older.

Fag. Queer. Pervert. The names were knives with the power to shred lives. He'd seen what happened when other kids got labeled. He'd done everything in his power to avoid it. In high school he'd become a track star, a debate team captain, the boy who never lacked for a date or a girl willing to let him touch her breasts and cunt.

In college it was more of the same. He'd continued to run track though he'd traded the debate team for the school paper. There'd been fewer girls but the ones he did go out with, he'd fucked, wanting to convince himself he was straight.

After he graduated there'd been his first teaching job, followed by a second one when he'd moved back home because his mother was starting to show the signs of the disease that would come to define both of their lives. Even if he hadn't already been steeped in years of denying his core self, he wouldn't have acknowledged his sexuality then, not in his devoutly religious mother's house.

On the outside, he'd been the successful son his mother had wanted. But on the inside, with each year that passed, he'd had to work harder and harder to suppress the truth of what he really was. Gay.

Trey grimaced. What a word. Gay. There was nothing about being homosexual that made him even remotely happy, much less lighthearted and carefree. Then again, when had he ever allowed himself to act on a same-sex attraction? Never.

Maybe it was time to stop pretending. Maybe when this was over and it was safe to involve someone else in his life…

Trey rubbed his chest. The dull ache was still there months after the funeral even though the truth was he'd lost his mother years ago to frontotemporal dementia—FTD to those unfortunate enough to have someone they love suffer from the fatal condition that shrinks the lobes in the brain controlling personality and speech.

It was a relief to know she was at peace now. She would have hated knowing what she'd become. Only his memories of how much she'd loved and sacrificed as she'd raised him on her own had helped Trey hang on as the disease turned her into a verbally abusive and embarrassing stranger.

A flash of lightning followed by the crack of thunder made him open his eyes. The cop driving grunted and said, "They might as well have sent you to Alaska. Christ, who picked this place?"

Trey didn't have an answer as he looked out at Hohoq. It was supposed to be his refuge but seemed more like a dreary prison. He counted five buildings and prayed the mist pressing in on the police car was hiding the rest. A glance was enough to extinguish any hope for a bookstore or a library. He'd probably end up grateful for a TV getting more than one or two channels.

The car slowed to a halt in front of an old-fashioned sign swinging on heavy chains. *Sheriff.*

"Grab your stuff," the cop said as he cut the engine and placed his hand on the door handle. "As soon as I make the official handoff, I'm out of here."

"Sure thing. I know you're in a hurry."

"Bet your ass I am. My wife'll kill me if I'm not back and on the plane to Vegas with her."

Trey rubbed his chest again, this time as twinges of envy slid through him. He wanted what the cop had, a nice heterosexual lifestyle with a wife at his side both at home and out in public.

He wanted it, but he knew it wasn't going to happen unless he was willing to spend the rest of his life living a lie— or unless he stopped letting what others think define how he lived. There *were* cities where it'd be no big deal to be openly gay. There *were* liberal school districts and communities where people understood being gay didn't equal being a child molester—far from it, and the statistics proved the point. Most of the sick scum who preyed on children were heterosexual.

Trey snagged the single duffle bag he'd had time to pack in his mad rush to get out of the house and into an informal protective custody arrangement. Maybe when this was all over he'd take a trip somewhere and...what...hit a gay bar, check out the personals? Yeah, right.

His virgin ass was so obvious it glowed. He'd attract every predator in town.

He opened the car door and was hit with a blast of wet icy wind. It was enough to bring Trey's thoughts clearly back to the here and now.

Survival. That was key. Even with his heaviest jacket on, he felt like he was freezing by the time he made it the short distance into the sheriff's office. His cop escort was already making the handoff to a man Trey figured was the sheriff, though he was surprised at the thick braid accompanying the Native American features.

"He's all yours," the cop said. "No sign of Patricia Veron, but that doesn't mean she won't surface for some payback."

"So expect trouble?" the sheriff asked, the answer lost on Trey as another man stepped into the room.

Trey stiffened, cock-first. He buried his hands in his pockets and was grateful the jacket was long enough to cover a boner that'd scream fag if any of the other men noticed it.

Stop fighting it. If you'd accepted it earlier you'd never have been sleeping with Patricia Veron and none of this would have happened.

Trey ducked his head and tried to get himself under control. *Think small town and just how notorious cops are for being close-minded when it comes to queers.* It didn't help. In that split second of awareness an image had burned into his mind and his cock wasn't going to let him forget it.

Tenino was having a hard time paying attention to the conversation between the city cop and Tekoa. His gaydar was pinging and his cock was at attention and ready to serve in the line of duty. It was the last thing he'd expected when he stepped into the office.

He'd been dreading hauling a stranger out to his cabin, but now...blond hair, blue eyes, a neat ponytail he could already see himself freeing and spreading out across the sheets on his bed... Tenino could hardly wait for introductions.

Ever since his cousins Ukiah and Tekoa had found their mates, he'd been feeling the need to settle. He didn't hold out any hope he'd have a mate in the truest sense of the word, a forever lover who could join him in flight when the storm called and the Thunderbird spirit rose. For that to happen he'd have to find one among The People, which didn't seem likely since not many of them were bisexual, much less one hundred percent gay like him.

His heart ached when he thought too hard about not having that ultimate spiritual connection, so mainly he *didn't* think about it. He lived. He had sex when he could get it. He'd even spent some time as a cop in Los Angeles and San Francisco, but in the end the pull of the land had been too strong. Now he was back to stay and ready to begin and end each day in the arms of a longtime lover, though finding one was proving to be difficult.

Tenino studied the blond who seemed to be trying his best to ignore his presence. Shy? He'd never found it attractive in men though it could be kind of cute in women.

He could make an exception for the blond. Besides, the blond was going to find it hard to stay shy at the cabin. The place was small. They'd be bumping into each other every time they turned around.

Tenino grinned. Bumping and grinding wasn't going to be a hardship.

He tried to remember exactly what Tekoa had told him about his soon-to-be guest. It hadn't been much. Friend of a friend asking a favor, the possibility of some danger so Tekoa didn't want the stranger at his cabin or at the lodge his brother Ukiah owned. Both places had women there now.

That's all Tenino remembered. He shrugged off the need for more information. It'd come. The grin widened. Hopefully *he'd* come.

The blond looked up at the mention of his name. Trey.

The sound of it stroked over Tenino's cock. He closed his eyes briefly as the image of him lying on top of Trey, whispering the name as he thrust, flashed through his thoughts. Tenino extended his hand when Tekoa made the introduction. Trey's eyes met his and slid away quickly. His shoulders hunched just enough to make him shrink inside his coat.

Tenino turned to shake hands with the cop. The cop's face was flushed and his expression said it wasn't because of the heat in the office. He'd caught the way Tenino was devouring Trey with his eyes.

Tough shit, Tenino thought. *Deal with it.*

"You going to be okay here?" the cop asked Trey. "If you're not good with this, you can ride back with me."

"I'm good," Trey said, emotion churning in the pit of his stomach while his heart raced like a rabbit's.

The cop didn't waste any time leaving. Trey looked everywhere except at Tenino, until Tenino said, "The cabin's remote, might as well grab something to eat in town. You hungry?"

Trey's eyes met Tenino's. White heat flashed though him along with the skittering, nervous fear that came with standing at the edge of a high dive before jumping to the water below. "Cabin?"

Tenino's smile was pure sin. "Can't put you somewhere it'll be easy for the bad guys to find you. So are you up for some dinner?"

"Yes." It was all Trey could manage and thankfully Tenino turned his attention to the sheriff. "What about you? You eating in town or waiting 'til you get to your place?"

"I don't think food will be on the menu by the time I get back home."

"Torture me why don't you?"

The sheriff laughed. He placed his hand on Tenino's shoulder. "Your turn's coming."

"I'm not like you."

"I never thought I'd find what I needed either. But look what dropped in my lap. Look what happened with Ukiah. Your turn's coming. Maybe it's already here."

Tekoa's glance flicked to Trey and back to Tenino and made the ball of want and trepidation grow in Trey's stomach. His cock grew harder at the words. His breath grew a little short. He'd always considered himself good at reading between the lines—or at least he had until the desire for a straight lifestyle had blinded him to the truth about Patricia Veron and her family. It almost sounded as if—

He shook his head, cleared it, reminded himself he was in a nowhere town with a couple of law-and-order types. Just because he was ready...make that *close* to ready...to accept his sexuality did not mean the first guy who got his heart racing and his cock head slick with arousal was gay.

It was going to be bad enough having to share a cabin with Tenino. The last thing he needed was to act like a sixteen-year-old with a crush. Yeah, Tenino's smile had caused what little blood remained in Trey's head to shoot south, but thinking about it with his big head *instead* of his little one, Trey realized Tenino was probably envisioning inviting some women over and having some fun.

Trey wasn't vain about his looks. He'd never had trouble attracting the opposite sex. He'd just lacked the true desire to do it. And he could see how his blond-haired, blue-eyed appearance was a great contrast to Tenino's darker one.

The color in Trey's face deepened when he realized both Tenino and Tekoa were looking at him, maybe waiting for him to answer some question he hadn't heard. He picked up the duffle, said, "I'm ready."

Apparently it was the right response. They left the office, only stopping long enough to throw the duffle into a Jeep with the sheriff's department logo on the side of it before walking to a nearby restaurant and claiming a table next to the window.

The rain hadn't arrived yet, but it was coming. Flashes of lightning streaked across the sky and the peals of thunder arrived in shorter increments of time. The mist was heavy and gray, giving the town a mystical appearance and making Trey think of Native American myths and rural folktales.

"So what do you do when you're not hiding from dangerous ex-girlfriends?" Tenino asked, drawing Trey's attention away from the strangely mesmerizing scene outside the diner.

"I teach. Elementary school."

Tekoa grunted. "You're lucky the Feds approached you and asked for your help instead of hauling you in as a suspect."

Trey shivered. He fought to keep the bile from rising in his throat and the nightmare scenarios that had him waking in a cold sweat from returning and destroying his hard-earned calm. All it took was suspicion to ruin a reputation and a career, to make life a living hell.

He gripped the menu to keep his hands from shaking. He wasn't in the clear yet, wouldn't know if he'd really survived until he was back home and applying for a teaching job.

The first thing he'd done after the Feds laid out their evidence and asked for his help was to call the principal at the school where he taught and arrange a meeting. They'd agreed on a plan of action, so the school wouldn't be hurt and neither would Trey when the story broke about the Verons.

The Feds had done as promised. They'd made a point of telling the media Trey was never a suspect and had been instrumental in helping them build their case and shut down a child pornography operation.

But there was no going back to the way things were. Trey knew that.

Even though his principal had tried to talk him into staying, Trey couldn't shake the need to move on. It was time to put some distance between himself and the city where he'd grown up denying his sexual orientation. It was time to leave the house he'd inherited from his mother, along with the guilt that came with being gay.

"Yeah, I was lucky," Trey said, putting the menu on the table, his appetite gone.

Their waitress arrived and took Tenino and Tekoa's orders. When she looked at Trey he said, "Nothing for me."

"Get him what Tekoa and I are having," Tenino said. "Otherwise he's going to regret not eating once I get him to my place."

The waitress lifted an eyebrow. There was no missing the speculation in her eyes.

Heat, confusion, the wild pounding of his heart kept Trey silent just long enough for the waitress to collect the menus and leave. He licked his lips, dared a glance at Tenino.

Their eyes met and held. Trey's chest tightened. He fought the urge to grip his penis through the denim of his jeans at the bold, confident look on Tenino's face—as if Tenino *knew*, as if he *wanted*.

Trey glanced away first. Conversation was beyond him and thankfully Tekoa and Tenino seemed comfortable with silence.

A foggy mist settled more heavily outside. The wind created the illusion of movement, caused imaginary forms to take shape in the swirling grayness. A memory pushed to the surface of Trey's mind as a dark, birdlike shadow appeared and disappeared along with a peal of thunder.

Hohoq. It was one of the names for the thunderbird.

Remembering it made Trey look at the scene outside and see it as more than a stark, desolate prison. He loved collecting stories of supernatural beings and occurrences. And over the years, he'd found the promise of a good ghost story, the working of a legend or folktale into a lesson plan, helped his students learn and gave them an incentive for good behavior.

Lightning flashed, followed quickly by thunder. The shadow wings reappeared and seemed to spread further, as if the thunderbird was drawing closer, just as the storm was.

He knew there were a variety of beliefs when it came to thunderbirds. In some cultures they were protectors. In others they were the Creator's messengers. At least one tradition held they lived as men but could take the form of a thunderbird when necessary. In almost every belief system the beat of their massive wings caused the thunder while lightning shot from their eyes.

Trey rubbed his chest as an odd sensation struck, making him think of talons reaching, sinking in, surrounding his heart and taking its measure, choosing to leave him alive and gifting him with a warmth that whispered of happiness and home, that felt like anticipation and hope.

When the waitress returned with a hamburger and fries, his stomach growled. Hunger returned in a rush and Trey started eating, very much aware of Tenino on the other side of the table.

"So what's your take on the situation, Trey? Is there likely to be trouble?" Tenino asked.

Trey looked up to witness Tenino stabbing a fry in a pool of ketchup. It made him think of blood.

"If Patricia finds out where I am, then yes. The Feds now think she might have killed before, more than once, to keep her family's secret safe. She'll feel responsible for bringing them down and she'll want to get even with me for betraying her. Her sister committed suicide when the story broke."

This time Trey couldn't hide the way his hands shook slightly. Patricia had nothing to lose. If she found him, it would end only one way — with one of them dead.

Revulsion filled him. He blocked his mind to the image of himself in bed with her. His hands lowered to the plate, but before he dropped the burger, Tenino reached over and snagged a fry, then a second one.

"Eat up. Weather's getting worse. We need to get out of here."

Trey found himself lifting the burger, eating. He tried not to think about how intimate it seemed to have Tenino casually helping himself to the fries — and failed. Even without looking at the sheriff's deputy, he was acutely aware of the other man's every move, every glance.

In self-defense Trey turned his head to look out the window. A pickup truck with a camper shell on the back pulled to an angled stop in front of the diner. He had only a glimpse of a beautiful blonde before the man driving pulled her to him and they fogged the car windows with the passion they shared.

Longing filled Trey and made him ache. Finally the couple parted. The man got out, blond and beautiful like the woman. He walked around the truck and opened the door. After helping her out they lingered, kissing again, their bodies pressed tightly together and their arms locked around each other.

Trey's cock pulsed, jerked at the sensuality, the sense of connection radiating from the couple. He barely registered Tenino saying, "Now that Clay and Jessica are back, I guess we shouldn't expect to see you unless there's an emergency."

He barely noticed Tekoa leaving the diner. And then the sheriff was on the other side of the glass.

The woman smiled as she left her blond lover's arms and slid into Tekoa's. Tekoa's lips took hers in kiss every bit as intimate and dominating as the one he'd interrupted and she clung, softened, seemed to melt against the sheriff. He lifted his head, said something to the blond and the blond laughed, leaned in, touched his mouth to Tekoa's.

The brief kiss sent shock waves through Trey, made him grateful the tablecloth hung down far enough to prevent total humiliation as he gripped his erection to keep from disgracing himself. His face heated. His heartbeat became erratic. He felt as though his entire world had just shifted on its axis.

Chapter Two

ℰ

Tenino's stomach clenched. He doubted Trey had any idea just how expressive his face was. Fuck! He wished he hadn't seen half the emotions Trey revealed.

No wonder his cock was standing at attention and his gaydar was pinging. Trey wanted what Tekoa had, a female lover and a male one.

Tenino polished off the last of Trey's forgotten fries. He tried to keep his eyes from devouring the blond across the table and his imagination from stripping him. It was impossible.

For the first time since walking into the office and seeing Trey, Tenino hoped Patricia Veron got picked up by the Feds soon. Otherwise it was going to get tense in the cabin.

"Ready," Tenino asked, standing abruptly and shooting a scowl at the waitress, a cousin whose eyes were practically dancing and whose fingers were no doubt tingling with the urge to get on the phone and tell everyone he'd left with a delicious blond.

Any other town and he'd have to worry about talk being unsafe for Trey, but not here. The People of the Thunderbird didn't reveal sensitive information to outsiders.

Trey rose and reached for his wallet. Tenino nearly groaned at the sight of the hard ridge pressed against the front of Trey's pants. "Don't worry about it," he said. "Meals are part of the pay here."

They were greeted by rain when they stepped outside. The street was empty save for the Jeep. They hurried to it but still managed to get wet. Darkness was coming close on the heels of the storm, blending in so there was almost no differentiating the dusk with the gray of clouds.

Tenino concentrated on driving. Argued with his cock about acting on the attraction to Trey.

He was a fool. He knew he was a fool. Yeah, he loved watching Tekoa interact with Jessica and Clay. Loved the open sexuality when the four of them got together to play poker or watch a movie. Fuck. He loved Jessica. She was gorgeous, sinfully submissive when her men wanted that from her. She was a wet dream waiting to happen and if he'd been straight or bi, he'd have been green with envy that she belonged to Tekoa and Clay.

Tekoa and his brother Ukiah had both been given mates not originally of The People. Otherworldly cups had appeared almost as soon as they'd met their mates, the mystically created liquid inside proof of the Creator's blessing. Drinking it had united Clay's and Jessica's spirits with Tekoa's, Marisa's with Ukiah's, and allowed for a full joining so they became Thunderbird.

Tenino sighed. He was gay and not straight or bi. It'd rip his heart out to share a lover with a woman. So what chance did he have of gaining a true spirit mate when their physical union would never produce children? How would it serve The People? The Creator?

And still he couldn't stop himself from catching glimpses of Trey out of the corner of his eye. Usually he found the call of the wind and rain irresistible. Usually he couldn't wait to get home, to stretch out in front of the fireplace and let his spirit escape the confines of human flesh to become Thunderbird.

It was the overpowering need to take flight, to feel his spirit deeply connected to the Creator's and to the land The People protected, that had brought him back to Hohoq. But as the air warmed in the Jeep and Trey's scent invaded his senses, images of stretching in front of the fire with Trey, of kissing and touching, soaring with passion instead of with the storm, filled Tenino's mind.

On some level he noticed the scenery as it passed on either side of the Jeep. He was aware of the slashing rain, the wind, the thunder and lightning, the presence of Thunderbirds high above them. But on another level, it was like driving through a tunnel with home marked by a light at the far end.

He rolled to a stop in front of the cabin. The rain was coming down in sheets, the blackness of night complete.

Tenino slid from the Jeep and raced to get under the porch roof. He had the door open by the time Trey grabbed his duffle and got to shelter. A flick of his hand over the switch and the inside of the cabin lit up.

His eyes went to the fireplace mantle and the Thunderbird image Ukiah had carved into it. There was no half-filled cup waiting as there had been for Tekoa when he took Clay and Jessica to his home.

Tenino swallowed his disappointment. Reminded himself he'd been a fool to hope there would be one—especially since Trey had a thing for women.

He stripped his jacket off and hung it on a peg next to the door. "I'll get a fire started," he said, the smallness of the cabin closing in on him with a coziness that promised an unrelenting ache in his cock unless he came to terms with Trey's presence there.

For the most part it was one room with the kitchen separated by a counter and the start of the bedroom delineated by a carpet. The couch was oversized, plush, the TV an energy-consuming extravagance that had made more than one of the elders shake their head and mutter about the foolishness of youth, especially when they saw the collection of video games making up his "library".

Tenino pointed toward an open door. "Bathroom's there," he said, crossing the wooden floor and kneeling on the thick, woven rug in front of the fireplace.

Even with his back to Trey, Tenino was acutely aware of Trey taking his jacket off. In his mind's eye he went further, saw Trey peeling down the wet jeans, then the rest of his clothing before stretching out in front of the fire in a sexual offering.

Yeah, this was going to be a problem, Tenino thought. He got the fire going, the task second nature, so often performed it didn't require nearly enough of his attention.

Trey disappeared into the bathroom, came out barefoot and wearing sweatpants. He stopped by the duffle he'd put on a chair and dug out a book.

Tenino's jaw clenched when Trey claimed a spot at the end of the couch closest to the fire. He needed to figure out a way to handle this. For the next week or so, this was his job, keeping Trey safe. But short of having a tracking device on Trey, there was little chance of Patricia Veron finding him — which meant there was little danger of anything except dying of blue balls.

His hands curled into fists as he fought the urge to unzip and give himself some relief. Fuck!

An icy-hot bolt shot through his cock at the word. Tenino closed his eyes, took a deep breath then regretted it as the light scent of Trey's cologne made his chest tighten.

Deal with it, he told himself. *There are two choices here.*

Kick back, have some fun. No commitments. No expectations. Just go with the flow, take what was offered even though doing casual with Trey would only make the cabin seem empty and the loneliness worse when he was gone.

Or he could hold out. He could fight the attraction and spend a lot of time jerking off in the shower.

Tenino grimaced. Yeah, that idea held a lot of appeal.

He turned away from the fire. Trey's head was down, his attention seemingly on the book he was using to shield his erection. Tenino was willing to bet his badge that if he asked, Trey wouldn't be able tell him what he was reading.

Why couldn't Trey be butt-ugly? Or a flamer? Either would have made things easy.

Instead Trey was perfectly masculine. He was lean, mouthwateringly fit without the muscles of a guy who did serious bodybuilding. And the blond ponytail was about to drive Tenino crazy. He had a thing for long hair. He loved freeing his braid and having a lover comb his fingers through it. He loved doing the same to a lover.

Tenino shook his head slightly and admitted to himself he didn't have a clue how to proceed. Say something about the chemistry that had him harder than he'd been in a long time? Don't say anything?

It's not like they were in a gay bar or set up by friends. They were snugged up in his cabin with one bed, one sofa and a whole lot of togetherness. Which meant he was going to be totally miserable in his own place if something didn't give.

Tenino took a deep breath, opened his mouth and let the first words that presented themselves out. "Look. No surprises here. I'm gay. I—"

"I'm not," Trey interrupted, swamped by deep-seated panic and reacting with denial before he could stop himself.

It was a stupid thing to do. As soon as the words were out Trey regretted them.

He was wearing baggy sweats and using a book to shield his hardened cock from view. Did he think Tenino was so clueless he hadn't noticed?

"Okay, bi then," Tenino said.

Trey managed to look up. To meet Tenino's dark eyes. "I'm not bi."

Even *he* heard the absolute truth in those three words. And the force with which he'd delivered them was like slamming a conversational door shut.

Tenino's eyebrows went up. Trey's heart thundered. His face flamed and his thoughts raced.

Maybe it's time to stop pretending, a small internal voice whispered. *Here's your chance. The two of you are going to be sharing a cabin. He's safe, a lot safer than anyone you'd meet in a bar or online.*

Trey's fingers tightened on the book. His breath grew shorter. Sentences formed, dissolved, reformed. But his throat closed, preventing any possibility of retracting his earlier denial, of openly admitting his sexual preference. He closed his eyes and ducked his head, not wanting to see himself labeled a coward in Tenino's eyes.

Shock. Heat. Lust. A nearly overwhelming need to dominate scorched Tenino and just about cost him his control.

Tenino stood abruptly, before he gave in to the temptation to force the truth out of Trey. Gay. Not just gay, but probably a virgin.

Tenino retreated to the bathroom, admitting to himself he was very close to having most of his brains reside in his cock. Most of his blood was already there.

He stripped and stepped into the shower stall, went for hot water because there were only two cures for what ailed him and in his mind, taking a cold shower wasn't an option. He lathered his hands, gave in to the fantasy it was Trey's hand circling his erection, Trey's hand cupping his balls.

Fuck, he had it bad. But short of handcuffing Trey—

Exquisite agony raced through Tenino's cock as the scenario of cuffing Trey to the bed and gaining a confession played out. Shit, it'd be the sweetest confession he'd ever heard, made in the midst of gasps and pleading and moans.

Tenino groaned as he imagined using his mouth and hands to work Trey into admitting the truth. He'd take it slow at first, build the need, the anticipation, make Trey's first time so good the only place he called home was the cabin and the only bed he wanted to be in was the one in the next room.

There were teaching jobs close enough to Hohoq for Trey to commute back and forth. It could work, for both of them.

Tenino closed his eyes, slid his hand up and down on his cock. His buttocks flexed. His thighs bunched. The need for release built.

He began panting, thrusting through the tight fist of his fingers, the movements growing sharper, more violent, finally gained relief as his semen escaped in ropy jets, coating his belly and chest.

Tenino swayed, lightheaded. He freed his cock and testicles in favor of pressing his palms to the tile of the shower wall until he regained his strength.

Damn, if that was what happened when he came just fantasizing about Trey, then the reality of coming *with* Trey was probably going to make him pass out. A husky laugh escaped. He'd deal with it. Because one thing was for certain, Trey wasn't staying a virgin for long. And if Tenino had his way, Trey's first male lover was going to be his last one.

Tenino pushed away from the shower wall and lathered his hands again, this time to clean up the semen on his chest and abdomen. Now that he'd gotten a little relief he could think again, though he was very careful to keep his thoughts from straying into fantasy.

He needed a plan. The trouble was, he'd never been in a situation like this one. His past lovers had all been experienced, some openly gay, others more discreet about it — but none of them in denial about wanting another man as a partner instead of a woman.

Growing up, his sexual preference wasn't an issue, at least among those belonging to the Thunderbird. There was even a name for it among The People. Two Spirited.

He'd never denied his sexuality. Yeah, he'd kept it private when he was a cop in LA, and to a lesser extent when he was in San Francisco. It'd just been easier that way. So he didn't hold Trey's denying being gay against him.

Hell, the guy had just helped the Feds bring down a family dealing child pornography. Trey was probably terrified it was going to destroy his career despite being innocent of anything but sleeping with a woman and pretending he was straight. On top of that, he had his female ex-lover out to kill him.

He was willing to cut Trey some slack. *Some* being the operative word. A phone call might come in tomorrow morning saying Patricia Veron was in custody. He had to make every minute count.

Tenino grinned. He could do that. In fact, he'd consider it his personal mission to get Trey so hot and bothered he had to retreat to the shower and jerk off—either that or face up to the chemistry between them and let Tenino show him just how much pleasure there was in accepting his sexuality and letting another man touch him.

A pulse of need went through Tenino's cock with the thought. He hardened again. For a split second he was tempted to take himself in hand and give in to the fantasy of imagining Trey on his knees, blond hair freed from his ponytail, mouth delivering sweet torture and mind-blowing ecstasy as the water cascaded over them.

The grin turned into a grimace as the need built and Tenino realized his plan was going to involve a whole lot of suffering—for Trey *and* for him. He turned off the water and got out of the shower, toweled off briskly then frowned at the jeans.

No way was he putting them back on. He wrapped the towel around his waist. *Don't want to spook the schoolteacher,* he thought, the grin returning.

How perfect was that? A cop and a schoolteacher paired up and playing house together?

A snicker escaped. It was better than a moan of pain. 'Cause as soon as he opened the bathroom door and saw Trey look up long enough to get an eyeful, fire streaked through his cock and up his spine.

212

Tenino crossed to the area that served as his bedroom and quickly put on some sweatpants. He left the shirt off, mainly because *more* clothing didn't seem desirable and the thought of the material touching his skin was unbearable. And then there was the fact he had a good body and he wanted Trey to see it — up close and *very* personal.

It wasn't vanity speaking, just self-awareness and a confidence that came with being completely comfortable in his skin. The Creator had blessed him with nice looks to begin with. Being a cop and taking physical fitness seriously had honed that body into something other men had found attractive in the past, though what he really wanted was for one particular man — Trey — to find him irresistible in the present and the future.

Tenino rubbed his palm over his nipple. His penis jerked and his abdomen quivered. Oh yeah, this plan was going to involve a whole lot of suffering.

"You play video games?" Tenino asked, plopping down on the couch, guessing he was right on the edge of violating Trey's personal space.

Trey closed the book. It was absolutely pointless to pretend he could read a single word, much less a complete page with Tenino in the room, shirtless and sitting so close.

"Some," Trey admitted. He didn't prefer them over reading, but he enjoyed them and they gave him a way to connect with his students, especially the boys. From time to time he'd found it very useful to take his PlayStation in and use minutes of playtime as part of a reward system for achieving certain academic and behavioral goals.

"What about a game then? We can even keep it tame, something like racing cars."

"Yeah, sounds good," Trey said, hyperaware of Tenino's smooth bare chest and tiny, hardened nipples, of the erection not any more hidden by sweats than his was.

Tenino rose from the couch to cross the room for the game controllers. Trey took a shaky breath. He felt exactly like what he was, a virgin on a first date.

Just go with it. Just ease into it. Let Tenino make the first move. Because there was no doubt in his mind Tenino would make a move. He may have backed off for the moment, but Trey didn't think it would last—he hoped it wouldn't last.

Nervous anticipation fluttered in Trey's belly. Fantasies had assailed him the entire time Tenino was in the shower. He imagined himself going into the bathroom, stripping, stepping underneath the hot spray of water and admitting he was gay, admitting to the attraction as soapy hands explored and lips touched for the first time.

He'd be a fool to ignore this opportunity, to keep denying the truth about his sexuality. He wasn't a kid anymore, didn't have to worry about schoolyard bullies. Hell, at the moment he didn't have to be scared about what acting on his fantasies would do to his career. He was unemployed, in hiding—free for the first time in his life to accept who he really was, and act on it.

Tenino returned to the same place he'd claimed previously, close enough Trey was swamped with heat and the scent of soap, with renewed images of Tenino as the water caressed his body. Trey took the offered game controller, looked away quickly when Tenino stretched his legs out and used the coffee table for a foot rest, his relaxed position making his erection press boldly against the front of his sweatpants.

Trey's fingers tightened on the game controller. He saw a subtle dare in Tenino's gesture, a blatant acknowledgement of attraction. But he couldn't make himself lift the book off his lap and place it on the table next to the couch. Instead he used it as a shield, a place to rest his forearms as he manipulated the game controls.

His face flamed when Tenino laughed softly. But thankfully Tenino seemed content to talk about the game, to guide Trey through an overview so they could begin racing.

Trey relaxed, found himself smiling, joking, letting his competitive spirit rise to the surface. He lost, more than once, but made Tenino sweat for his victories.

It was past midnight when they finally quit, when Tenino tossed his game controller onto the coffee table next to Trey's then reached over and plucked the book from Trey's lap.

Trey's breath caught at the intensity of Tenino's gaze, the purpose written on his face. His heart thundered in his ears as his lips parted slightly and his penis pulsed. He didn't fight when Tenino pushed him backward onto the couch cushions. It seemed like the most natural thing in the world to stretch out, to have Tenino position himself on top, groin to groin, hard cocks lined up, separated only by soft material.

"You still want to claim you aren't gay?" Tenino asked, his lips a breath away from Trey's.

Chapter Three

ဢ

Trey shivered, nearly moaned as exquisite sensation surged through him in molten waves of needy heat. His hips lifted, his cock rubbed against Tenino's in silent acknowledgement, but Tenino didn't relent.

"I can cuff you, work a confession out of you if that's what it takes," Tenino threatened, his breathing a little ragged, his hips bucking. "Answer my question, Trey. You still want to claim you aren't gay?"

"No," Trey whispered and couldn't stop himself from admitting everything though he knew Tenino was smart enough to have guessed. "I'm gay. But I've never acted on it before."

Tenino's smile was dark, nearly feral. "You ready to?"

Trey answered by lifting his head and pressing his lips to Tenino's, by swallowing Tenino's moan of surprised pleasure.

Firm lips yielded but Tenino made Trey fight for control of the kiss. Tongues slid against one another, cocks straining, leaking.

Emotion swamped Trey. If there'd been even a hint of a doubt about his sexuality remaining, it burned away in the heat scorching him.

It felt so good to have Tenino lying on top of him, their cocks pressing together as their tongues thrust and retreated, tangled. It felt better than anything he'd ever experienced, so profoundly right he knew he'd never look for pleasure in a woman's arms again.

His hands went to Tenino's hair, undid the braid. His heart thrilled at the way Tenino shivered at having his hair played with.

Trey swallowed Tenino's groan and wanted to coax more of them from him. His fingers combed through black, silky locks, the tips sliding over deeply tanned skin and firm muscles.

Tenino's hips jerked in response. He roughly freed Trey's ponytail, his elbows sliding forward so more of his weight was on Trey. His fingers tangled in Trey's hair, their grip radiating power, desire, possessiveness as his tongue grew more dominant, more insistent.

Trey moaned, shuddered. Lust pulsed between the two of them in time with the rapid, thundering beat of their hearts. His hands slid underneath the waistband of Tenino's sweats, encountered only taut, smooth buttocks.

Tenino lifted his mouth from Trey's. "You're driving me crazy," he said, rolling onto an elbow, reaching down to grab the bottom of Trey's t-shirt and pull it up.

The need to feel skin against skin had Trey's hands leaving their exploration of Tenino's buttocks. The shirt was tugged off. Pure pleasure coursed through him when Tenino reclaimed his earlier position and their chests touched, heated flesh to heated flesh.

More arousal escaped through the slitted tip of Trey's penis. He wanted to push his sweats downward, do the same to Tenino's. For the first time in his life, Trey felt empowered, emboldened by the rigid length of his cock, the erection he'd gotten because of another man.

Tenino's lips covered his again, the kiss carnal, forceful, and Trey speared his fingers through Tenino's hair, loved the way Tenino didn't hold back. Tiny hardened nipples touched, rubbed against each other, sent icy-hot spikes of torturous pleasure straight to Trey's penis. He groaned when the kiss ended, nearly whimpered when Tenino kissed downward, found an ultrasensitive nipple and bit.

"Please," Trey gasped, arching his back, tightening his fingers on Tenino's hair, not even sure what he was asking for.

Dark satisfaction glittered in Tenino's eyes. His smile said he understood what Trey wanted and intended to give it to him.

Tenino's tongue swirled over the nipple, his teeth demonstrating just how close pain and pleasure were to one another.

Trey's hips jerked. He spread his legs and felt his face heat at the unconscious invitation to be fucked he'd just issued. Feelings of vulnerability fluttered through his chest but didn't have time to spread as Tenino's firm lips and wet tongue continued to trail downward.

Anticipation built, a need so pervasive that when Tenino's hand reached the waistband of Trey's sweats, he lifted and in one smooth movement his pants were off and his cock was free.

"Please," he moaned again as Tenino's breath struck naked flesh. Repeated it when a firm masculine hand gripped him.

"I like the sound of you begging," Tenino said, tightening his fingers, making Trey's buttocks clench and his hips surge upward so he thrust through the fist of Tenino's hand.

Tenino's silky hair caressed Trey's thighs, teasing over his belly. It made Trey lightheaded to see Tenino between his legs, mouth so close to where he was desperate to feel it.

Trey moaned, remembered the times he'd closed his eyes when a woman took him between her lips, the times he pretended it was a man instead, then felt guilt and shame afterward when he was limp, spent. Never again, he promised himself. Never again.

He cried out, shuddered as Tenino's tongue lashed him, as Tenino's mouth closed around his cock head. There was no hesitation in Tenino. There was nothing soft in his touch, in the stroke of his tongue or the pull of his lips.

Take no prisoners.

The thought came to Trey as Tenino sent wave after wave of exquisite agony and unbearable pleasure through his cock, as he panted, writhed, tangled his fingers in raven-black hair and began begging again, uncaring about anything but gaining release.

Trey thought he might die when Tenino's free hand found his testicles, prevented him from spewing his seed. "Let me come," he gasped.

Tenino answered Trey's pleas by sucking mercilessly, by rubbing his tongue over Trey's cock head. He knew what was driving him, what was making him draw out every sound of pleasure he could from Trey.

His instincts were dark and primitive, something he'd never experienced with any other lover. He wanted Trey. Now. Forever. And if making Trey a slave to passion was what it took to keep him there after Patricia Veron was taken into custody, then so be it.

"Let me come and I'll go down on you," Trey said, his breathing fast, his voice husky.

The promise of having Trey on his knees, of fucking through utterly kissable lips as he gripped long blond strands of hair, shredded Tenino's control. He took Trey deeper, swallowed, reveled at the way Trey's body shuddered, jerked in violent release before going lax, his thighs still spread, a virgin yet to be taken.

Tenino rolled to his feet, stripping the sweatpants off. He stayed standing as blue eyes traveled over him appreciatively, grew heated at the sight of his cock full and proud against his abdomen.

Without a word Trey slid from the couch, his movement smooth, masculine, reminding Tenino of a lithe, golden panther. Trey's fingers gripped Tenino's cock. His breath whispered over the exposed tip and sent lust roaring through Tenino.

"You're not circumcised," Trey said.

A drop of arousal escaped, winked from the tip of Tenino's penis as the foreskin pulled back further. He was tempted to ask if being uncircumcised bothered Trey, but Trey killed the words by ducking his head, licking over Tenino's ultrasensitive cock head.

He grunted, dug his fingers into Trey's hair as he'd fantasized about in the shower. "Don't tease," he said, and knew it was the wrong thing to say when Trey smiled.

"What? Don't return the favor?" Trey asked, rubbing his thumb against the tip of Tenino's penis, tightening his grip, pumping, the foreskin heightening the sensation and making Tenino moan.

Liquid heat pooled in Tenino's belly, his testicles. His buttocks flexed, his thighs bunched. He trembled with urgent need as Trey tormented him, proving the saying that payback was hell—though in this case, it was torturous ecstasy.

Tenino hunched over and scraped his fingernails over Trey's much lighter skin. He commanded. Threatened. Finally begged as Trey did to him what he'd done moments earlier, took him to the edge of release time and time again, only to make him wait as the lust returned, built, became a raging inferno leaving him convinced he'd die if he didn't come.

He nearly passed out when Trey relented, couldn't have controlled the violent jerks of his hips or held back his shout of victory if he'd wanted to. He might not have managed to collapse onto the couch if he hadn't been standing next to it.

"Damn," Tenino said, arms going around Trey, shifting so Trey lay on top of him, their mouths nearly touching. "You sure you've never been with a man before?"

"I think it's something I'd remember," Trey said.

Tenino grinned, loving the way Trey blushed just enough to make him look adorable, loving the way Trey was sensitive, maybe even a little shy, without being the least bit feminine.

He couldn't resist lifting his head, pressing his mouth to Trey's, coaxing Trey's lips into parting, his tongue into coming out to play. He didn't usually like being on the bottom, didn't typically let himself be fucked, but as the heat built between them, Tenino knew he'd let Trey go where few other men had gone, he'd let Trey take him anally because what he wanted with Trey transcended the physical. What he wanted from Trey originated in the soul. He wanted a spirit mate, a forever lover.

Tenino's hands glided over Trey's back, stroking, caressing, putting into touch what was too early to put into words. His legs widened, his cock hardened to rub against Trey's.

It was a guilty, probably perverse pleasure, but he loved a circumcised cock when it came to a lover. He just didn't want to be a circumcised lover himself.

"I'd ask if that was okay for you," Trey said, laughter in his voice, "but you're looking very pleased with yourself. You remind me of one of my students whose gotten away with something and can barely stand to keep it to himself."

"One of your students, huh? Tell you what, if you get a wild hair to pull out the paddle and play teacher, I'm going to pull out the cuffs and play cop."

He laughed when Trey reddened. But Tenino's cock hardened completely when Trey said, "That's the second time you've mentioned cuffing me. Do you... I mean... Is that something you like to do in the bedroom?"

Images of having Trey completely at his mercy pressed in on Tenino. Until he'd met Trey, bondage hadn't gotten much screen-time in his repertoire of fantasies to jerk off to. But now...

Tenino looked at the blond Adonis above him, shivered at the feel of the hot body lying along the length of his. He didn't need to see or be a shrink to figure out why cuffing Trey really appealed to him. The thought of Trey leaving, going back to his life somewhere else made a knot of cold dread form in Tenino's chest.

Trey's expression changed to a mix of hesitancy and budding confidence, mischief and carnal intent. It mesmerized Tenino so he didn't realize what Trey was up to until Trey's fingers encircled both of their penises, held them together so they throbbed, burned, sent heated shards of pleasure up Tenino's spine.

"I have ways of making you talk," Trey joked, stroking from base to tip.

"Do your worst," Tenino managed, short of breath after only a single torturous touch. "Just remember, payback is a bitch."

"A bitch you say? Look who's on the bottom."

Tenino's hips jerked as Trey used his hand as if it were a sheath fucking both of them at the same time, as Trey made sure he felt the way their testicles touched, Trey's position and weight saying he was the alpha male in the relationship.

A moan of pleasure escaped from Tenino. If Trey wanted to be the aggressor this round, it worked for him. He'd already accepted he would let Trey fuck him if Trey wanted it, needed it.

Tenino speared his fingers through blond hair. He guided Trey's head down and took his mouth in a kiss demonstrating the one on the bottom still had plenty of power.

Thoughts of the lubricant and condoms stashed in the coffee table drawer flickered through his thoughts, but what Trey was doing felt so good, so right, Tenino couldn't put a stop to it.

His testicles pulled tight against his body in warning. White-hot need built. Seared. Burned away control.

He came in shuddering surges that seemed to last forever, that felt as if they'd been wrenched from the depths of his soul. He knew absolute joy when Trey's movements mimicked his own, when ropy jets of Trey's semen mixed with his own so chests and abdomens held evidence of the pleasure they'd found with one another.

Tenino had never experienced anything like it. The beginnings of love settled into his heart in an irony he was self-aware enough to appreciate. In the past, the mention of any emotion beside the desire to fuck like rabbits early on in a relationship would have sent him running, same as it'd probably do with Trey.

"Shower," he said, not wanting to spook Trey with too much too soon.

Trey followed Tenino to the bathroom, didn't even consider they would take separate showers. The view from behind was every bit as enticing as the one from the front, every bit as tempting.

He loved the color of Tenino's skin, the firm muscles created by genetics and honed by choice and dedication to his job. Everything about Tenino was gorgeous, lust-inspiring. And as Trey studied the curve of Tenino's buttocks, the sleek shape of them, he felt the blood rise to his cheeks at the same time far more of it flooded his cock.

The night had already proved better than any fantasy, more satisfying than any other sexual experience. He couldn't imagine ever needing a glossy pin-up or gay porno flick to make him come, not when he had the memory of Tenino to make him hard and help him find relief. And yet...he was curious about fucking, about being fucked.

Tenino turned and caught him staring. With the sweep of his eyes downward, Tenino made him realize his hand had unconsciously gone to his cock, that he was fondling himself as he wondered about taking Tenino anally and being taken the same way.

"Insatiable, huh?" Tenino joked, stepping forward, covering Trey's hand with his, guiding it up and down Trey's cock. "Glad to know I have that effect on you."

Trey moaned softly when Tenino kissed him. He closed his eyes, basked in the sensation coursing through him as their tongues slid against one another in an imitation of a far more carnal act. His heart flooded with emotion, rejoiced in the easy camaraderie that settled around him so trust wasn't an issue between them.

"I'm not usually on the receiving end," Tenino whispered against Trey's mouth long moments later. "But for you I'll make an exception. Is that what you want, Trey? To fuck me?"

Trey's cock throbbed, grew fuller, responded with escaped arousal. He answered the question honestly, knew the time for denying his desires, his sexuality was long past. "Yes, I want to fuck you."

"Then consider this foreplay," Tenino said, opening the shower stall door with his free hand and reaching in to turn on the faucets before using their joined hands on Trey's penis to guide him underneath the heated water.

They kissed. They explored with soapy hands, neither of them in a hurry to leave the steamy intimacy of the shower.

Trey savored every moment, committed each touch to memory as the lust between them built until he was panting, shivering. "I'm going to come," he said, buttocks clenching, fighting against it, his hand circling his cock and tightening painfully to prevent it.

He was barely aware of getting out of the shower, of drying off and somehow making it to the bed. He moaned when Tenino came down on top of him.

Trey spread his legs, welcomed the feel of hard cock against hard cock, of heated skin and smooth, firm muscle. Soft, desperate sounds escaped as he thrust upward, slid his erection along Tenino's as his mouth sought and found a masculine one.

Tenino's groan was music to Trey's ears. The slick wetness and throb of Tenino's cock, a victory for Trey and an aphrodisiac that tempted him to roll Tenino to the bottom, to kiss downward so he could use his lips and tongue, the suction of his mouth to make Tenino come.

Insatiable, Tenino had called him, but Trey knew it was more than that. What he was feeling transcended just the physical. Being in Tenino's arms was like coming home.

Trey parted Tenino's lips with the thrust of his tongue, speared his fingers through Tenino's hair and held him tight, loving the feel of Tenino's weight and heat. He wanted to be fucked. He was ready for it. Needed it. With a moan Trey canted his hips, offered himself and knew without a shadow of a doubt that taking the next step was as necessary to him as breathing.

Hot, primal lust invaded Tenino. It filled his mind with a red haze and his body with feral, clawing hunger. He felt savage, possessive—so close to being out of control it scared him.

Every instinct was to take, to fuck, to dominate. The sounds Trey probably wasn't even aware of making were driving him crazy, feeding a predatory instinct Tenino usually felt only when he became Thunderbird.

He deepened the kiss, settled more heavily on Trey. He fought the desire to pin Trey's hands to the mattress and force promises from him.

The faint rhythm of a drumbeat worked its way into Tenino's consciousness, pounding to the beat of his heart and pulsing through his penis in warning. His foreskin retracted. His cock head throbbed and grew slick with arousal.

He panted, fought the urge to find the tight rosette of Trey's anus and enter virgin territory. He wanted. *Needed.* But the drumbeat grew louder and the ancient singing began, bringing hope—and fear.

He'd never heard the call to free his Thunderbird spirit and join with the storm while making love to a partner. If he gave into the lust riding him, he risked a revelation that might freak Trey out and send him running.

It took supreme willpower to roll away. But doing it made the phantom drumbeat and song fade away, leaving only the harsh sound of his own breathing and Trey's low moans of pleading.

Tenino's skin was coated in a fine sheen of sweat. His hands shook slightly as he opened a drawer and pulled out condom.

"I'm safe," Tenino said, hating the idea of anything separating the two of them, but knowing he had to do this right, for Trey.

He opened the condom, nearly had to take himself in hand to keep from coming when Trey's hips arched off the bed as if pleading with him to hurry up and slide the latex over engorged flesh. "This will make your first time easier," Tenino managed, trying to throttle back, ease away from the wild emotions buffeting him like storm winds. "It is your first time fucking something besides a woman's cunt, right?"

"Yes," Trey admitted, feeling panic threaten to ruin the moment with performance anxiety and leave him totally humiliated.

Tenino leaned in and initiated a kiss. "I could make it easy for you. I could take you instead, but since you've driven me crazy from the first moment I saw you, I'm going to make you wait, maybe even make you beg before you get my cock inside you."

Trey was already there, willing to beg. He opened his mouth, but the words were lost in a shudder of vicious pleasure as Tenino expertly slid the condom over his shaft. He clenched his buttocks, tried to suppress the moan and the telltale blush that had Tenino's eyes flashing with surprise and his face becoming a mask of feral satisfaction.

"First time anyone's done that for you?" Tenino asked.

Trey's testicles pulled more tightly against his body. Raw need throbbed through his cock in reaction to the predatory purr in Tenino's voice. Somehow he managed to say, "Yes."

Tenino pulled a small plastic bottle from the drawer. Trey's fingers clutched the sheet as Tenino coated the condom with lubricant. He shivered in anticipation, barely recognizing himself. The need coursing through him was tangled with so many different emotions, with a desire to experiment, to play a different role.

His lips parted immediately when Tenino straddled him and bent down for a carnal kiss that had Trey's hips lifting off the mattress, his cock searching for a tight orifice to fuck. "Please," Trey said.

"Yeah, that's a good start," Tenino said, reaching between them, his hand gripping Trey's cock and guiding it so the head pressed against the tight ring of muscles Tenino rarely let another man breach.

Heat scorched through Trey. He panted, lifted, fought to push through Tenino's firm grip and into the tight heaven he was so close to.

"Let me fuck you," he said, shivering, knowing even though his penis was the one that would gain the relief of penetration, he wasn't the one in control.

Tenino's rough chuckle validated the thought but it also freed Trey from helplessness by serving as a challenge. He released his stranglehold on the sheet and took Tenino's cock in hand.

Trey loved the feel of hot satin over throbbing hardness, the wetness of arousal and the knowledge that he was the reason for it. "Better start moving up and down on my cock or you're going to lose your chance to be on top," he said, amazed he could tease when all he wanted to do was thrust until he came.

"You think you can take me?" Tenino asked.

"Anytime, anyplace."

The challenge had the desired effect. "Do it then."

Tenino rolled away in a smooth movement. He spread his legs and Trey positioned himself on top.

Reality telescoped in. Time seemed to stop for an instant, as if in recognition of the importance of this particular moment.

Dark eyes met blue ones. Hearts beat in sync.

Black hair spread across the sheets. Blond hair hung down to form an erotic curtain enclosing the two of them, trapping them in an intimacy that made the breath catch in Trey's throat.

He touched his lips to Tenino, craved a deeper connection as he began working himself into Tenino's anus. It was exquisite, nearly unbearable. Trey panted, grew slick with sweat as he worked himself in one slow inch at a time, let Tenino's reaction control the depth of penetration, the speed and force of it.

He loved having Tenino's cock trapped between them, fevered velvet over hardened desire. He loved having his own cock held tightly inside Tenino.

Trey shuddered when he was all the way in. Instinct took over.

He began thrusting. Slowly at first, then faster — harder, his heart soaring as he swallowed Tenino's guttural moans, as he reduced Tenino to thrashing, fighting, coming.

Afterward they showered again then returned to bed, sliding under the covers this time. Wood crackled in the fireplace, the glow of flames providing light as well as heat, a comfort that felt like home.

Trey closed his eyes and fell asleep almost immediately. Tenino rolled to his side, looked down at the blond in his bed.

A soft chuckle escaped. Damn, Trey'd blown him away tonight, going from denial to glorious acceptance of his sexuality. Now all he had to do was convince Trey to stay. Everything inside him insisted that he had to keep Trey in his world.

It was crazy. They barely knew each other even if the chemistry between them was explosive, more powerful than anything he'd experienced before.

Instinct? A gut read like he used in the line of duty? Was that the reason he felt so sure about Trey? So determined to keep him in Hohoq and share as much of his life with him as he could?

Hope rose inside him as he remembered both Tekoa and Ukiah telling him how desperate they'd been for a physical and spiritual union as soon as they first saw their mates. Didn't he already crave the same thing with Trey?

Tenino's cock stirred, partially filled. But before his thoughts could veer to the carnal, a ripple of uneasiness passed through him as his eyes went to the Thunderbird image carved into the fireplace mantle.

He'd prayed for a sign from the Creator, had wanted to return to the cabin with Trey and find a cup waiting, filled with the honey-gold drink that would allow Trey to become one of The People. He'd hoped it would be for him as it'd been for Ukiah and Tekoa. Only now he realized that Ukiah had found Marisa slipping over death's edge and chased her spirit back into her physical body, Tekoa had found Clay gravely injured, had done a sing for him, touched him with spirit energy and the power of their ancestors.

Tenino rubbed his hand over his chest, tried to recall the legends about the Creator changing those not born of The People. There weren't many of them. Then again, in the days when the Thunderbird flew freely and widely, the land had yet to be invaded and conquered by people fleeing Europe. The cultures and way of life giving birth to the Thunderbird and to those who could see and join with it in spirit flight had yet to be decimated and nearly destroyed.

A shiver slid down Tenino's spine, spread into his gut with the fear the cup might only appear if Trey were gravely injured or near death. He looked down at Trey and knew he'd do everything to keep him safe, even if it meant they might never fly together, their spirits one with the Thunderbird.

Chapter Four

ഓ

Trey woke to the smell of bacon cooking and coffee brewing, to a masculine voice talking quietly on the phone and memories guaranteed to cause a morning erection. He opened his eyes as Tenino ended his call. Need coiled in his belly and pulsed through his cock when Tenino turned toward the bed.

"Sun's up," Tenino said.

"So am I."

Trey felt the telltale heat slide into his cheeks, guessed it was probably going to take a while for him to be totally natural when it came to interacting with a male lover. Tenino's appreciative chuckle was positive reinforcement. And the dark hungry look that came after had Trey's heart rate speeding up as Tenino crossed the room to stop next the bed.

"So you're claiming to be up with the sun," Tenino said, grabbing a fistful of covers and pulling them back, exposing Trey's nakedness and the throbbing truth of his hard-on.

Tenino took possession of Trey's cock, measured the length of it as he slid his hand up the shaft. "Damn, you make me crazy," he said, fingers tightening so Trey's hips lifted in silent pleading.

Without warning Tenino put a knee on the bed and bent down. Firm masculine lips claimed Trey's penis. The wet heat of Tenino's mouth and relentless command of it chased every thought from Trey's mind, obliterated every need except to come.

He gripped the sheets, panted, fought to make it last. But he was no match for Tenino or the clawing hunger raking his insides. He gave up the battle with a cry, shuddered in release before settling into a weak heap of sweat-slick skin and lax muscles.

"You don't expect me to get up after that," Trey said when his breathing steadied.

Tenino laughed. "You're lucky I've got breakfast cooking on the stove, otherwise I'd take that as a personal challenge. Trust me, I could definitely get you up again if I set my mind to it."

Trey grinned. He knew he probably looked like a teenage boy experiencing his first crush but he couldn't help it. He'd never really allowed himself to think about what it might be like to live with a male lover, to actually have a relationship. When he'd allowed himself to confront the truth of his sexuality at all, it'd been more like a quick, illicit fuck, a short fantasy engaged in while he was sleeping, or if he was awake, then when his mental resistance was too low to prevent it from happening.

Now he was finding he enjoyed the camaraderie, the teasing banter, the being with someone where there were no pretenses. He liked it just as much as the sex.

He was heading for heartbreak by falling in love with Tenino. Trey knew that. He'd made the classic mistake, fuck first and wonder what it means afterward. But it's not like they'd met under normal circumstances. And a guy like Tenino... If he'd wanted a live-in lover, he'd have one already.

"You're thinking too much," Tenino said and Trey was glad to have his meltdown interrupted.

"Comes with being a teacher."

"Better get dressed. I'm about to throw some eggs on. How do you like yours?"

"Over easy."

Trey snagged the sweatpants from where they lay near the couch then hit the bathroom before joining Tenino at the kitchen counter. "Looks good," he said, taking in the egg, bacon and toast piled on two plates.

Tenino pointed to the coffee maker. "Help yourself. There's some milk and OJ in the fridge."

Trey got some coffee then grabbed his plate and took a seat at the table across from Tenino. "So what's the plan for the day?" he asked, contemplating for the first time that while he was bare-chested and wearing only sweats, Tenino was dressed in jeans and a flannel shirt.

"You know how to handle a gun?" Tenino asked.

"If you mean other than very, very carefully? No."

"Then that's first up. I want you to know how to protect yourself."

Trey's stomach did a funny little flip-flop at the same time his heart flooded with something that could only be labeled hope.

"Sounds good," he said, ducking his head, concentrating on eating for fear his expression would reveal his rapidly escalating and out-of-control feelings for Tenino.

They finished breakfast, their conversation intermittent, ranging from discussing Xbox games and football to their jobs.

Despite Tenino's claim the sun was up, it wasn't visible through the clouds shrouding the land. "How cold is it outside?" Trey asked, drying his hands on the dishtowel and studying the scene outside the window above the sink as Tenino put the last dish away.

"Not too bad. You can probably get by with a t-shirt and a long-sleeved one over it. We're not going far, just to the other end of the clearing. If you get cold, you can come back for your jacket."

Trey draped the towel over the rack and returned to his duffle bag. He fished through it, pulling out articles of clothing and smiling when his hand touched the smooth surface of a ceramic pig.

He hefted the pig out with both hands. The thing was heavy. It was also eye-watering yellow and decorated with purple flower-shaped spots.

Tenino snorted from across the room. "I don't believe it," he said, leaving the gun safe he'd unlocked and walking over to stand next to Trey. "That your emergency stash?"

"Could be. It's full of dollar coins. Only way I can keep myself from accidentally using them as quarters."

"Yeah. I hate that. More than once I've tossed a quarter into a tip jar then realized it was a dollar." Tenino reached out. "Let me hold that thing."

Trey handed it off.

"Whoa," Tenino said, pretending he could barely hold the pig up. "I can see why you packed it. And the paint job, great camouflage. Who'd guess a yellow pig with purple flowers would hold a fortune?"

Tenino turned the pig in his hands, laughter giving way to quiet seriousness when he read the words written in childish script. *For Mr. Masters. The world's best best best teacher. From Tanya K. Ward.*

"She died over Thanksgiving break of a type of kidney disease that runs in families," Trey said, remembering a little girl with a bright smile and a hundred tiny braids. "Her older sister is still alive thanks to a transplant, but her younger one didn't reach three. I couldn't risk leaving it in my house and having Patricia come back and destroy it. I can hardly believe it survived the first time."

Tenino's expression became all cop. He set the piggy bank on the floor, in between the chair legs. "What do you mean by 'You can hardly believe it survived the first time'?"

Trey's eyebrows drew together in puzzlement. But his stomach did the same funny little flip-flop it'd done when Tenino said he wanted him to be able to protect himself.

"Patricia trashed my place. That's why I'm here. The Feds don't need me to testify as a witness or anything. They'd pretty much made their case before they approached me. But there were a couple of links in the distribution chain they couldn't pin down. Finally they figured out it was because the guys only dealt with Patricia. That's what I did for them mainly, glued myself to her side, passed on anything I heard or saw.

"They weren't even sure how deeply she was involved in the business until they raided the place. Mainly they were after her father and two uncles. When the Feds missed Patricia, they thought she'd flee the country, or at least go into hiding.

"But day before yesterday I came home to find almost everything important to me destroyed. All my pictures—of my mom, of me, of the classes I've taught—were burned in the fireplace. Anything that couldn't be burned was ruined some other way. The pig escaped because somehow one of my shirts ended up on top of it. Patricia knew it meant something to me. She went to Tanya's funeral with me."

Trey didn't resist when Tenino's arm slipped around his waist and pulled him close. "You did the right thing helping the Feds, even if it cost you."

"I know," Trey said, leaning into the embrace, accepting the comfort offered and feeling closer to Tenino than he'd ever felt to another person—male or female. "I'd do it again. The Verons needed to be stopped."

He sought Tenino's lips, found them. Said with his kiss what he didn't dare put into words.

Tenino's moan was a sweet harmony. The press of his erection against Trey's hard cock was a validation that touched his soul. Fantasies of spending the rest of the day in bed started to take root until Tenino said, "Target practice first, fun second. And if I remember correctly, today is the day you're going to beg me to fuck you."

"What if I start begging now?" Trey asked, his hands curving around Tenino's muscular buttocks, his fingers digging in, preventing Tenino from stepping away, from escaping the rub of hard cock against hard cock.

Tenino laughed, had the advantage because Trey was naked from the waist up. His fingers found Trey's nipples, squeezed and sent icy-hot flashes of painful ecstasy streaking through Trey to make his hips buck, his penis leak.

"Start begging now and I'll think you want to come any way you can, even if it means having to change your pants," Tenino said.

"What about payback being a bitch?"

"I think I proved last night I can take it. Didn't I?"

Images flashed through Trey's mind, of lying on top of Tenino, of thrusting, fucking another man for the first time. Coming.

Trey's hands dropped away from Tenino's ass. He stepped back. His cock pulsed in protest but his heart soared when Tenino's expression revealed that the loss of contact cost him too.

"Let's get going," Tenino said, voice husky, face taut.

Trey dressed in warmer clothing while Tenino gathered what they needed. At the doorway Tenino thrust a bag containing aluminum cans into Trey's hands, along with a rifle.

They stepped outside. Trey followed Tenino around to the back of the cabin, laughed when he saw the size of the satellite dish. "And who says bigger isn't way better."

"Hey, I live alone in the middle of nowhere. I get tired of playing with myself."

Trey gaped. Found it difficult to imagine Tenino surfing live porn sites to jerk off.

Tenino read his expression and grinned. "Get real. I don't pay to peep and I don't hook up online to masturbate. I'm talking Xbox live. World gaming. You've got a dirty mind for a teacher."

"You set me up by saying you got tired of playing with yourself," Trey grumbled.

Tenino stopped. He hooked his fingers into the waistband of Trey's jeans and pulled him forward. "Yeah, well now that

you're here, playing with myself isn't going to be necessary—
unless I do it so you can watch. I don't intend to make it easy
for you to leave." He delivered a quick, hard kiss that left Trey
dazed.

Did Tenino mean what he said? Did he want more than a
short-term hookup? Trey's thoughts and emotions bounced
around like a ball while his cock pleaded with him for release.

He licked his lips and would have shoved his hands into
his pockets, or better yet into the front of his jeans to give
himself some relief, if he hadn't been holding a sack of cans
and a gun. The thing with Tenino had happened so fast, blown
a lifetime of denial away.

Trey felt totally out of control but it didn't scare him. He
felt alive, truly alive. Now if only he had the courage to
actually ask Tenino straight out what he meant, where he
wanted this thing between them to lead.

They walked in silence though the land wasn't silent.
Birds called in the damp mist. A breeze whispered through
trees, making shadow figures dance and merge.

The pounding of Trey's heart seemed to be echoed by the
distant beat of a drum accompanied by chanting. He shook his
head, smiled at his own flight of fantasy. Laughed silently as
an internal voice intoned, *Blond-haired, blue-eyed Anglo
schoolteacher relies on Native American warrior for protection in a
remote wilderness.*

How clichéd was that? Even if the warrior wore a badge
and dressed in flannel and jeans instead of buckskin and
beads, and the teacher was male instead of female.

At the far end of the clearing was a tree stump, tall and
wide enough to serve as a table. Tenino put the ammo bag and
guns he was carrying on it then headed to where two wooden
frames waited for targets to be clamped onto them.

Trey followed with the sack of aluminum cans. As Tenino
unrolled and put up the paper targets with their human-

shaped torso image in the center, Trey placed the cans on small logs.

When they returned to the stump, Tenino was all business. He was as tough as any instructor at a police academy firing range and Trey fell a little bit more in love seeing that side of him.

Trey thrilled each time he made an aluminum can jump into the air or skip across the ground. He basked in Tenino's praise each time they stopped to check the paper target and found he'd hit it.

Time held no meaning. The outside world was far removed as they shot a wide variety of guns and enjoyed each other's company.

"So where's the closest bookstore?" Trey asked after they'd fired the last round of bullets and removed their ear protectors.

"Are you hinting you'd rather be reading a book than shooting guns?"

Trey slapped his hand over his heart, tried for an affronted expression. "What! You think I don't enjoy manly pursuits like decimating aluminum cans and pretending to kill people? Next you'll be expecting me to wear pink and put on mascara."

Tenino snickered and snaked an arm around Trey, pulling him against the front of his body. "I bet you look good in pink," he said, pressing his lips to Trey's, sliding his tongue in for a very thorough, very arousing kiss.

Trey groaned, rubbed his cloth-covered erection against Tenino's. The phantom singing he'd imagined as they crossed the clearing returned, only louder this time. The drum beat in time to his heart, in time to the need pulsing through his cock.

In his mind's eye, Trey saw the two of them standing bare-chested in this spot under a summer sky, shedding their clothing, driven by a sudden urgency to fuck after target shooting. He shivered and ran his hands over Tenino's back.

"Damn," Tenino said when their lips parted to allow for breath.

"Should I start begging now?" Trey asked.

Oh yeah, Tenino thought, teaching Trey how to handle a gun had definitely flipped some switches he hadn't known were there. "Let's get back to the cabin first," he joked, because if he didn't get some relief soon, he was going to be the one begging.

They packed up the guns and spent ammunition, collected the shredded aluminum cans and took down the bullet-ridden targets.

"I like it here," Trey said as they retraced their earlier steps.

"Wait'll you see the rest of it." Tenino remembered Trey's earlier question about a bookstore and wondered how far would seem too far, then shrugged it off. The internet was a great equalizer.

They stepped into the cabin. Tenino sighed when he realized that as much as he wanted sex, he couldn't turn his back on years of training or fail to show Trey the right way to do things. "Put the guns on the kitchen table. I'll get the cleaning kit."

The distinctive smell of solvent and gun oil soon filled the air. Tenino loved the scent of it, usually found it relaxing, but watching Trey working the cleaning rod, thrusting it in and out of the gun barrel along with the bore brush was torture.

Erotic images crowded in, memories of the night before. Yeah, he wasn't usually on the receiving end when it came to his partners, but the intimacy of having Trey above him, of watching Trey's face as it showed every emotion, including how much he liked to fuck, had made it incredible, something Tenino could see himself doing, again and again.

He stood up as soon as the guns were clean. Kicked off his shoes and unbuckled his belt, nearly panting when he saw the heat in Trey's cheeks, the flash of lust.

"There's something about guys and guns," Trey joked, sliding out of the chair and onto his knees.

Tenino nearly came when Trey finished what he'd started, unbuttoned the top button and pulled the zipper down, freed his cock so it stood full and proud, more than ready to see some action.

"Now," Tenino managed, thoughts of making it to the bed or the thick rug in front of the fireplace gone in an instant as he thrust his fingers through Trey's blond hair and urged him to close the distance, to suck the organ he'd so thoroughly aroused and then exposed.

"Is that an order?" Trey teased.

Tenino gasped, shuddered as heated breath followed by the quick flick of a tongue sent delirious pleasure through his shaft. "Do it," he managed, applying pressure with his hands, promising retribution with his voice. "If I have to cuff you, you won't be able to wear pants or sit for a week."

Trey snickered and the sound of it made Tenino grin despite the way his cock throbbed with savage eagerness and his balls were tight, aching with the need to empty.

"Sounds like you do have a fetish for bondage," Trey said. "Maybe I'll even let you indulge in it."

Whatever Tenino might have responded with was lost as Trey's hand circled his straining length, as Trey's mouth claimed everything his fingers didn't. Tenino moaned, thrust. There was no thought, no chance to reclaim it. Need tangled with desperation and hope, allowed for only one response, the yielding of all control.

He panted, shuddered. Whispered Trey's name as he fucked through a fisted hand and knew the ecstasy of masculine lips and a carnal tongue, of giving himself over to someone who seemed perfect for him, someone he was determined to keep in his life for a long time.

Tenino's hips bucked. His thighs bunched. He tried to draw it out but Trey made it impossible.

Trey's lips and tongue seared him. Drove him into a frenzy that could only end one way.

Tenino shouted as he came. Lava hot waves of exquisite ecstasy shot through him as jets of semen erupted, leaving him lightheaded, swaying, his heart thundering in his chest and his fingers clenched mercilessly in Trey's hair.

"Damn." He wished he could do better but he couldn't. He was lucky to manage the one word.

Trey's hot mouth left him. Pride kept Tenino from whimpering, or worse yet, passing out from the pleasure still resonating through him like a tuning fork.

"Damn, you're good," he said, this time managing a grin as Trey stood, face flushed, blue eyes holding knowledge and confidence, so different than what they'd held when the two of them first met.

"You make it easy."

It seemed the most natural thing in the world to pull Trey forward, to capture the lips that had just blown him away. He tasted himself, reacted to it by hardening again, by guiding Trey to the bed.

Tenino was barely aware of sliding the handcuffs from his back pocket, of locking them onto Trey's wrists then using a piece of cloth to secure them to the headboard.

Chapter Five

ℬℭ

Trey knew he should be freaked out, shocked at being tethered to the bed, his arms raised above his head, his back against the mattress. But the look on Tenino's face, the hunger and relentless determination, the burning lust was enough to have him lifting, making it easy for Tenino to strip the jeans and underwear away.

His breath caught when Tenino opened the drawer of the nightstand, pulled out a condom and the lubricant. His anus tightened defensively, like a virgin afraid of penetration.

He noticed he was shivering, but the race of his heart, the wild pounding in his cock didn't let him label what he was experiencing as anything other than anticipation.

Tenino dropped to his side. His shirt was unbuttoned, as was Trey's. His eyes roved over Trey's bare skin, caressed it with a heat that almost made Trey whimper. He moaned when Tenino's fingers found his nipples, tightened on them, sending shards of painful pleasure to a cock already leaking.

"Payback's a bitch," Trey joked, only to pay the price as his balls tightened in remembrance of what it was like to lie on top of Tenino, to thrust into a tight, dark place.

"You could say that."

Tenino's hand moved downward, claimed Trey's cock. He loved the way it throbbed against his palm, leaked, jerked.

Part of him wanted to lean down, suck it into his mouth and reduce Trey to mewling whimpers. But the part of him that'd cuffed Trey to the bed was after something else — complete and total submission, complete and total acceptance of the relationship being forged between them.

Yeah, he'd enjoyed letting Trey fuck him and they'd revisit the scenario again—maybe even often because he was finding he could be more flexible than he'd thought possible—but fundamentally he wasn't wired that way. At his core he was dominant.

He wanted to be the man on top, the man shoving his cock into his partner's ass, making him scream and come.

Tenino brushed his thumb over Trey's cock head. He smeared the liquid arousal over the smooth head, silently calling himself a pervert for liking Trey's circumcised penis, for thinking it made Trey seem more vulnerable—as if Trey's virgin status wasn't more than enough to bring out some primal urges.

Damn. The thought of being Trey's first was mind-blowing.

The thought of anyone else fucking Trey was enough to make Tenino crazed, and told him more clearly than the constant erection and ever-present threat of a terminal case of blue balls that this attraction to Trey was serious, different than anything he'd ever experienced.

He'd never been the jealous type. He didn't like to look closely at it now—but there'd been stretches in his life where a quick, anonymous fuck or blowjob suited him fine.

No names. No commitments. Nothing except a physical release that didn't involve his own fisted hand.

Tenino wrapped his fingers around his own cock. He slid up and down, worked his penis in the same rhythm he worked Trey's and seriously thought about letting go and coating Trey's belly with come.

He reduced Trey to writhing, begging. But truth be told, he brought himself close to doing the same.

How torqued was that? Trey was the one in cuffs while he was the one who was supposed to be in control.

Tenino just about lost it when Trey willingly spread his legs, started begging to be fucked. It took heroic effort to release Trey's cock, then his own, so he could squeeze lubricant onto his fingers.

Trey jerked when Tenino pressed lubricant-coated fingers to the tight ring of his anus. "You could have warmed the stuff up first," he joked in an effort to hide his sudden nervousness.

"It'll warm up soon enough," Tenino said, eyes so fierce they reminded Trey of a bird of prey. "Bear down. Push out."

Trey's cheeks flamed but he complied. He moaned as Tenino breached him, opened him, stretched and prepared him, Tenino's fingers finding a place Trey hadn't known could be the source of so much pleasure and stroking over it until he was panting, fighting the restraints.

He almost cried out when Tenino rolled away. But his heart rate sped up as he watched Tenino put on a condom.

Nervousness dimmed the haze of passion. Trey shivered when Tenino settled on top of him, pressed a condom-encased cock head to his entrance.

His buttocks clenched protectively while his penis pulsed in eagerness, responding to the expression on Tenino's face, the determination. "Don't fight it," Tenino said, his fingers going to Trey's nipple, tightening hard enough to make Trey moan and ache for something more.

Trey forced himself to relax, to push out as Tenino pushed in. It was exquisite, nearly unbearable. Earth-shattering.

He tugged against the restraints. He used them to keep from tensing up again even as he wished his hands were free so he could spear his fingers through Tenino's hair.

Trey shook as inch by inch Tenino slid into him, took him. Only Tenino's hand returning to Trey's cock, taking control of it, kept him from coming before Tenino was all the way in.

No erotic fantasy could compete with the sight of Tenino above him, his face a mask of agonized pleasure, his tanned body coated in a thin layer of sweat, straining to go slow rather than to give in to the urge to fuck.

There was no going back. No return to denial.

Trey felt disgust in himself for all the years he'd wasted. For the lie he'd lived and the dishonesty he'd brought to his relationships with women. But he didn't wallow in self-recrimination. There was no point in it and on some level, he knew all the choices of his past had led to this moment, this man.

"Kiss me," Trey managed, wanting the ultimate intimacy, needing it, knowing he was lost when Tenino's lips touched his, when their tongues tangled as Tenino forged deeper and deeper.

Sensation rode Trey. Emotion consumed him. Hope overwhelmed him.

He was helpless, the handcuffs only symbolic. He wanted Tenino, now and forever.

One moan after another followed as Tenino began thrusting. Trey couldn't have fought the pleasure even if he'd wanted to. Nothing had ever felt as good, as right as having Tenino on top of him, fucking him, finally letting him come before coming himself.

The sound of rapid breathing filled the air. Beneath it a phantom drumbeat echoed and raced in time to Trey's heart.

He forced his eyes open and found Tenino's face inches above his. Their gazes held as Tenino's cock softened inside Trey, neither of them speaking, as if they both wanted to hang on to the closeness and delay the moment when their physical connection would end.

"You okay?" Tenino finally asked, his voice whisper-soft, rough-edged.

"Yeah. Better than okay."

"Good." Tenino dipped his head, planted a quick kiss on Trey's lips before rolling to his feet and disposing of the condom then freeing Trey from the handcuffs.

"I need a shower," Trey said, grinning as he sat up. "So does the sheriff know you use police-issue equipment like that?"

"I got a little carried away," Tenino admitted, his face reddening just enough to make it totally endearing to Trey.

"Well, I won't say anything," Trey managed with a straight face. "But I'm thinking my silence should come at a price."

"Oh yeah?"

The rough dark edge to Tenino's voice had Trey's cock stirring, ready to harden again. "Yeah. Like next time you're in the mood to play a little bondage game, you're the one who gets cuffed."

White teeth flashed in a face made erotically savage by the look in Tenino's eyes. "Any time you think you can take me down, go for it."

Heat coursed through Trey. Images of wrestling naked, fighting for the dominant position had him taking himself in hand.

Tenino's cock hardened in response. His hand mimicked Trey's, slid from base to tip. Made Trey want to go down on his knees the way he'd done when they'd finished with the guns.

"I thought you were hot to get to the nearest bookstore," Tenino said, the rough timber of his voice like a phantom hand reaching inside Trey, stroking.

It took Trey a second to remember asking where the closest bookstore was when they'd finished shooting. He circled his cock head with his thumb, rubbed over the slit, challenged. "Guess it can wait until this gets old."

Tenino snorted, leaned down and found Trey's testicles with his free hand, took possession and made Trey gasp as pleasure spiked through him. "You think this could ever get old?"

Trey fought the urge to flop backward, to cant his hips and spread his legs. One fuck and he already felt like an addict where Tenino was concerned.

The phone rang, saving him from himself though he shuddered, ached when Tenino's hand left him.

"To be continued," Tenino said, pressing a quick kiss to Trey's lips. "That's probably Tekoa checking to make sure everything's okay. If we're staying here, one of us should bring in some of the wood stacked outside so I can get the fire going in the fireplace. It'll cut down on how long the generator has to run later to charge the batteries."

Trey laughed but stood so he could get dressed. "One of us being the poor city slicker who you think doesn't know how to deal with a fire in the fireplace."

"Do you?"

"How hard can it be?" Trey said, choosing those particular words with care.

Tenino's grin made heat flare in Trey's chest. "Good question. We'll have to see just how hard things can get."

Tenino walked to the desk, totally at ease with his nakedness. Trey remained motionless, unable to look away from the firm muscles and autumn-brown skin of the man he hoped would be his first lover, and his last.

As if sensing Trey's eyes on him, Tenino picked up the phone, turned, took himself in hand even as he spoke into the receiver, said, "Oh yeah, the schoolteacher and I are getting along just fine. Any word from the Feds?"

Trey blushed, quickly pulled on sweatpants and a shirt, then his shoes. The rumble of thunder greeted him when he stepped outside. He found the wood and gathered an armful of it, inhaled deeply, loving the smell of clean air and evergreens, damp earth and the approaching storm.

He'd spent most of his life in the city though he'd hiked in areas set aside as preserves. But compared to here, those places seemed…tame, refined, less…

Trey frowned, struggled to pinpoint the difference and found it when the low clap of distant thunder was followed by the phantom drumbeat, as if this land was so ancient and primordial it had a heartbeat, as if it was a place of magic like those captured in legends and folktales.

He'd underestimated it when he'd gotten his first look at it through the window of the police car. Now it spoke to him, called to him in a way he couldn't ignore and didn't want to.

Tenino was hanging up the phone when Trey stepped back inside.

"Any news?" Trey asked, going to the fireplace and setting the wood on the hearth.

"Nothing good, at least when it comes to Patricia Veron gunning for you."

Trey stood, turned to watch as Tenino came toward him. "What does that mean?"

"A fight broke out in the prison cafeteria a little while ago. One of her uncles was shanked while the guards were distracted. I think it's safe to say he was probably the target all along. Child molesters aren't popular. Doesn't look like he's going to survive it."

Trey started to ask which uncle but didn't. He had met both of them, liked them. But that didn't make him feel bad about one of them being attacked in prison.

A long time ago they may have been the innocent victims, but they'd grown up and ruined lives. They'd perpetrated horrendous crimes on children.

Trey glanced down Tenino's still-naked body and saw the phone call had impacted him just as thoughts of Patricia and her family had killed his erection. He turned, reached out to touch the thunderbird carved into the mantle, changed the topic. "I can see how this land gave birth to the thunderbird. There's something about it, something almost mystical. I keep imagining I'm hearing a drum, and sometimes there's chanting."

Surprise ripped through Tenino, followed by sheer happiness. Both Ukiah's mate Marisa, and Tekoa's mate Jessica, had heard the heartbeat of The People before drinking from the Creator's cup.

"We call it singing," he said, keeping his voice level, matter-of-fact, when what he really wanted to do was question, cross-examine, secure every bit of evidence proving Trey was meant to be his permanent partner.

"Sorry," Trey said, heat rising to his cheeks, making Tenino curse silently in fear of shutting the conversation down.

"No offense taken." His fingers settled on the mantle next to Trey's. "Ukiah made this."

"Your cousin, right? The sheriff's brother?"

"Yeah. He's an artist. Also operates a lodge, complete with private cabins, for people who come here to hike and rock climb but don't necessarily want to rough it in tents. These days he's got a waiting list and there are always people begging to stay during the winter when he closes down.

"The land has a way of holding you, making it almost impossible to leave. I managed it once. Worked as a cop in Los Angeles then in San Francisco. But I couldn't stay away. I won't leave again."

Trey nodded, ducked his head so his blond hair completely hid his expression. Tenino wanted to reach over, pull the strands of gold back, or better yet, pull Trey against him and prevent him from hiding. Shit, it'd all happened so fast. It was way too soon to talk about something that transcended the pleasure of fucking and was more about the spirit than the body.

He grimaced. In a minute he was going to start reciting poetry. How fast would Trey run if he started doing that?

Trey surprised him again by saying, "Hohoq is one of the names of the thunderbird, isn't it?"

"Yeah. The Thunderbird is important to those of us who live here. Roughly translated, we're called People of the Thunderbird."

"There are a lot of different beliefs when it comes to them." Trey's voice held a hint of a question as well as caution, as if he didn't want to risk saying or straying into something sensitive.

Tenino couldn't stand it. He curled his arm around Trey's waist, forced him to turn so they could look into each other's eyes. "Don't pussyfoot around and worry about political correctness with me. I'm a gay cop. You think I can't handle anything you can dish out?" He leaned in, tempering the words with a kiss meant to tell Trey he'd endure a hell of a lot of accidental insults in order to keep the lines of communication open.

Trey met his kiss with equal passion. Nearly drove him to the rug with desperate longing.

Tenino fought the lust, knew this conversation was more important than physical release—even if his penis didn't agree. "What is it you want to know?" he managed, needing to close his eyes for a second so Trey's lips and the feel of their cocks touching—hardened once again even if they were separated by the thin material of Trey's sweats—didn't distract him.

"Just wondering what the thunderbird means to you, I guess," Trey said.

Tenino wasn't sure how to answer, wished now he'd spent at least a few minutes thinking about something beyond sex with Trey. "The Thunderbird serves the Creator by guarding the land, just as The People protect and care for it."

It was the best he could do, the truth as much as he could tell it. Once his people had been so much more, but...

Tenino turned his thoughts away from anger and bitterness. The past couldn't be forgotten. Neither could it be changed or those who lived today be held responsible for what their ancestors had been a part of or allowed to happen. He was one of The People. He was Thunderbird. But he was also American. A cop. A man who enjoyed technology yet still revered the natural world.

"I want to show you something," he said, the impulse riding him as if it were the Creator's wish.

Tenino moved away, got dressed then went to the table. He picked up several guns and took them to the gun safe. Without a word, Trey collected the rest of them and came to his side, handed them to him so he could put them in their proper places.

"Does the sheriff's department have budget problems?" Trey joked. "Looks like an arsenal in there."

Tenino laughed. "Hazard of the trade. I don't know a single cop who settles for just his on-duty piece." He closed the safe.

"Won't do you much good if you have to get to them quick," Trey said.

"If I need this much fire power, I'm in deep shit. I've got my service piece and the shotgun in the patrol car. The chance of someone breaking into the cabin is remote but I don't like to take unnecessary risks. Last thing I want is for one of my guns to turn up at a crime scene."

Tenino picked up a shoulder holster he kept on top of the safe next to the on-duty one holding his service piece. He put it on then slid the .45 caliber from its usual holster, checked the safety before placing it into the shoulder piece. He didn't expect trouble, but that didn't mean he wouldn't be prepared for it.

He started to step away from the safe, thought better of it and laughed at the strange twists and turns of falling in love. His hand went to the keypad on the safe, hit a series of codes before asking, "When's your birthday?"

Trey told him and Tenino keyed in the number. Felt ridiculous at putting so much meaning into trusting Trey with access to the guns, but there was no avoiding it. The only other person who knew how to open the gun safe was Tekoa.

"Just in case I'm not here and you need protection, it's keyed for your birthday," Tenino said, managing to sound casual. "Just hit TM first so it'll match the user with the code."

Trey shivered visibly. "Hopefully that's not information I'll ever need to use."

"Yeah, well, that's the plan. Better grab your jacket. A storm is moving in. I think we can make it to the place I want to show you and back before it hits."

Chapter Six

🆚

Curiosity ate at Trey as he followed Tenino outside. He expected them to take the Jeep with the sheriff's seal on the side but instead Tenino stopped only long enough to retrieve the shotgun from its rack before proceeding to a stand-alone garage.

The doors opened sideways rather than rolling up. "ATV's on this side," Tenino said, grabbing the handle on the left, pulling to create an opening just wide enough to get a four-wheeler out.

"Just one?" Trey asked, his cock reacting to the idea of riding with his arm around Tenino's waist and his front pressed to Tenino's back, even if the little kid in him wanted his own ATV.

"A guy can only ride one at time. But if you hang around, there's room in the garage for two."

"Sounds good," he managed, his voice little more than a croak.

Tenino nodded, just enough to let Trey know he'd heard the admission that the thing between them extended beyond staying safe from Patricia Veron.

The shotgun went into a sheath secured to the ATV. Tenino rolled the four-wheeler through the open doorway.

Trey closed the door. The ATV engine rumbled to life. He slid onto the seat behind Tenino, felt aroused and excited, happy in a way he couldn't ever remember feeling—like everything was falling into place and he was where he was supposed to be.

Within minutes Trey understood why they'd taken the ATV instead of the Jeep. They headed upward on a steep, narrow trail. It was dark in places, the path shaded by evergreen trees. He grunted when they hit a low spot, sending a shower of muddy water over their legs and making him wish he had jeans on instead of sweatpants.

"This is a shortcut," Tenino said a while later, slowing at a curve. "It'd take a couple of hours over fire roads and then some walking if we used the Jeep."

"I like it." Trey couldn't resist placing a kiss on the bare skin of Tenino's neck. "But I still want my own wheels."

Tenino laughed, gunned the engine. It felt like they were heading straight up the side of a mountain.

Trey's breath caught when they cleared the trees. Below was a valley, its vast tracks of old-growth forest containing redwoods that had probably been alive for thousands of years.

In front and around them, snowcapped mountain ranges stretched out. Tenino wheeled the ATV around and cut the engine. Trey slid from the seat, Tenino followed. They stood on a small rocky plateau that felt like an ancient gateway.

In the distance the storm gathered. Dark clouds formed and reformed, served as a backdrop for splintered bolts of lightning as thunder rolled across the land. Power vibrated through the air, primal, unstoppable, uncontainable — destructive and yet also life-giving.

There were no the words to adequately describe what Trey saw, what he felt. He could only nod when Tenino said, "Thunderbirds fly in this place."

The first drops of rain hit them, cold, gentle, though Trey guessed water would soon come down in violent, stinging sheets. In silent accord they both turned to the ATV. Tenino straddled the seat first. Trey slid on behind, wrapped his arm around Tenino's waist again, heard the phantom drum beat and looked backward as the ATV kicked forward.

He saw an old man on horseback where no man or horse could be—feathers braided into hair and horse's mane. Both man and beast otherworldly, the land personified. And then the image was lost to the darkness of the trail and wildness of the Tenino's descent.

Trey was clinging to Tenino by the time they got to the smooth, wide trails leading into the small valley where the cabin was. His heart raced with the same exhilarating fear a roller-coaster ride gave him.

The adrenaline spiking his system needed an outlet and he knew just what form it should take. His arms loosened so his hands could go to the front of Tenino's jeans.

"I take it you like living on the edge," Trey said, exploring the bulge he found, deciding one wild ride deserved another.

"Shit," Tenino said, voice catching, a groan escaping as Trey measured the length and hardness of the erection protected by denim, then found the snap, the zipper, and freed them.

The four-wheeler slowed, bucked with the unintentional application of brakes. Sped up when Trey's hand slid underneath the waistband of Tenino's Jockeys and wrapped his fingers around Tenino's cock.

"Unfair," Tenino panted.

Trey laughed. "Definitely fair. Any jury would rule in my favor considering what you just put me through."

"You enjoyed it."

"And you're enjoying this," Trey said, exploring the soft skin and wet tip of Tenino's cock.

Tenino responded by hitting the gas, racing toward the cabin as if their lives depended on it. Trey laughed, decided to ease back because it would definitely ruin the day if one or both of them ended up in the hospital.

The rain was coming down with a little more determination by the time they reached the cabin. The flashes of lightning were closer, the thunder louder.

With a final stroke, Trey freed Tenino's cock, slid his hand from the warmth of the Jockeys. Tenino stopped the ATV in front of the closed garage. Trey got off, grabbed the door handle, pulled.

There was the sound of a gun firing.

Tenino jerked, fell forward, blood soaking into his jacket.

Trey reacted without thinking. He grabbed Tenino and dragged him into the garage.

The rain began falling in earnest, beating on the roof. It was muted by the thunder of Trey's heart, his frantic, harsh breathing.

Blood poured from a hole in Tenino's chest, leaked from the corner of his mouth along with bubbles of air. *No!* Trey cried, stripping his jacket off, covering the wound, applying pressure though he feared that just as much blood might be pooling underneath Tenino.

Footsteps sounded. Too late he thought about the shotgun in its sheath on the ATV.

His hand shook as he found Tenino's .45, took it from the shoulder holster. He needed to get to a phone, a car, to—

Patricia's voice interrupted. "You betrayed me. You ruined my life and destroyed my family. Now you're going to pay."

Trey found the gun's safety and pushed it into the disabled position. His hands were covered in blood. His mind became a white haze consumed with the will to survive, the absolute need to do whatever it took to save Tenino.

She never considered that he might have a gun and know how to use it. And even when she saw it in his hands, she didn't think he was capable of taking a life.

Patricia laughed, a sound holding a deep well of hatred, a thirst for violent revenge whose origins were anchored in the abuse she'd suffered as a child at the hands of her father and uncles. She smiled savagely as she brought the hand holding the gun up.

Their eyes met. Held for a surreal instant—all veneer stripped away—ended when Trey pulled the trigger of Tenino's on-duty piece.

A sob escaped, not for Patricia as she dropped to the ground and didn't move, but for Tenino who was also motionless. "No!" Trey shouted, the gun slipping from his grip as he bent down, pressed his palms to Tenino's torn and bloody chest as his mind scrambled for the right thing to do.

He covered Tenino's mouth with his own, forced his breath into Tenino's lungs. He worked frantically, felt the fabric of his soul rip with each exhalation of breath, with each press of palms against unresponsive chest.

The coldness of reality, of loss, brought agonizing pain and chaotic emotion, unchecked tears and audible sobs. He wished it were him who'd taken the bullet instead of Tenino, would have gladly given up his life if it brought Tenino's back.

"His spirit flies now," a voice said and Trey jerked, looked up and found the old man he'd seen earlier, feathers and beads braided into the hair on either side of his face, his deeply tanned skin bare except for a loincloth and moccasins.

"Help him, please help him," Trey said, knowing he was in the presence of a being tied to this ancient land, a primordial force given a physical form so he could comprehend it with his human eyes and mind. "Let me take his place."

The old man offered a wooden cup. "Your spirit calls to his, and his to yours. Drink and you will be able to find him. Your spirits are meant to soar together."

Trey took the cup between bloody fingers, drank the honey-gold offering without hesitation, uncaring that he didn't fully understand the old man's words. All that mattered was Tenino.

There was a wrenching sensation, followed by gray cold nothingness, and then by awareness of movement, as though he was the wind sweeping over a land shrouded by fog. He felt a presence, a mass of air moving to his side so they became twin jets of air streaming through nothingness together until slowly they merged and melded, became one—and the beating of a drum began behind them, its rhythm steady and insistent, commanding spirit back to flesh.

The pain was almost unbearable, a death and birth. Voices joined the sound of the drum. Heat burned away the chill of nothingness as the song rose and fell, reached a crescendo—stopped as Trey gasped, opened his eyes and cried at the sight of Tenino bending over him, his chest smooth where once it had gaped and bled out his life.

Tenino's gaze held raw emotion, making words unnecessary. He lowered his head, pressed his mouth to Trey's in a kiss that was primal, consuming.

Trey's arms went around Tenino, pulled him down so limbs tangled as tongues thrust and slid against one another, cocks filling with the frantic desire for physical intimacy. They were panting, shuddering when the need for air forced their lips apart.

Slowly Trey became aware of the rain pounding the roof of the garage, the thunder, the lightning flashes drawing his attention to the open doorway and Patricia's body. He thought he should feel a backlash of guilt and horror, but he felt only relief.

It was over.

"We need to call this in," Tenino said.

Trey shivered, wanted to protest when Tenino lifted off him but he knew Tenino was right. "Do you remember what happened?"

"Yes." Tenino offered his hand. Trey took it and was pulled up and into Tenino's embrace. "I know you came after me."

Tenino's mouth claimed Trey's again. The kiss started savage but moved seamlessly into a gentle melding of body and soul. It reached into Trey's chest and wrapped around his heart like the phantom talons he'd felt when he was sitting in the diner and watching the wing shadow of an imagined thunderbird.

Tenino pulled away just enough so they could look into each other's eyes and see the emotion there, the word neither of them was quick to say but each felt. Love. "You brought me back. Which means you're stuck with me."

"I can deal with that," Trey said. "There are worse things."

"Oh, yeah?"

"Yeah." Trey's gaze strayed to Patricia's body. He felt a stirring of pity, for the victim she'd once been. But it was overridden by horror at the monster she'd become, if not an abuser herself, then a person who knowingly lived on the wealth gained from child pornography, who willing participated in the business of selling it.

He shuddered, relived for a moment the horror of Tenino's death, of taking a life — revisited the nightmare path he'd ended up on because he denied his sexuality, pretended to be straight.

Oh yeah, there were worse things than ending up in Tenino's life, Tenino's bed. His heart swelled with happiness, with the promise of a future together. "Isn't there a Chinese proverb that says if you save someone's life, you've got to care for them forever?"

"You're the teacher, you tell me." Tenino grinned. "But if that means you do the cooking and housecleaning, I'm all for living by Chinese proverbs." He closed the distance between them touched his mouth to Trey's. "Let's call Tekoa and get this behind us. There's more about me you need to know, but I can't show you until after this is handled."

Tekoa arrived a little while later, after Tenino and Trey had showered and dressed in clean clothes. He listened as Tenino spoke in their native language, wrote down what would become their official statements, what the law and those not of The People could understand and accept as truth. He took photographs before bagging Patricia's gun and Tenino's service piece, as the coroner, a grizzled bear of man who arrived behind Tekoa, bagged the corpse.

"Any idea how she found you?" Tekoa asked as they stood in the cabin after the coroner's vehicle had driven away with Patricia's body in it. "You make any phone calls out? Tell anyone where you are?"

Trey shook his head. "No calls."

"Only way she could have found us is with a tracking device," Tenino said.

"The pig," Trey said, understanding in that instant how the bank had survived Patricia's rage when nothing else of sentimental value had.

He'd thought she missed it because one of his shirts was draped over it but instead she'd known he'd take it with him when he returned to find his house trashed.

Tekoa's eyebrow lifted when Trey retrieved the ceramic pig and returned with it. He held it belly up, removed the stopper then held the bank over the table.

Dollar coins spilled out first, rolling and bouncing and clinking, empting from the bank to reveal a GPS tracking unit.

"Damn," Tenino said. "I held the thing in my hands and missed the possibilities."

Tekoa bagged the tracking unit and left a few minutes later, just as the violent edge of the storm reached them.

Lightning flashed, splintered the sky above. Thunder shook the cabin.

"Alone at last," Tenino said, need as powerful as the storm filling him.

It took sheer willpower to keep his clothes on and his hands off Trey long enough to light a fire in the fireplace, but he managed it—just.

"You know you drive me crazy," Tenino said, standing, reaching for Trey, pulling him forward and groaning when their cloth-covered erections touched.

"Me? I'm not the one who died."

Tenino felt Trey tremble, heard the catch in his voice of delayed reaction setting in. He crushed it with a kiss meant to leave no room for anything but lust.

Tongues battled. Hands roamed, tormenting and teasing until driven to work in fevered accord so clothing was stripped away and skin touched.

They sank to the floor to the thick rug, rolled, wrestled, built the passion with rough and tender caresses, with wet tongues and heated lips, the sting of teeth and scrape of nails.

Hair slid from its binding, added to the sensuality until they were both panting, anxious for release.

Tenino could feel the storm raging outside, issuing the same ancient call first answered by his ancestors. He guided Trey onto his hands and knees, used liquid arousal to prepare the way until Trey was rocking backward, his voice and body telling of his willingness to be entered.

It was ecstasy, a joining of flesh and spirit as Tenino slid into Trey, his cock unsheathed, free of any barrier. He reached around, gripped Trey's penis, loved the way Trey moaned, pulsed in his hand, gave himself completely over to a passion he'd denied before arriving in Hohoq.

"There's no going back," Tenino said, remaining still, fighting the urge to thrust.

"I don't want to."

"Good."

Tenino began moving then, sliding in and out, fighting for breath, for closeness, for the merging of two into one, for the ultimate release.

It came as semen jetted through his cock, through Trey's, heralded by the roar of rain as spirit sheared away from flesh with a clap of thunder.

They became pure energy, power gathering until it took the form of brightly feathered Thunderbirds, their wings outstretched, riding the thermals in the valley they'd seen through human eyes earlier.

This is real, Trey said, his mental voice awed, humbled, excited.

As real as the cup you accepted and drank from.

Tenino reached out and touched Trey's feathered back with his talon. *You asked what the Thunderbird meant to me. Now you know the truth of it. In the eyes of The People, you're one of us now. My partner and lover.*

With those words, desire stirred in Trey and he became aware of his human form lying on the rug in front of the fireplace, Tenino curled around him in a silent embrace. He faltered, felt the powerful, winged shape start to become insubstantial, torn between the call of the storm, the exhilaration of flight and the need to talk, to meet Tenino's eyes and hold him, to rejoice in both of them being alive.

We have a lifetime to fly together, Tenino said, turning, guiding Trey back toward the cabin, wings moving in sync, hearts beating in unison, two spirits made whole and forever joined.

Also by Jory Strong

✺

Carnival Tarot 1: Sarael's Reading
Carnival Tarot 2: Kiziah's Reading
Carnival Tarot 3: Dakotah's Reading
Crime Tells 1: Lyric's Cop
Crime Tells 2: Cady's Cowboy
Crime Tells 3: Calista's Men
Death's Courtship
Ellora's Cavemen: Dreams of the Oasis I (*anthology*)
Ellora's Cavemen: Seasons of Seduction I (*anthology*)
Ellora's Cavemen: Seasons of Seduction IV (*anthology*)
Elven Surrender
Fallon Mates 1: Binding Krista
Fallon Mates 2: Zeraac's Miracle
Fallon Mates 3: Roping Savannah
Familiar Pleasures
Supernatural Bonds 1: Trace's Psychic
Supernatural Bonds 2: Storm's Faeries
Supernatural Bonds 3: Sophie's Dragon
The Angelini 1: Skye's Trail
The Angelini 2: Syndelle's Possession
The Angelini 3: Mystic's Run

About the Author

୨୭

Jory has been writing since childhood and has never outgrown being a daydreamer. When she's not hunched over her computer, lost in the muse and conjuring up new heroes and heroines, she can usually be found reading, riding her horses, or hiking with her dogs.

Jory welcomes comments from readers. You can find her website and email address on her author bio page at www.ellorascave.com.

Tell Us What You Think

We appreciate hearing reader opinions about our books. You can email us at Comments@EllorasCave.com.

Why an electronic book?

We live in the Information Age—an exciting time in the history of human civilization, in which technology rules supreme and continues to progress in leaps and bounds every minute of every day. For a multitude of reasons, more and more avid literary fans are opting to purchase e-books instead of paper books. The question from those not yet initiated into the world of electronic reading is simply: *Why?*

1. ***Price.*** An electronic title at Ellora's Cave Publishing and Cerridwen Press runs anywhere from 40% to 75% less than the cover price of the exact same title in paperback format. Why? Basic mathematics and cost. It is less expensive to publish an e-book (no paper and printing, no warehousing and shipping) than it is to publish a paperback, so the savings are passed along to the consumer.

2. ***Space.*** Running out of room in your house for your books? That is one worry you will never have with electronic books. For a low one-time cost, you can purchase a handheld device specifically designed for e-reading. Many e-readers have large, convenient screens for viewing. Better yet, hundreds of titles can be stored within your new library—on a single microchip. There are a variety of e-readers from different manufacturers. You can also read e-books on your PC or laptop computer. (Please note that Ellora's Cave does not endorse any specific brands.

You can check our websites at www.ellorascave.com or www.cerridwenpress.com for information we make available to new consumers.)

3. *Mobility*. Because your new e-library consists of only a microchip within a small, easily transportable e-reader, your entire cache of books can be taken with you wherever you go.

4. *Personal Viewing Preferences.* Are the words you are currently reading too small? Too large? Too... ANNOYING? Paperback books cannot be modified according to personal preferences, but e-books can.

5. *Instant Gratification.* Is it the middle of the night and all the bookstores near you are closed? Are you tired of waiting days, sometimes weeks, for bookstores to ship the novels you bought? Ellora's Cave Publishing sells instantaneous downloads twenty-four hours a day, seven days a week, every day of the year. Our webstore is never closed. Our e-book delivery system is 100% automated, meaning your order is filled as soon as you pay for it.

Those are a few of the top reasons why electronic books are replacing paperbacks for many avid readers.

As always, Ellora's Cave and Cerridwen Press welcome your questions and comments. We invite you to email us at Comments@ellorascave.com or write to us directly at Ellora's Cave Publishing Inc., 1056 Home Avenue, Akron, OH 44310-3502.

MAKE EACH DAY MORE *EXCITING* WITH OUR

ELLORA'S CAVEMEN

CALENDAR

www.EllorasCave.com

erridwen, the Celtic Goddess of wisdom, was the muse who brought inspiration to storytellers and those in the creative arts. Cerridwen Press encompasses the best and most innovative stories in all genres of today's fiction. Visit our site and discover the newest titles by talented authors who still get inspired - much like the ancient storytellers did, once upon a time.

CERRIDWEN PRESS

www.cerridwenpress.com

Discover for yourself why readers can't get enough
of the multiple award-winning publisher
Ellora's Cave.

Whether you prefer e-books or paperbacks,
be sure to visit EC on the web at
www.ellorascave.com
for an erotic reading experience that will leave you
breathless.

1888859

Made in the USA